THE RIPPER GENE

c.1

THE RIPPER GENE

MICHAEL RANSOM

A TOM DOHERTY ASSOCIATES BOOK
NEW YORK

THE RIPPER GENE

Copyright © 2015 by Michael Ransom

A Forge Book
Published by Tom Doherty Associates, LLC
175 Fifth Avenue
New York, NY 10010

www.tor-forge.com

Forge® is a registered trademark of Tom Doherty Associates, LLC.

The Library of Congress Cataloging-in-Publication Data is available upon request.

ISBN 978-0-7653-7687-9 (hardcover)
ISBN 978-1-4668-5207-5 (e-book)

Forge books may be purchased for educational, business, or promotional use. For information on bulk purchases, please contact the Macmillan Corporate and Premium Sales Department at 1-800-221-7945, extension 5442, or write to specialmarkets@macmillan.com.

First Edition: August 2015

Printed in the United States of America

0 9 8 7 6 5 4 3 2 1

For Jennifer, Michael, and Chloe

ACKNOWLEDGMENTS

First and foremost I would like to thank my publisher, Tom Doherty, for ultimately enabling all of this to happen. I would also like to thank my senior editor, Bob Gleason, who has believed in me for a long time and who ultimately took me under his wing in so many ways and has really given me the chance to become a bona fide novelist. I'd like to thank Kelly Quinn and Elayne Becker at Tor-Forge for their support and answers to my endless questions as a new author. And I would like to thank all of the wonderful people at Tor-Forge who absolutely epitomize publishing as art. I am forever indebted to Tor-Forge for giving me this opportunity.

I'd also like to thank all of my friends and colleagues at literally hundreds of different pharmaceutical companies, biotech start-ups, diagnostic manufacturers, academic centers, and even government agencies (you know who you are) who have spoken with me about the science in my present and future books, and who have always encouraged and supported my writing aspirations over the years. I especially thank Jonathan Day for relentlessly arranging a fateful meeting with the ever-gracious Doug Preston, who introduced me to my wonderful friend and future agent, Susan Gleason.

I freely and happily acknowledge that I'm deeply indebted to Susan for believing in me for so many years before we convinced anyone else in the rest of the world to give this book a chance. And I look forward to many more lunches and drinks in Manhattan at Harry's as we discuss our current and future plans! Those meetings often keep me going when the workload seems too great.

I'd also like to thank the organizers and members of several writing organizations who over the years have enabled venues and workshops that have helped me and other beginning writers in our craft, most notably ThrillerFest, the Author's Guild, and Mystery Writers of America. Your support of writers and writing is invaluable and does not go unappreciated. At the same time I'd like to thank several of the SACs (special agents in charge) at the New York FBI field office for providing their time and valuable insights into their day-to-day activities and realities of life as an FBI agent. Their dedication is truly admirable, and they deserve to be main characters in books like these!

I thank my mother for her strict insistence on grammatical correctness when I was young, and my father for passing along his wisdom and incredible humility over the years. I'm just beginning to appreciate it. Thanks to my sister and brother as well, who I will not humiliate in my acknowledgments this time around. I also must thank so many close friends over the years who have intimately known me and my books and discussed them with me at length, and my current friends, especially those in Kinnelon, many of whom went so far as to read my manuscript and give me the feedback that at times propelled me to the finish line. Again, there are too many of you to name, so you know who you are, and I am indebted to you.

I also thank my wife, Jennifer, and my children, Michael and Chloe, for believing in me, for encouraging me, and for simply always being there for me on this incredible journey. I'm indebted to you forever and love you more than words can say.

For those of you who are interested in the controversial and intriguing scientific premise of *The Ripper Gene*, there are many scientific publications in the literature, but I would recommend *The Anatomy of Violence* by Dr. Adrian Raine, a colleague of mine who is a full-time professor at the University of Pennsylvania.

Finally, to stay in touch with me, I would ask each and every person who finds the premise and/or the story here interesting to leave me some feedback at www.MichaelRansomBooks.com, and I will get back to you. I'm already looking forward to our next writing-reading endeavor together, and wish you all happy trails (and reads) until then!

He who himself begins to loathe,
grows sick in flesh and spirit both.

—THEODORE ROETHKE

THE RIPPER GENE

PROLOGUE

HALLOWEEN 1983
CROSSROADS, MISSISSIPPI

Every Halloween the ladies from Crossroads Baptist took us to different church members' houses for trick-or-treating so no razor blades, rat poison, or liquid Drano would end up in our candy. My mother was always one of the chaperones, and that night she rode in the front seat of Mrs. Callahan's station wagon with us.

The car rolled steadily beneath swaying fingers of Spanish moss as we left the swamps. Glowing faces floated in the backseat around me as we bounced over the rutted, gravel road. A ghost, a cowboy, a ballerina, a ghoul. One kid even wore a devil mask beside me.

I wore a knight's costume, replete with a wooden sword and a breastplate of armor made from an aluminum trash can. The lid served as my shield.

Mara, my twelve-year-old girlfriend, sat beside me. She was dressed like a princess, a silver tiara glinting atop her raven-black hair in the moonlight. We'd stolen a kiss in the bathroom of the church basement earlier, during the apple-bobbing contest. There, in the darkness of the backseat, I could still taste the cinnamon from her glossed lips. The memory of kissing her, somehow finding her mouth with my own in that dark and forbidden bathroom, had sent pulsating waves of excitement through my young torso for the entire night.

We continued along the gravel roads, not speaking, just stealing glances in the moonlight. No man-made lights or lampposts punctuated the pine-choked countryside surrounding us. Out the windows a million stars spread across the Milky Way like a white paint explosion on a midnight-blue canvas.

Just as Mara leaned toward me to finally speak, the car slammed to a halt, screeching in the gravel and sliding a good twenty feet on the road. All the kids toppled to the floorboard and after a moment's silence, Mrs. Callahan's voice whispered in the dark. "Oh my God. What's that?"

I poked my head above the backseat just as my mother replied, the thick curls of her black hair spilling over the seat and filling my view. "Oh, just some young boys horsing around up there. Wait. Is that blood, Margie? Drive on up."

Mrs. Callahan shifted into drive, but didn't take her foot off the brake. "Probably just a Halloween prank, Mrs. Madden. We best go on around." Mrs. Callahan's eyes were so intensely focused ahead that I craned my neck away from my mother's hair to follow her gaze.

Two teenage boys, both in white T-shirts and jeans, stood illuminated on the road ahead. One of them turned toward us, shielding his eyes with a hand, the front of his T-shirt stained a deep red. A moment later the other boy staggered and fell sideways into the shallow ditch along the far side of the road.

"Margie, I think they're really hurt," my mother said. "Maybe they were in a car wreck."

Mrs. Callahan's eyes narrowed and her voice fell to a growl. "Ain't no cars around here, Mrs. Madden. Why don't we just go to the next house and call an ambulance?"

I inhaled the air behind my mother's hair. She used Prell, and her hair smelled just like the green liquid in the bottle. She faced Mrs. Callahan, but caught sight of me out of the corner of her eye and cupped my chin in her hand as she spoke. "It wouldn't be Christian, Margie. Drive on up, and I'll roll down the window and ask them what happened. Go on."

Mrs. Callahan eyed my mother as if to speak, but instead released the brake and we rolled slowly forward in the night, approaching the boys. The one boy still lay facedown in the ditch, unmoving. The other one stumbled at the edge of the road, moving in circles back and forth as though tracing the symbol for infinity.

My mother rolled down her window.

The boy who was still standing was crying. His blond hair hung in front of his face, and he whined, "Help us, please. There's another boy on the other side of the hill. He ain't moving, either. We had an accident. We were riding motorcycles."

My mother unlocked and opened her door. "Margie. You stay with the children—" she began, but Mrs. Callahan's hand shot across the seat and clutched my mother by the sleeve of her white sweater.

"Mrs. Madden. Really. I don't know."

My mother leaned back inside and smiled. But it wasn't the genuine kind; it was the kind she always used whenever she was about to end a conversation. I knew it, and Mrs. Callahan knew it, too.

"Margie, these boys are hurt," she said, "and I'm a nurse. It's the only thing I can do. Y'all go on up to Nellie's. Call nine-one-one and the ambulance. Then call Jonathan and let him know I'm all right. Leave the children at Nellie's for the time being. When the police get there, bring them here. We'll be waiting right here on the side of the road. Hopefully that poor boy in the woods isn't hurt too bad."

"Mama," I said.

"Hush. Go on up with Mrs. Callahan and I'll help these boys, then I'll see you and daddy up at the house. I love you, Lucas."

The memory always goes fuzzy then. The next thing I remember is my mother's face receding into the dark woods as Mrs. Callahan drives away. I press my face against the glass of the window, a tear trickling for some reason over my cheek as the one bloodied boy holds my mother's wrist and leads her into the overgrown grass and small trees. My mother looks back at me one last time, smiling the way only women can, the one that's sad and frightened and turned in the wrong direction but is supposed to reassure you that everything will be fine.

It's the last time I'll ever see my mother's face.

They disappear into the woods.

And just before our station wagon crests the hill, I see the other previously mortally wounded boy suddenly stand up in the ditch, not looking at all as sick and hurt as he'd appeared before. He looks furtively about to make sure no one is watching, then runs into the woods, sneaking behind my mother and her bloodied companion.

I wrestle and thrash in the car, begging Mrs. Callahan to stop, until she finally screams at the top of her voice, swearing at me with a stream of profanities that stun us all into silence, screaming at me to be quiet because I'm scaring the other children. She drives faster and I can still hear the sounds of children crying all around me as the dark forest envelops the empty gravel road behind us, separating me farther and farther from my mother, forever.

ONE

Anna Cross was a beautiful young woman, but if you looked at her long enough, her countenance soured, tainted by the pathos that only a wide-eyed dead girl could possess.

I started to stand, but found it difficult to remove my gaze. It was hard to imagine the young girl alive, before the crimson letter *A* adorned her otherwise unblemished forehead. The cuts covering her chest, arms, and legs were deep and nearly perfectly straight, but my eyes kept tracking back to her slender face and the obscene letter *A* smeared across her forehead—the tip of the *A* poised perfectly beneath her blonde widow's peak.

I noticed, too, that her left hand clutched outward conspicuously in cadaveric spasm, as though she'd prepared to scratch a chalkboard in the moment before she died.

The headlights of a lone car on Highway 49 shimmered through a distant line of pine trees in the gray dusk, and the delayed Doppler of its high-pitched engine eventually droned behind. I remained in a crouched position beside the body, not yet willing to leave.

"So what do you make of it, Agent Madden?"

I shifted my weight slightly toward the sheriff's voice behind me.

The young girl's body had been discarded fewer than two hundred yards from the highway. She was still clothed in a blue-jeaned skirt and short, black tank top but propped in a sexually suggestive pose nonetheless, leaned carefully against an ancient oak stump in a small clearing in the woods. Her forearms rested on her parted knees and her head was cocked slightly to the left, as though she were a careless, sultry model adorning the cover of the latest men's magazine.

"Pratt," I asked, instead of answering, without looking in his direction. "The fingers of her left hand look like she was holding something but there's nothing there. Did your guys find anything I haven't seen yet?"

In the gathering twilight the sheriff walked in a half circle into my line of view and stood there like an older Elvis in silhouette, his jelly-doughnut belly hanging over a thick utility belt. He adjusted the brim of his hat and managed to laugh and cough at the same time. "Well, now that you say it, before you got here one of the boys picked up an apple a few feet away from the body."

I breathed in a short breath.

The sheriff's voice went up a notch and he held out his hands in placating fashion. "Don't worry, though. I had him bag it right away, all nice and proper. He signed and dated the Baggie, just like he's supposed to. We can get it for you, if you want to see it." His voice tapered off as he recognized that he'd just offered to make evidence from the crime scene available to me.

I was the criminal profile coordinator for the FBI's New Orleans field office, normally lending my profiling skills to murder cases out of New Orleans and surrounding parishes. The recent retirement of the coordinator in the Jackson field office meant that I'd be pulling double duty in Mississippi for a while. Based on the circumstances of the present crime scene I wasn't sure I was needed for this case, but I still wanted to cover all the bases.

I let a few more awkward seconds pass. "Yeah," I finally whispered, holding back my anger with a calmness that I'd always found far more effective than shouting or spewing profanities. "That might be a good idea."

His two deputies paced the perimeter of the taped-off crime scene, eavesdropping and casting sideways glances every few seconds to see my reaction. I assumed it was the one on the right who had picked up the apple, since he seemed more invested in the outcome of our discussion. He was looking over about twice as frequently as the other one.

I pursed my lips and finally smiled up in Pratt's direction. "Why don't you come with me for a second, Sheriff, so we can discuss this further in private," I said. I walked over and lightly clapped him on the shoulder.

We left the crime scene and walked toward the edge of the woods. The leather of Pratt's ancient belt and unused gun holster creaked as he followed along. "What's on your mind, Agent Madden?" he asked when we stopped.

I kept my voice low, but now let my exasperation seethe through every word. "You know good and fucking well what's on my mind."

"I—"

I flipped open my pocket notebook and took out a pen. "First. Did that deputy mishandle the apple? Did he pick it up bare-handed?"

Pratt held up his hands again and shook them downward in the negative, eager to defend himself and his crew. "Hell, no. I teach my men better than that. He had on gloves, and the apple's in an evidence bag, all signed and dated, everything's in order."

"Okay, that's good. Anything else removed from the crime scene? Anything?"

Again the placating hands. "No. As soon as I found out he removed that apple, I had them shut it down immediately. Nothing else was disturbed."

I let out a barely audible sigh of relief. I needed only one more answer. "Okay, last question. Did your deputy get pictures of the crime scene before he picked up that apple?"

The beat before Pratt cleared his throat told me the answer before he even spoke.

"Oh, for shit's sake." I held up my finger to emphasize my next statement. "If that apple has the perp's fingerprints or saliva on it, and we're not able to use it in court because of some sort of evidence loophole . . ." I stared at him a moment longer and let the empty threat sit in the air, then left him without another word.

The two deputies leaped to attention as I reentered the clearing.

"Which one of you found the apple?"

The one I'd guessed, a blond kid in his midtwenties with a splotchy mustache, stepped forward. "I did, sir."

"Show me exactly where you found it."

"It was right here." The deputy stepped a few feet away to the right of the body and pointed. I pulled out my pad and jotted down the approximate location of the apple next to the body. At that moment Pratt glumly reappeared.

I spoke without looking at him. "Go get me that apple, Pratt. I want to see it tonight, before it's transferred to the forensics lab."

He stopped midstride and, without another word, turned ninety degrees and walked back through the woods toward the police vans.

I was still angry, but as I watched him walk away I thought of something my chiropractor once told me, that anger only clouded the mind because it knotted the body. I fully endorsed that statement, as an expert in knotted body management. I used my hands to turn my head in either direction, attempting to release the tension in my neck. Anger never got me anywhere. Suppressed anger was even worse, and I'd had to employ it maximally to this point.

Later, I'd have to figure out a way to smooth things over with the local sheriff.

"Who do you think did it?" the young deputy beside me asked.

I flipped the pad closed. "Honestly? I think we're looking for a guy who thought it imperative to smear a bloody letter *A* onto his girlfriend's forehead. I thought of Hawthorne's *Scarlet Letter* when I first saw it. Maybe that's what the killer wanted. Or maybe *A* for *apple*? Or *A* for

Anna? Who knows? Whatever the meaning, it seems like a 'Find the boyfriend, find the killer' sort of case to me."

"You think her boyfriend did it?"

"Boyfriend, husband, significant other. You just don't see that kind of overkill every day. It's usually associated with the victim and assailant having known each other. Lot of hate and anger, usually."

The young officer shook his head. "I guess so," he said, still staring at the body.

"So," I said loudly, "we'll assume boyfriend unless we find other evidence that tells us differently. Let's get back over to the sheriff and wrap this up, okay?"

He nodded with that same blank stare, but then his face lit up. "You know, there was one other thing about that apple I forgot to mention."

"What was that?"

"It had a slit in it, about two inches long. I didn't look close because Sheriff Pratt yelled at me to bag it and take it to the van."

"I'm sorry, did you say a slit?"

"Yes, sir."

After a few moments I realized the deputy was still staring at me, waiting for a pronouncement or some sort of response. And I wasn't about to reveal my thoughts.

"Okay, duly noted. Let's head back," I said, offering a forced smile that fell away as the younger man turned and made his way through the forest ahead of me.

I shook my head imperceptibly. I didn't want an apple in this case. I'd initially hoped the apple might harbor a careless perpetrator's DNA.

I had to fly back to Quantico in a couple days to give my yearly lecture at the FBI Academy. I didn't need this complication in my life, not now. Full of self-pity, I looked back at Anna Cross. Her decomposing eyes stared through me until I looked away, ashamed.

In the distance I saw the shadowy form of the sheriff stomping toward me in the dusk, the apple in the plastic evidence bag swinging in time with his angry steps.

In less than ninety seconds my profile had been turned upside down—something sinister waited inside the apple left in that young girl's dying grasp. An apple containing a thin, rectangular slit in its peel? I knew what lay inside.

I just didn't know why.

TWO

The next morning I found a yellow sticky note on my office door at the New Orleans field office: "Come find me when you get in." I tossed my jacket and satchel on the desk and headed down to the labs.

When I entered, Terry Randall, the head of our forensics unit, swiveled on his stool and held out a petri dish containing the razor he'd removed from the apple.

"Hi, Terry. What have you got on it?"

"As much as we're going to get, I think, which isn't much. But I'll take you through it." He motioned for me to sit beside him.

I'd discussed the case with Terry briefly last night and had made sure the apple was waiting on him in the laboratory this morning. He was my go-to guy in the New Orleans office, and my clear successor. He had rotated through our forensic laboratories while getting his doctorate at Tufts, and I'd hired him straight out of graduate school. He was the co-inventor of a genetics-based behavioral prediction algorithm we'd developed while he was in his PhD program, and we'd been a team ever since.

"Okay, first things first. The razor in the apple was a Gillette—no shit, the most common razor manufactured in America. The lot number came from a batch of razors that were cut and subsequently shipped out to thirteen different states and ninety-four different store chains. Seventeen in Mississippi alone. It's a black hole."

"We knew checking the razor manufacturer was a long shot, but at least now we know. Any trace evidence? Fibers, anything?

"Nothing. It's like the perp wore a giant Glad sandwich bag. We literally haven't found anything foreign from the crime scene yet. The guys haven't gone through all the vacuum bags though. Maybe something will still turn up."

"Anything else?"

"The apple may be our best lead. You asked me to find out what kind it was? It's something called an Ein Shemer. I called a local horticulturalist this morning and he identified it from the photo I e-mailed him. They're warm climate apples. They can be grown in Mississippi, and are actually pretty common down here. The guy didn't want to commit to a firm number, but he guessed there were probably several hundred orchards in Mississippi and Louisiana alone."

"So he agreed it was picked, not purchased?"

"We can't be one hundred percent sure until we do further analysis, but that's what he thought after seeing the photo. The extended stem and leaf, the overall poor quality—it was just his hunch but he thought we were probably right, that it likely came from a local orchard rather than a store, based on its appearance."

I stood. "Is that everything then? By the way, it's a whole lot further than I thought you'd get in the span of a morning."

"Yeah, that's it for now. We're still working here. The only fingerprints lifted from the apple match those of the victim, and all of the bloodstains found on her body and clothes match her serotype. No sexual intercourse of any kind on the body, no bite marks, no saliva or semen. Looks like at least the typical forensics are going to be a dead end."

This last batch of information suddenly gave me an idea. "Hey, did they swab the letter *A* smeared on her forehead and check its serotype?"

"Hmm. I think so, but hold on, let me check the coroner's report."

He thumbed through a file on the end of the lab bench before looking back up. "Actually no, the CSIs didn't swab that area. I'm surprised they didn't. Maybe they just forgot."

I looked at my watch. "Listen, I need to finish up a couple reports today and I have to prep those slides for the lecture at the academy tomorrow. Do me a favor and call the morgue right away and find out whether they can still get a blood sample from that letter *A* on the body. It's just a hunch, but I want to know whether the blood used to smear that letter on her forehead came from Anna or from someone else."

"Consider it done." Terry raised an eyebrow. "You think it's not the victim's blood?"

"I don't know. But now I remember what struck me as odd at the crime scene last night. I remember thinking it was strange that none of the cut marks that were visible on the victim's body were smeared or smudged, which should have been the case if the killer had used the victim's blood to draw that *A* on her forehead. It's a long shot," I said, "but I want to know whether her blood or someone else's was used."

Terry tilted his head with a small shrug of his shoulder. "Okay, we'll look into it. I hope we can still get a sample. I'll call the morgue right now."

"Thanks, Terry. Call me in my office if you find anything."

I went back down the hallway and sat behind my desk. Yes, there were two reports to be written and that lecture wasn't going to prepare itself . . . but Anna Cross's murder had suddenly gone to the top of the list. I had too many unsolved cases in my life, my own mother's murder being the first in a long line of too many failures, and I still held out hope that at least Anna Cross's demise would be an easily solved crime.

My mother, in fact, had been slain in the very same county twenty-plus years before. That sudden realization probably explained why this case was bothering me more than most.

Unfortunately, the interviews with Anna's family last night hadn't helped. They'd revealed that she'd been focusing on law school, hadn't been with anyone for more than a year, and that there had simply been no bad blood in any of her past relationships. We'd already phoned the last three boyfriends, dating all the way back to her senior year of high school, but each of them had provided an airtight alibi. Each of the three boys had been in public most of the night and they all lived with roommates or girlfriends who'd verified their whereabouts last night. The old boyfriends were looking more and more like a dead end.

At least the boyfriends that her family actually knew about. I kept reminding myself that it was still *theoretically* possible that Anna had been in the midst of an affair. And if she had been, then she just might have issued an ill-advised ultimatum that had turned sour in that worst of ways.

Suffice to say I thought it was still entirely possible that it was a boyfriend thing, just a boyfriend about which the family had no knowledge or clue.

In fact, the number of slashes was powerful evidence that still argued for a killer with passionate knowledge of the victim: Monsieur X. Young Anna bore a total of twenty-three slash marks on her body. Because of this overkill, I'd assigned one of Terry's people to call every female friend in Cross's e-mail and phone lists. While families were often unaware of their beloved's illicit relationships, girlfriends usually weren't.

The remaining details of the crime scene continued to gambol in my mind, and whether I liked it or not, the rest of the evidence added up in favor of a carefully orchestrated modus operandi rather than a crime of passion.

First, the postmortem sexual posing—although atypical—suggested we were dealing with a sexual stalker. The atypical posturing was problematic—clothes were usually only placed back upon victims killed by someone who felt instant remorse and who wanted to restore the victim's dignity. Nonetheless, after her reclothing, Anna Cross's legs had been spread-eagled in a sexually evocative way that most body-posturing sex offenders preferred to do with naked corpses. At best, the reclothing of the body followed by the sexually suggestive posturing was an indecipherable motif.

Second, there was the bloody letter *A* smeared on the victim's forehead. It could have stood for any number of things. *A* for *Anna*, or *A* as the first letter in the alphabet? Or *A* for a grade? Or, my original gut reaction, *A* for *adultery*? Again, if it stood for *adultery*, it pointed to someone with an intimate knowledge of the victim, who felt betrayed. Still a possibility, and maybe those phone calls to girlfriends would give us a lead.

It seemed to me, however, that everything pivoted around the apple, the third and final piece of evidence that argued against a crime of passion. Young Anna Cross had been holding the ultimate symbol of Halloween in her hand when she died. Not just any apple, but an apple with a razor intentionally embedded in it. And that one tiny aspect created the profile of a killer who didn't just leave behind a victim, but left behind a tableau—a victim posed in a sexually suggestive position, yet strangely reclothed, and forced to hold an apple with a razor in it.

I hated to admit it, but everything suggested we weren't dealing with a crime of passion, but the work of a serial killer with a message, or a messianic calling, or some other horseshit, that had only just begun.

I caught myself. My mind was already making a mad dash for the finish line long before all the evidence was analyzed. There truly was nothing to do but wait on the interviews and the remaining laboratory analyses.

I finally shook myself from my thoughts and logged into the FBI server to prepare the monthly report for my boss, Jim Raritan, since I'd see him after my lecture in Quantico the next day. After a moment's hesitation, I decided I wouldn't include the Anna Cross case in the write-up. Despite my misgivings, there was still a decent—if not overwhelming—chance that we were dealing with a one-off sort of killing here. I hoped so.

The little voice inside my head told me I was being a fool for wishful thinking. I tuned it out.

I had work to do, and a plane to catch.

THREE

The next day I shifted uneasily in my seat as Dr. Bob Canner, a legend around Quantico's Behavioral Analysis Units, introduced me to the FBI Academy.

"Today it gives me great pleasure to introduce a former student of mine, Dr. Lucas Madden, to you. Many of you have discussed his cases during your course work, but he's probably best known for his pioneering studies that link violence and genetics. His best-known work is his discovery of the 'ripper' gene, which turned out to be a gene encoding a key dopamine receptor expressed in the brain.

"More recently he's proposed that we may be able to predict distinct patterns of violent behavior based on genetic differences in neurological genes, using a method dubbed by the media as his very own 'Damnation Algorithm.' He comes today to speak to us on that topic, and how advanced next-generation DNA sequencing tools may one day be used in the behavioral profiling of serial killers. Please join me in welcoming him today."

I stared across the sea of attentive faces during the applause. I relished my once-yearly lecture for the Advances in Criminal Profiling series but hated the title of this year's talk. Some horse's ass at CNN had nicknamed our method the Damnation Algorithm, and it had stuck. I'd given up fighting it several months ago.

I took the podium. "Thank you, Bob. Today I hope to convey how a small bit of genetic information from a killer can be used to predict behavior in most, if not all, cases. A process otherwise known as the so-called Damnation Algorithm. First slide, please."

The class swiveled its attention to the large drop-down screen on my right, depicting a veritable rogue's gallery of serial killers. The curly hair, prominent forehead, and elongated eyebrows of David Berkowitz, the charismatic Hollywood smile of a cocksure Ted Bundy, and the half-lidded, drug-baked eyes of a mustached Jeffrey Dahmer were among some of the most recognizable.

"It's a well-known fact that serial killers come in a bewildering array of combinations and exhibit disparate patterns of behavior depending on whether they are, for instance, experienced or inexperienced, organized or disorganized, whether they're souvenir takers or not, and myriad other well-defined behavioral observations."

I clicked to the next slide, in which the photos of the same thirty killers were now rearranged in a branched tree according to the overall similarity of their DNA profiles. "We've now shown that newer genetic analysis tools based upon next-generation sequencing can actually cluster these serial killers into groups of similar violent behaviors, based on their DNA patterns alone. Importantly, we don't just look at single nucleotide polymorphisms, as scientists did in the past. We can now investigate many different aspects of human DNA—its methylation patterns, microRNA binding sites, copy number variants, insertions, and deletions, just to name a few. When we examined the totality of genetic differences that can be observed, we found that key differences between violent offenders mapped to several dozen human genes . . . all of which are linked in one way or another to neurochemical signaling in the brain.

"Properly used, the new algorithm is designed to take an unknown suspect's DNA—the kind you might recover from a crime scene—and assign a predicted behavioral pattern to aid in the capture of the offender."

I flicked to the next slide and noticed a complete silence in the room. The faces in the audience seemed thoroughly receptive.

It was going to be a good lecture. I could feel it.

Afterwards I faced the audience in a standard question-and-answer session.

After a few normal chatty questions broke the ice, a dark-headed kid in the front asked a more targeted question. "So how did you get DNA from Ted Bundy? Or any of the other convicted killers who were executed long before you ever even came to the Bureau?"

"Great question," I acknowledged, leaning over the podium. "The honest truth is that we had to be inventive. Most of these guys weren't what you'd call 'altruistic.' They didn't donate their bodies to science, but they did have habits we could exploit." I paused, scanning around the room. "And even more importantly? We were lucky. We were fortunate to have had incredibly visionary predecessors in the original Behavioral Science Unit who had the foresight to preserve things like cigarette butts and chewed gum from these offenders, in case they might be of use someday. Sure enough, we eventually picked up the DNA for a lot of these offenders from saliva traces on cigarette butts or wads of gum. I never dreamed Juicy Fruit would help us design a genetic algorithm to test serial killer behavior, but it did."

The audience laughed in unison. I prepared to thank everyone for coming, when another voice sounded in the hall.

"But does all this genetic analysis really add value to a behavioral profile?" A female agent stood and spoke from the upper rows. "Most of these genes are just linked to general violent behavior, not any specific type. Seems far-fetched to believe that genetics in a few genes can accurately predict serial killer behavior. Have you tested it yet?"

I glanced up, perturbed, but only because she was partly right—we hadn't tested it in the real world yet. "Not yet, but we plan to test it in an investigation soon. I'll tell you what: we'll let you know what we find, since you seem to be so skeptical." I smiled, and a few chuckles from the amphitheater ensued.

But by this point it was clear that the entire audience was expecting a verbal sparring contest. The majority of eyes in the auditorium suddenly tracked back toward my interrogator, as if she were a tennis player about to return serve.

She started to speak again, but I preempted her by addressing the whole crowd in a loud voice. "I'm sorry, but that's all the time we have for questions today. I do again thank you for your attention." I cut my eyes toward the rear of the room. "I hope that you all keep an *open* mind when it comes to the genetics, and biology, of behavioral profiling."

I stepped down from the podium as the audience delivered a final round of applause. At the bottom of the steps Bob Canner waited on me, a tremendous smirk across his lips.

"How's the hot seat?" he chuckled, glancing toward the back of the amphitheater. I followed his gaze. As the audience dispersed, my challenger now spoke with several other persons gathered around her. She threw her head back with an unflattering expression of disbelief, the kind that would accompany the word *dumbass* with great vigor and conviction.

"I think I had a detractor," I said. "Perhaps several."

Bob laughed. "Oh, you certainly got a nice dose of our Agent Woodson. I think she challenged the theory of gravity one day. Until I threatened to throw her out the window to prove my point." He winked at me.

"I can only imagine."

Bob waved his hand. "Oh, she's one of those scientist types, like you. Always questioning, always looking for the best explanation, not just the first one. Right up your alley."

"Not *my* alley."

Bob moved in front of me and I had to quell the urge to tilt my head to keep a line of sight on the admittedly attractive agent in the upper rows.

"But Lucas, she's the one graduate from last year's class given a permanent position within BAU-2, to help with the overflowing caseload. She's intuitive; she's already put together two profiles in missing person cases that led to arrests. I'm telling you, she reminds me of you. She's as sharp as they come."

I smiled as insincerely as possible. "Well, that's *really, really* neat. But we should get moving. What's next on the schedule?"

"What's next, you ask?" Bob repeated my question with glee. At that moment he turned his head back in the direction of the upper amphitheater. I stepped around him in order to see up the steps, not terribly eager to find out what sort of slander was probably still taking place in the rear of the auditorium.

Unfortunately, Agent Woodson crashed directly into my path as she descended rapidly down the steps and leaned down to hug Bob. Her forehead met the side of my head at full speed, sending both of us staggering backwards. "Ow!" she exclaimed, placing her palm against her forehead and leaning forward on the bottom step of the amphitheater as Bob steadied her.

"Oh, Jesus, I'm sorry," I began to say, before a blinding white light flashed in front of my eyes.

It was silent for a moment longer, and then we all laughed. Up close, she had blonde, shoulder-length hair, green eyes, and a thin, prominent nose. Her skin was a light tan, offset by the cream-colored, high-collared blouse she wore beneath a navy blue blazer. She was surprisingly tall as well, only three or four inches shorter than me. No wonder we'd bumped heads when she'd stood on the next to last step.

"My interrogator," I managed to say. "I'm sorry to make your acquaintance this way." I extended my hand while continuing to rub my temple with the other.

"I guess it's a good thing we FBI agents have hard heads," she said, still smiling. "Your interrogator? Well, I suppose so, in the flesh." She accepted my hand. "I hope my questions didn't bother you," she said, looking nervously between Bob and me. "It only meant I was interested."

I waved her comment off. "Not at all," I said. "The questions are always welcome. It was a Q and A session, after all."

She smiled at that remark, and held on to my hand for a few seconds longer. Then she released it, and along with it seemed to relinquish any interest in pursuing our debate further.

Bob spoke up beside us. "So, Lucas. You had asked what was next?"

I glanced at him, having momentarily forgotten anyone else was in the amphitheater with us. "That's right."

"Well," he said, still grinning, "Agent Woodson requested a lunch meeting with you after your lecture, so for the next hour she's all yours." He looked back and forth between us, questioningly. "That is, provided you don't have concussions?"

We both laughed at that.

"However," he said, "before that, I do need to speak with her for a minute or two in private, if that's okay."

"Absolutely," I said. "I'll wait here."

Woodson held up a finger to indicate she'd be right back, then followed Bob out into the hallway without a word.

I found myself slightly unnerved by Agent Woodson's sudden shift in attitude from the lecture. Maybe my caution was warranted, maybe it wasn't. She seemed just a little too eager to make a name for herself in the eyes of her peers and her instructors, maybe just a little overzealous.

Then again, it reminded me of someone I knew all too well, around the time I was preparing to leave the academy myself, just as Bob had intimated.

It turned out that Agent Woodson's company wasn't just tolerable, but actually enjoyable. Over lunch she took a genuine interest in both my personal and professional history. After we took a seat in a private room of the lunch cafeteria, she asked me to explain in more detail how I really came to discover the ripper gene and join the FBI.

I gave her the canned story of how I'd gone to medical school but didn't want to be a doctor. How I saw a study that showed the amygdala regions of the brain lit up in normal people exposed to terrifying scenes of mutilation, but how the same horrific scenes led to no responses in serial killers. How I'd studied the works of neurobiologists at Penn and other institutions, who'd insisted there was a biological basis for violence, no matter if people didn't want to admit it. How my own thesis research led me to look for a genetic basis explaining why the wiring of limbic brain regions of serial killers seemed so different from those of normal persons when visualized by fMRI and other imaging techniques.

"That's when you discovered the ripper gene?" Agent Woodson asked.

"Exactly."

"Great name for the gene, by the way."

"Thanks. We eventually showed that ripper encoded a dopamine transporter that localized to the amygdala region of the brain. It was the perfect culprit. Most people carry normal copies and as a result have normal transmission in the amygdala. In other words, they like pictures of bunny rabbits and are repulsed by mutilated corpses. But in the small set of unfortunate individuals carrying two dysfunctional copies of the ripper gene, dopamine transporters are turned on like crazy, depleting the available dopamine in their brains and causing a signaling defect in their amygdala. They respond no differently whether they're looking at a rabbit in a garden or a torture victim in a basement."

Woodson shook her head in wonderment, but didn't say anything.

"Anyway, my thesis showed that deficits in ripper gene function were present in more than seventy percent of the serial killers I tested. The prevalence in the normal, nonincarcerated human population is around two percent."

Woodson whistled. "Impressive stuff. But that's weird. You'd think scientists would have seen that significant of an odds ratio long before, in classical genome-wide association studies. I mean, if the mutation rates were that different between normal persons and serial offenders. Don't you find it surprising that someone hadn't already found it?"

"Aha, but that's just it," I said. "Notice that I said, very intentionally, *deficits* in ripper gene function. Not *mutations.* That's why the new DNA tools are so important. Different DNA methylation patterns can completely turn genes off or on, but scientists weren't paying attention to methylation back then, just to DNA sequence. We came along and showed that methylation of the DNA was just as important as its sequence, and when you looked at the sum total of the myriad types of DNA variation, genetic differences of many types across multiple loci became relatively strong predictors."

Woodson nodded as she followed the logic. "Cool," she said softly, and took a sip of her coffee. She seemed to be studying me for a moment, as if making a judgment call of some sort in her mind. "So how did you become involved with the FBI?" she asked suddenly. "Did you apply straight out of graduate school?"

"Oh no, I'd planned on becoming a professor. But my career took a U-turn when Bob came to Harvard's psychology department to give a lecture entitled 'Behavioral Profiling and the Criminal Mind,' which was absolutely fascinating. Come to think of it, I took him to lunch after his lecture." I raised my eyebrows.

Woodson smiled.

"Anyway, six months later my stethoscope was collecting dust on a bookshelf while my ass was getting whipped back into shape at the academy in Hogan's Alley."

Woodson nodded in knowing agreement, about to reply, when a knock on the private dining room door interrupted us.

"Madden? Is there an Agent Madden in the house?"

I knew the voice but couldn't quite place it. When the door opened, however, voice and face blended into one. Parkman. Alan Parkman.

I'd worked with him once before. I'd been in Quantico back when he'd been Special Agent in Charge in Philadelphia. Back then, Parkman had taken it as a slap in the face that Jim Raritan had assigned anyone, much less me, from the BAU to *his* case.

My first day in Philly, Parkman greeted me in city hall, reiterating how he didn't need some Southern-fried "behavioral fucking profiler" wasting FBI time on the case. Just as the mayor walked past, I reminded Parkman that I'd been called in because he had failed to nab a seven-time rapist who operated in "broad fucking daylight."

We solved the case, but needless to say, Parkman and I didn't play racquetball together after that. With the cruel irony that sometimes accompanies us in life, Parkman eventually took my place as a "behavioral fucking profiler" in BAU-2 when I voluntarily requested a transfer down to New Orleans. He liked to think that he actually chased me out of Quantico, even though he'd had nothing to do with it.

Now, Parkman leaned through the door, hanging on to the door frame with one hand, sweeping the room with his eyes. He'd always reminded me of a Wild West gunfighter, with his slicked-back black hair, handlebar mustache, and tiny black eyes. The only thing missing was a black ten-gallon hat.

He smiled when he saw me. "Raritan's looking for you," he said, looking from me to Woodson and back to me again. "And come to think of it, he didn't look too happy, either." His smile grew even wider. "In fact, I think he looked downright *pissed*. Well, see you later, Madden."

The door closed behind him.

I looked across the table to Woodson. "Well, looks like I have a date with the big boss earlier than I expected," I said, standing up and placing my napkin on my plate. "It was a pleasure meeting you."

Woodson smiled and stood as well. "Nice meeting you too, Agent Madden. Good luck with Big Jim; sounds like you'll need it." She extended her hand and I shook it. "See you around," she said, and then vanished through the door before I could reply.

I stared after her for several seconds. Despite our bout in the Q and A session after the lecture, I'd warmed up to her considerably over the course of our lunch. But there were more important things to deal with, and chances were very good that I'd never lay eyes on her again.

I latched my briefcase, exited the dining room, and headed to the cafeteria exit, in the direction of Jimmy "Big Jim" Raritan's office. Unless Parkman was just messing with me, I needed to find out exactly why my boss was so pissed. By my calculations I had about five minutes for soul-searching before I arrived at his office.

I had one phone call to make before that.

FOUR

I called Terry while walking to Raritan's office, and he unfortunately confirmed that the CSIs hadn't swabbed the letter *A* from Anna Cross's body, and that the body had already been cleaned up by the coroner's office. We had no chance of swabbing the letter and getting DNA from that letter *A* now.

I hung up, disappointed that we'd missed the opportunity. Though it was ninety-nine percent likely that it had been her own blood, I couldn't overlook the fact that we'd seen no smears in any of the cuts found on her body that could have indicated the source of the blood used to draw the *A*. It seemed we'd never know.

As I knocked on Raritan's office door, I suddenly questioned the wisdom of withholding the Anna Cross case from the quarterly report I'd submitted the day before. But I had no time to consider it further, as a guttural utterance devoid of emotion emerged. "Come in."

I entered and found the hulking man leafing through a filing cabinet in the corner of the room. Big Jim Raritan. Six foot five, three hundred pounds. A former Oklahoma Sooner who played defensive end for the Pittsburgh Steelers for four years before his anterior cruciate snapped like a piece of jerky and forced him into early retirement.

Now he was head of the FBI Academy's fabled Behavioral Analysis

Unit 2, or BAU-2 as it was called, the unit responsible for serial, spree, mass, and other murders. He took over after Bob retired, and in so doing immortalized himself on a short list of famous profilers who'd headed the various incarnations of the original Behavioral Science Unit ever since it was founded in 1972.

The seemingly exaggerated limp in Jimmy's walk belied the massive power of muscles hidden beneath the two-piece suits that were now his uniform. He motioned me into a chair and sat behind his desk. "Agent Madden. Good lecture today. Please, take a seat."

I did. "So, what's on your mind, Jimmy? Parkman made it sound like I'd find a raving lunatic in here."

Jimmy waved in exaggerated fashion. "Oh now, I might have been a little out of sorts when Alan ran into me earlier. I'd just found out about an aggravating new problem. But I'm all better now, Lucas, because I'm looking directly at the man who's going to help me resolve it." He peered at me another second, just long enough to make me wonder whether I should say something, before he continued. "But we can get to that in a moment. First, let me know what's going on down in your neck of the woods. Any new activity? Anything we should be putting into ViCAP?"

The Violent Criminal Apprehension Program, or ViCAP, was a database that stored characteristics of crime scenes and allowed investigators across the country to query it for similarities between crimes in different locales. For the database to work, it had to be populated. Whenever any FBI field agents came across a crime that seemed linked to the work of a serial offender, we needed to enter the data concerning certain characteristics of the crime scene into the ViCAP database.

As Raritan's words worked through my brain, I realized that I hadn't entered the particulars of the Anna Cross case into the computer system yet and was reminded of my decision to withhold the case from the quarterly report.

"Nothing new," I finally said. "Looks like we'll have enough physical evidence to get an easy conviction in the serial arsonist case down in the Quarter." I shrugged. "It's been quiet. That's all I have on my end."

Jimmy just kept looking at me, or through me, perhaps, and finally tossed a file onto the desk between us.

"What's that?" I asked.

He raised his eyebrows, as if noticing the file for the first time himself. "Oh, that? That's the Anna Cross file we received earlier today from the Stone County Police Department down in Mississippi." He shook the file so that the black-and-white photos fell to his desk. The top photo was a face I knew all too well already, Anna Cross's eyes fixed in death, with the massive bloody *A* smeared prominently across her forehead.

My stomach dropped. "Oh, that case. Well, that actually occurred in Mississippi. They just brought me over last night to check it out. I thought you just wanted to know about anything new in my Louisiana jurisdiction, so—"

"Don't give me that horseshit, Lucas. What's the matter with you? Why isn't this in ViCAP already? Can you tell me that?"

"It's an isolated murder, Jimmy. Overkill. I think it's probably just some jealous lover." I shrugged. "We'll support the investigation, if it comes to that. But the cops down there are trying to locate an ex-boyfriend as we speak."

Raritan rubbed his hand over his mouth and chin in what appeared to be an exaggerated attempt to keep his composure. "I see," he said. Then he flipped through the photos again, pulling one out. "So what's this? What do you make of this?"

I glanced down at the picture to find a photograph of the apple from the laboratory, and the razor extracted from it. I sighed. "It's the apple we found next to the body. It had a razor in it."

Raritan leaned back. "An apple with a razor in it. And you're looking for boyfriends? Let me ask again, in a different way that you may better understand. So what the hell's wrong with you?"

"I don't know, Jimmy. I guess I just hoped—"

"This 'hope' you refer to," he said, cutting me off midsentence, "is a real pain in my ass, Lucas, every time. For such a good profiler, getting you to start working on a serial murder investigation is like pulling teeth. Why is that?"

"It's not that simple," I said.

Raritan slammed his fist on the table. "Yeah, I know it's not that simple, and I don't care. And I'm tired of these slow starts of yours. What are you doing down there? Trying to wish, or hope, crimes out of existence? We can't go through this shit again, Lucas."

I cringed. Whenever anything resembling a problem surfaced, it always came back to the Juan Alvarez case. Arguing with Raritan about profiling seemed exactly like what it would be like to fight with a wife over a onetime, one-shot affair. The slightest problem would resurrect it, over and over, whether relevant or not.

Whenever there was the slightest hint that I'd made an error in judgment, I'd inevitably be taken to task, straight back to the case of Juan Alvarez. As I stared across the table at Raritan I knew I'd never live it down.

And it was probably for the best. I didn't really want to live it down. I'd nabbed my serial killer in that case all right, right away. In fact, I'd caught Juan Alvarez so quickly that he'd hung himself in his cell under the accusations. After which the real killer continued to strike again, and again, and again.

His family had screamed for my head, rightfully so, with every murder that continued to be committed after Alvarez's suicide. We didn't catch the actual killer until three more children were killed.

"Well?" Raritan intoned.

I steadied myself before speaking. "Don't worry, Jimmy. I'll get this information into ViCAP as soon as I get back. It only happened twenty-four hours ago."

Raritan eyed me. "Now that's closer to what I wanted to hear. You know as well as I do that you have a killer on your hands, and not some random boyfriend. Quite possibly one who just came out of his shell. And if that's the case, it might be easier to find him, because he's more likely to trip up. So do us both a favor: quit screwing around and get on it, all right?"

I held up my hands. "Hey, listen. Don't beat around the bush, Jimmy. Just come out and tell me like it is." I waited for a smile, but received none in return. I gave up and stood to leave. "Okay, okay. You got it. Anything else?"

"Just one more thing." Raritan suddenly wore a tight-lipped smile that suggested he struggled to suppress even more unbridled rage. He motioned toward a newspaper lying on one of the chairs. "I almost forgot but, yes, there is one more thing. You see that over there?"

"Newspaper?"

"Yeah. That's quite a news story about you and your Damnation Algorithm in there."

"Oh yeah? That's good, right? I didn't realize this had come out today. You mind if I take this copy?"

Raritan's smile grew broader, but at the same time somehow less genuine. "Oh no, not at all. And after you read it? Send me a memo with how you propose that the FBI and the Vatican begin to make amends, now that you've managed to officially offend the Catholic Church all the way up to the pope."

"What?"

Raritan held his hand up and closed his eyes. "I'm not even taking the time to discuss this further. Next time, stipulate that the Bureau gets to review a copy of the interview before you go pontificating, and I use the word with every single ounce of irony intended, about the long-term implications of your scientific discoveries. I'm up to my elbows in other people's assholes over this."

"Can I just say one thing?"

"Nope, no, you can't. Not anything at all. I have a three o'clock." Raritan extended his hand with the most lifeless enthusiasm I'd ever seen in a proffered handshake.

I made a point to roll my eyes as we shook hands. "Always a pleasure, Jimmy."

"And I feel the same. You take care now, Lucas, and don't forget to write."

FIVE

Late that afternoon I slumped into a seat in the exit row of the plane back to New Orleans to ruminate on my heartwarming and "life-reaffirming" visit with Raritan. As I recalled our conversation, I realized that I still hadn't had a chance to read the news article.

I fished the folded paper out of my briefcase and read:

DNA-BASED ALGORITHM DEEPENS DIVIDE BETWEEN SCIENCE AND RELIGION

The article described our recent publication in *Nature Genetics,* which had shown correlations between genetics, epigenetics, and serial killer behaviors—the basis for the so-called Damnation Algorithm, the exact same data I'd just covered in my lecture. Although the reporters had only interviewed me on the scientific aspects of our discovery, the article primarily highlighted the controversy our discovery had created by implying that the moral choices an individual makes might already be prewired in their very own DNA.

I groaned as I read further.

> The research has been characterized in various circles as ranging from dangerous to blasphemous. A high-ranking official at the Vatican spoke under conditions of anonymity. "These results are unsubstantiated and the researchers have

made claims which are not validated in a larger population. Quite simply, a person's moral fate is not predestined by his or her DNA."

That may be, but Madden and colleagues remain unfazed.

I wondered for a surreal moment who, exactly, had told them I remained unfazed? The article went so far as to end by advising its readership *not* to look at their DNA, because after all, "you might not like what it's telling you."

I folded the paper and crammed it into the seat pocket in front of me. I tried to block it from my mind, because I had far more important things to worry about than asinine news reporting. My number one priority was to get the Anna Cross case into ViCAP.

Not because Raritan had essentially threatened my livelihood if I didn't, but because I knew that we were dealing with a potential serial offender. Every moment mattered.

I tried with only moderate success to sleep during the rest of the flight. I dozed a few times, but thanks to my spat with Raritan, every time my eyes closed, the memories of the Alvarez case returned.

Back then I hadn't been content to wait; everything had to be now, now, now. We always needed convictions yesterday. And I was good at bringing them in. I was advancing rapidly in Quantico when Juan Alvarez crossed my path. He was a young man who, based on a behavioral profile I'd put together, was arrested for the murders of three young children in Washington, DC. While awaiting trial he hanged himself in his cell, unable to bear the guilt of suspicion. He wasn't on a suicide watch.

Upon hearing the news I felt relieved—my hunch had been correct. But the very next day, the telltale bite mark showed up on a fourth child victim. And later, on a fifth. And ultimately a sixth.

Juan Alvarez had been innocent, and I might as well have tied the noose around his neck and killed those next three kids.

After that I began dreaming nightly that Juan Alvarez had come back from the grave, the sheet still tied around his broken and disjointed neck, to drag me back down into his coffin.

A month after his suicide, I woke up with a fever just shy of 106 degrees and managed to somehow dial 9-1-1. The EMTs found me naked in my kitchen, water running and ice cubes on the floor. I spent three weeks in the hospital, barely surviving a severe case of viral-induced encephalitis. I'm certain that the guilt I felt in the wake of that case had liberated some latent virus buried deep within my own DNA.

When I finally recovered, I requested a transfer from the hectic world of the BAU. I couldn't bring myself to stop being a criminal profiler, but I realized I could limit my casework by taking what would appear to be a demotion and becoming a state profile coordinator instead. At my request, they sent me to the Louisiana field office.

I never recuperated fully, though. And every now and then the young man I killed sometimes returns in my dreams.

I woke up with a jolt when the plane touched down in New Orleans.

Anxious to get home, I gunned the Explorer out of short-term parking. As I made my way onto the Twin Spans I looked at the clock: it was seven o'clock. If I hurried, I'd cross Pontchartrain without incident and be in Bay Saint Louis within the hour. I'd have the data for the Cross case entered into ViCAP well before midnight.

I was on the far side of Slidell when my cell phone rang—a 228 area code from Mississippi. The voice on the other end belonged to Donny Noden, an old friend of mine and the sheriff of Harrison County. Donny had worked for the DEA before switching to local law enforcement, and we played poker occasionally.

He paused uncharacteristically after we exchanged hellos, and I realized he wasn't making a social call. "We, uh, we just found another body down here, and we figure you better come on over and take a look. Looks like the same deal as that Anna Cross case."

"You're sure, Donny?"

He gave me a few more details. I cursed myself silently in the rearview mirror for allowing another girl to die before classifying the Cross murder as the work of a serial killer. The exit for Bay Saint Louis came and went, and I continued east along I-10, trying desperately to ignore the guilt that threatened to consume me as I drove.

An hour later I found myself following yet another deputy through a forest. I spied Donny at the far edge of the illuminated crime scene and walked over.

"Here she is," he said, stepping aside to reveal the newest victim.

I knelt beside the young woman, who sat in the same fully clothed posture as Anna Cross had, hands reaching out and resting on spreadeagled knees. The gray flesh of this girl's face gave off a sickly glow: she'd been exposed far longer than the first victim before being discovered. Abnormally thick black reading glasses were perched perfectly on the bridge of her nose. Several swaths of her blonde hair had already begun to fade back to their natural, darker hue.

This time, however, the bloody word *TAN* sat perfectly centered upon her forehead.

One of the CSIs told us her name was Jessica Harrison, a twenty-three-year-old resident of Silver Run, Mississippi. Her driver's license had been found in her back pocket, along with a folded clip of cash. The seventy-eight dollars still on her person had all but nullified the possibility of a robbery-murder.

The victim had been leaned against a large tree stump just a few hundred yards from the highway. The signature of the killing was almost identical in every way to the Cross murder scene, except for the word *TAN* atop the new girl's forehead.

And, this time, the yellow-green Ein Shemer apple was still clutched in the dead woman's hand. Closer inspection revealed a thin rectangular slit on the surface of its peel, too.

"Lucas," Donny's voice sounded behind me, "we had company earlier this evening."

I stood. "What kind of company?"

He shook his head, exasperation clearly evident in his tone. "Before you got here. A crew from *The Times-Picayune* shot some film of the crime scene before we had a chance to seal it off. They took off before we could stop them."

I raised my eyebrows. "You're sure they were from the *Times*?"

He nodded. "Yeah, we ran the plates. Anyway, bastards from the *Times* have already called, asking for more specifics."

"Shit," I said simply. "They'll definitely run something tomorrow."

Donny frowned, twisting the wrinkles of his face like a bloodhound's. "I'm sure they got pictures. They'll screw this whole hot damned investigation up," he said.

"Not necessarily." I looked back at Jessica Harrison's body leaning against the stump. The rigor mortis that caused her hands to sit extended like a beggar's palms also made the green apple clutched in her fingers plainly visible. It was almost a certainty that the news photos had captured the apple in the dead victim's hand.

"But we know they took pictures, Lucas. One of my boys saw them popping 'em with a magnification lens. They're going to give away the signature."

I faced him. "But we still have an ace in the hole."

"What do you mean?"

"They may know about the apple, and will probably tell the world. But they don't know about the razor inside. So even if they do publish photos, we can still weed out any whack jobs that try to claim responsibility. If the real killer does call to confess, or claim responsibility, or taunt us, he'll be the only guy who will mention the razors."

Donny nodded slowly as he listened, and a rare look of relief crossed his features. "I guess you're right."

I turned to take one last look at the body and saw the coroner kneeling beside her, unfolding a body bag. "Hey," I said, catching his attention, "we're done here. When the ME and the photographers are finished, she's all yours. Conduct a full autopsy, but do one other thing, too."

The man looked up and squinted, removing his small, gold-rimmed glasses and wiping them on his shirt. "What's that?"

"Make certain," I said, "that the blood from those letters on her forehead are swabbed individually into collection tubes and sent for DNA analysis. And make sure that a sample from each is sent to the New Orleans field office, too. Okay? Duplicate samples. These guys can give you the info for the second shipment address."

"You got it," said the coroner, replacing his glasses and unzipping the black bag the rest of the way. The muffled sound of thunder pulsed in the distance.

I turned to speak to Donny again, but he'd already moved away and begun conversing with his deputies on the far side of the crime scene. He caught my gaze, so I gave him the familiar two-finger wave from my right temple to signal my departure. He gave it back, but it looked strange and out of place next to the somber cast of his face. Somewhere along the way, a once-jovial gesticulation between friends had become suffused with world-weariness.

I knew that look: it was a look of dread. The same dread that anyone in law enforcement feels whenever they know they've uncovered a perp who's just getting started, just getting warmed up, and there's sure to be plenty of death and despair in the days and weeks to come.

I left without another word to anyone, just as a light rain began to filter through the tops of the trees.

SIX

The sound of a car engine outside my house woke me from a deep sleep later that same night. It took me a few seconds to realize I had driven back from the crime scene and fallen asleep on my living room couch.

Bright lights suddenly cut through the front windows and the sound of tires crunching through the gravel driveway followed. I grabbed my Luger from its holster on the coffee table and moved slowly toward the front door. A rapid series of footsteps clacked across the porch, and a sharp rap on the door echoed throughout the house.

My sister's voice called, "Lucas?"

A momentary relief at the familiar voice quickly gave way to a renewed sense of alarm. My sister lived in Picayune, and she usually didn't drop by for social calls after midnight. Something was wrong.

"Katie, what's the matter?" I asked, hurriedly unchaining the lock and opening the door. "Is everyone okay?"

Katie stared up at me from inside the soggy hood of a navy blue raincoat. She smoothed a wet lock of brown hair away from her forehead. "The girls are fine; they're at a sleepover."

"So what's going on?"

"Tyler just called me. It's Mara. She's disappeared."

I gave a dismissive laugh. "Are you kidding me? You came all the way over to tell me this in person?"

"Tyler's really worried, Lucas. He'd never admit it, but he needs your help." Katie pushed past me and I stepped aside.

"Let Tyler worry, then," I said, closing the door behind her. "It's not my problem anymore. Let him learn to get used to her disappearing acts."

Katie walked around the corner of the vestibule and vanished into the living room. "Come on, I'm frozen from the rain. Make me some hot chocolate."

I wanted to tell my sweet little sister that I was going to bed, that she was welcome to all the hot chocolate in the house and she could shut the door herself on the way out.

Instead, I sauntered into the living room behind her.

Katie called over her shoulder. "Be right back, I have to go to the bathroom." Her footsteps echoed down the hallway into the rear of the house.

I poured water into the teapot and set it on the burner.

Mara Bliss. I'd bumped into her shortly after I moved back down South to transfer into the New Orleans field office. She'd become an art dealer, a successful one, and matured into one of the most beautiful women I'd ever seen. Her deep brown skin had blossomed into a gorgeous complexion, so smooth and soft that it had the same magical effect as seeing a van Gogh—it drew you in, and dared you to touch it. The same day we ran into each other, I'd summoned the courage to ask her to dinner. Much to my surprise, she'd accepted.

Within weeks we were an item, and she single-handedly pulled me through the aftermath of the Alvarez case. For a short time, I thought we had a chance.

But Mara had tons of money, too much time on her hands, and a wild streak that I couldn't have possibly foreseen. She was an unpredictable woman, to say the least. One of her peculiar habits was simply what I called her "disappearing acts." She would leave for days at a time, claiming that she was visiting once-in-a-lifetime exhibitions at one art museum or another.

Toward the end of our relationship she began to spiral into deviant sexual behavior, begging me to follow. Unfortunately the quasi violence that she so craved in the bedroom became too reminiscent of the all-too-real sexual depravation I often battled for a living. Eventually, I had to get out.

The night we broke was memorable for all the wrong reasons. I mainly remembered the kinetics of her wild appearance, made all the more chaotic by her anger. Her brown skin shining in the moonlight, raven-black curls lashing back and forth, seafoam eyes, maroon lips bared in a sneer that made her look like a vampire. She'd gone wild when I broke with her, and immediately began hurling accusations of infidelity, demanding over and over to know who it was, who was I fucking, what whore I was fucking, what tramp. She'd screamed at me in a small park until I realized we'd probably never talk in civil tones again. I walked away from her, uttering one last good-bye that she couldn't have heard above the cacophony of her own hatred.

I never looked back.

Ironically, I learned later that she'd already been seeing my brother for at least a month before I finally decided to end things with her. What a fool I'd been. Last I'd heard from Katie, now more than a year later, Mara and my little brother were engaged.

Apparently Tyler didn't have the same kinds of hang-ups about S&M that his big brother had.

Katie's voice sounded in my ears. "Lucas. Are you listening? This isn't typical. She left with no warning whatsoever. She—"

"You're wrong, Kate. It's *completely* typical. She disappeared half a dozen times for days on end back when we were together. I finally got sick of it. Maybe Tyler will finally wise up, too."

"But nothing's gone. None of her bags are missing. It's like she just vanished into thin air." Katie poured hot water into her cup and sat down at the table across from me.

"Maybe she bought a new suitcase," I finally offered. "Maybe some new clothes. Who knows? Trust me—this is one of Mara's grand disappearing acts. Same old same old. If Tyler's too blind to see it, then he'll have to learn it for himself."

"If something's happened to her you'll never forgive yourself."

I was, in fact, pretty sure that I could indeed find a way to forgive myself, but I kept that to myself. "Okay, okay. I'll call Donny and have Harrison County Sheriff's Department look into it—I promise. But for now can we both just get some sleep? I can barely stay awake. In a couple of days this will all blow over. I guarantee it."

Katie fixed me with an accusatory stare. Every day she looked more and more like our mother. She'd possessed all the features of my father at birth, but through the course of adulthood she'd barreled toward an unavoidable genetic end point. A head full of darkening brown hair, luminous brown eyes and tan skin, cheekbones that arched higher with each passing day—all of her facial structures slowly morphing into something so similar to our mother's prominent features that it was, at times, unsettling.

"Everything will be fine," I assured her.

"Okay. I'm sorry. It's just that I can't stand to see Tyler so worried like this."

My sister's words stung me. I wondered momentarily if she or anyone else had ever felt sorry for me when I went through the same shit with Mara, but I held my tongue. I wasn't about to alienate the one remaining member of my immediate family who still talked to me. "I'll talk to them, I promise. If she hits the twenty-four-hour mark, tell Tyler to file a missing persons report. She's going to show up though, so please also advise him that I personally recommend he skip the missing persons report and just wait for her to pop back up." I held up my hands to ward off any further interjections. "I'll look into it tomorrow, I promise."

Katie took a final sip from her cup and stood. "You're a good big brother . . . despite the immensity of all your shortcomings."

"I'll accept that. Tell the girls I'll see them at their football game this weekend. Are you sure you don't want to stay over, leave in the morning?"

"No, no, I want to get back home. We'll see you this weekend." She kissed my forehead. "Good night, Lucas. Let me know if you hear anything about Mara."

"I will."

I walked her to the door. She walked down the front steps and I watched her until she drove out of the driveway and onto the road.

Back inside the kitchen I sat down at the table, wide awake. Talking with Katie had brought back too many memories of my mother. Desperate to take my mind off them, I tried to think about the case at hand.

For the time being, none of the evidence in the Cross and Harrison cases made much sense, and there was that one particular detail that was growing more troublesome by the moment. If I really was dealing with a serial killer, then it was one who left razored apples as a calling card in the same county where my own mother had been murdered in an apple orchard on a Halloween night twenty years before.

I stood up from the kitchen table and turned out the lights. It was stupid coincidence, nothing more. I couldn't let my imagination run rampant.

In fact, it was just good old shithouse luck, as my grandfather often used to say.

Nothing more. Nothing less.

SEVEN

I found three messages on my cell phone the next morning.

The first was from none other than Jim Raritan himself. Somehow he'd already found out about the second victim and wanted to know whether I was dealing with it, asked in an I-told-you-so voice even more annoying as a recording than in real life. He also wanted to know when I would schedule a briefing for local law enforcement. It was just Jimmy's way of telling me "No slow starts." I could handle it.

The second was a voice from the past. Charlie Bliss, Mara's father, left a terse message asking if I had any news on Mara's whereabouts. When Mara and I were together, Charlie had been a second father to me. But the moment Mara and I broke off, Charlie disappeared from the face of the earth. This was the first I'd heard from him in over a year.

The final message was from *The Times-Picayune.* A reporter wanted to know if I had any statements concerning the "Snow White Killer." I groaned. Apparently they'd put together the similarities between Anna Cross and Jessica Harrison, most notably the apples at the crime scenes and the black hair of the victims. In their endless pursuit of selling more papers, they'd come up with a catchy name for the murderer: the Snow White Killer.

I suspected it would stick. Everything I was involved with lately got a cute name tag to go along with it.

I set the cell phone on the nightstand and hoped that the rest of my day wouldn't annoy me as much as the first five minutes had.

On my morning drive to work I found myself thinking about Mara Bliss. She had been my first kiss, in a graveyard outside my father's first church in Crossroads, Mississippi. I still remembered every detail—the white moon hanging in the sky, the knee-high grass swishing around us, and the intermittent buzzing of cicadas surrounding us. I still remembered how that first silk-lipped kiss had stunned me into inaction, much as the kiss that Halloween night had taken my breath away a few months later.

I was amazed that I could still become lost in the memories of that first kiss, feeling my stomach drop away as she and I crouched only a few feet away from the sepulchre of her dead grandfather, in the middle of that graveyard. Little had I known at the time that in only a few months my mother would be murdered and buried there, too, laid to eternal rest only a few feet away.

The cell phone bleated in my pocket and jarred me from the memory. Ragged breathing greeted me from the other end, hard, desperate, and out of control. Then a hauntingly familiar voice filled my head. "Lucas?"

"Mara?" Though surprised to hear from her, I immediately breathed a sigh of relief as I realized I'd be able to put Katie's worst fears to rest in an I-told-you-so voice all my own. Mara's next words, however, stopped me cold.

"Lucas. I don't want to die like the others. Please don't kill me."

"What?"

"Please come back, Lucas. Please don't kill me like the other girl."

"Mara, what are you talking about?"

Alternating inhalations and deep breaths of sobbing came from the other end. "Lucas, you said you'd act like this, and you told me not to let you do it. You have to come back here and get me. You have to come back to Nana's house."

I tried to interject, but she spoke again.

"She wasn't moving. You told me to read what you wrote on her forehead, but I couldn't see it. Please don't kill me when you come back, Lucas. Please."

The phone line clicked off. A cloying horror rose in the back of my throat as I struggled to assimilate the one-sided conversation.

First, "Nana" was Mara's name for her grandmother. Her grandmother had died years ago, but she'd resided outside New Hope, only twelve or so miles away. Second, Mara had asked *me* not to kill her. In fact, she'd asked me not to kill her "like the others," which meant that for some inconceivable reason she thought I not only wanted to kill her, but that I'd killed someone else as well. Third, and most chillingly, she'd alluded to writing on another woman's forehead.

I swerved into the wide swath of marshy grass separating the north- and southbound lanes of I-10. I turned one hundred and eighty degrees and headed back up the interstate in the opposite direction, back toward Mississippi. New Hope was in Harrison County. I punched Donny's number on my cell phone. "Donny?"

"Speaking."

"It's Lucas. Listen. I just received a strange phone call, and I need to check it out. It was from Mara."

The silence on the other end reminded me: Donny wasn't a big fan of Mara Bliss. "I see."

"Donny. She's been missing for a couple of days now, and she just called me."

"And?"

"And she asked me not to kill her. Not to kill her like the others."

"What the fuck's that supposed to mean?"

"No idea. And that's not everything. She also said that she couldn't read what I'd written on another girl's forehead."

That information had the same effect on Donny as I'd experienced a moment before. "Holy shit. Where are you right now?"

"She said she's at her grandmother's house. I'm on my way right now."

"Where's her grandmother's house?"

"New Hope. Can you guys meet me over there?"

"What's the address?"

"I don't know, but I can remember how to get there. She lived on Wolf Road."

"Aw shit, in the bayou. You can get lost for years out there if you don't know where you're going. Alright, we'll figure it out and meet you there."

I hung up and pressed the gas pedal to the floor. The old familiar panic set in, the frantic despair I hadn't felt since Richmond almost three years ago.

A sign said New Hope was only eleven miles away. I pushed the Explorer to one hundred miles an hour, hoping the incremental increase in speed might actually help me save Mara Bliss.

From a killer who, for some unfathomable reason, she believed to be me.

EIGHT

Fifteen minutes later I pulled my SUV into the weed-choked driveway of her grandmother's abandoned house and jolted to a tumultuous stop. Red dust billowed in all directions as a swirling breeze swept across the yard. I opened my door and exited the vehicle, squinting my eyes but keeping them locked on the house ahead. I held my Luger in one hand, pointing it at the house in what must have seemed a ridiculous fashion, while clutching the two-way radio receiver in the other. Its curly cord tethered me to the dashboard of the parked vehicle like an astronaut on a space walk. I continued to stare at the dilapidated old house, debating whether to call Donny as he'd asked or to go on in alone.

The windows were boarded up tight, but the front door lolled unnaturally and ominously opened. As if it had been pried open only recently. Only thick blackness lay beyond it.

Where Mara, my childhood girlfriend and former lover, now by those strange twists of fate and fancy in adulthood my brother's fiancée, waited inside. A rumble of thunder shuddered in the distance, and I shivered.

I leaned back through the window of my SUV and tossed the radio back onto the driver's seat. I didn't have time to give Donny directions through the labyrinthine back roads of the bayou, and I didn't have time to argue with him about going in alone, either. They'd find the house, eventually.

Mind made up, I walked quickly through the front yard and up the decaying porch steps, pushed the front door open, and crossed the threshold into the house's dark interior.

I found myself in a long foyer. By the time I reached the other end of the hallway, the light from the open front door was a small rectangle of light behind me. I opened the hallway door to the dark inside of the house and waited for my eyes to adjust, but soon realized they never would. Every window in the house was boarded up. There was no light to be had, not even a sliver. I felt about and found a light switch on the wall and flicked it just in case, but did so to no avail. Out of options, I removed a penlight from my side pocket, flicked it on, and slowly advanced toward the small circle of white light shimmering on the far wall.

"Mara?" I said aloud, but her name came echoing back all wrong in the dark. "Murder?" bounced off the walls ahead.

The penlight soon illuminated a doorway across the room that I recognized as the basement door. Basements were an anomaly this far down South, especially in the bayou, but a few old antebellum homes still had fruit cellars. At that moment a thump, barely discernible, echoed from below. And at that moment I realized that ever since the phone call, I'd envisioned Mara underground in a basement somewhere.

Maybe, I thought, it had seemed so because of the echoing quality of her voice on the call. Or maybe it had just been the most frightening place I could have imagined her to be.

I pulled the door open slowly and stepped down the stairs, my boots creaking on the sawdust-covered steps of the cellar. With each step a new, unfamiliar odor of musk and dampness mixed with dozens of other smells mostly impossible to place (honeysuckle, formaldehyde, varnish?) became stronger and stronger. At the bottom the penlight revealed nothing but a rusted water heater. I heard a rustling sound and turned the flashlight to my right.

Huddled in the corner not twenty feet away, Mara sat cross-legged and shivering in a torn dress. Adrenaline released inside me as I realized she was still alive. A dark blindfold covered her eyes, and her wrists were handcuffed to a pipe along the concrete wall. She held a small dark object in her left hand, probably the cell phone from which she'd called.

Her head bobbed nervously back and forth as she strained to hear. She shifted her position on the floor, and the penlight revealed dozens of cuts and abrasions along her legs.

"Mara. It's me. Lucas."

She jerked her blindfolded head in my direction, her feet digging backwards into the dirt floor, compressing herself farther into the corner at the sound of my voice.

After a beat of silence, she began to scream.

The animalistic howl built in intensity and the pitch rose, until the dreadful wail transformed into a high-pitched, continuous shriek that refused to stop. The cellar filled with the sounds of terror.

I couldn't think. The only thing in my head was the screaming, echoing in the damp basement and growing louder each second. Goose pimples rose vehemently on the back of my neck.

"Mara!" I yelled, but to no avail. I couldn't even hear my own voice.

I gave up and scrambled to her.

When I grabbed her shoulders, the screaming finally stopped, as though some newer, deeper fear had taken her breath away. A moment later she coughed and began breathing in great, gasping sobs.

"Mara," I said, "we have to get out of here." I lifted her blindfold with my left hand and attempted a comforting smile as her eyes adjusted to the small beam of my flashlight. "Come on, let's go."

She looked at me, long black streaks of mascara running from her eyes. She was filthy. A gray film covered her body, her raven-black hair lay matted and tangled, and more cuts covered her arms as well as her legs.

The past and all its pain fell away in a moment, and the only thing I felt was compassion, and a desire to save her.

"Lucas," she whispered.

"Mara, it's okay. I promise."

She flinched. "Lucas," she begged, "please don't kill me."

I touched her face and she froze. "What are you talking about? I'm not going to hurt you. But we have to get out of here."

She nodded with a single shake of her head, but remained in a rigor mortis–like state inspired by my touch.

I peered at her a second longer, then looked back at her wrists. "Hold still," I whispered, "so I can get you loose." The handcuffs securing her wrist to the pipes weren't police issued but the cheaper kinds you could get in sex shops. I considered wire cutters from my car trunk, but noticed a weak U-joint in the pipe above her head.

"Lucas?"

"Stay still. I'm going to lift these handcuffs to a point where I can get them off this pipe, okay?" I illuminated the pipe with my penlight, moved her wrists over to the weak U-joint, and pulled.

The crumbling pipe gave way and we tumbled backwards as her wrists pulled free. The penlight fell to the floor, flickered off, and the cellar plunged into darkness. After we landed on the dirty floor Mara's body sprawled across me, her hair across my face. A pain seared through my ankle. I pushed her aside and groped for the flashlight until my fingers closed around it and flicked it on. The beam revealed Mara already sitting above me, staring down as I tried to sit up and speak. "Okay. Let's go, Mara. You're free."

She spoke in a hoarse tone. "No, Lucas. You said you'd do this. You know what you told me to do."

"Mara, I honestly have no idea what you're talking about. Just get off me so I can get up. We need to get out of here."

At that moment footsteps echoed above our heads, and the basement door swung open with a loud creak. I grabbed my Luger but couldn't extricate myself from my vulnerable position beneath Mara. As my fingers found the familiar handle of my gun, a flashlight from the top of the stairs illuminated us where we sat on the floor. I lifted the Luger into the air and tried to twist my torso around to face the light, but I couldn't break free of Mara's entangled limbs.

A voice I didn't recognize called my name from the stairwell. "Detective Madden? This is the Harrison County Sheriff's Department! Detective Madden?" Relief flowed through me. I managed to twist from beneath Mara and we both stumbled to our feet.

"It's me, we're okay," I said, but at that moment a tremendous thud in my back pushed me violently forward. It didn't hurt, and I turned to look backwards at Mara, wondering why she'd pushed me. I tried to inhale and heard a strange gurgling noise. I felt warmth descend and spread along my waistline. I felt like I was tipping.

I landed heavily on the floor a few feet away, face forward. I rolled onto my back. In the darkness I tasted the dirt of the floor and realized that I'd lost the flashlight again.

The warmth continued to descend into my lower back. A burst of light from behind me revealed Mara's face illuminated by the powerful police flashlights. A series of footsteps filled the air, and a strong voice called out, "Police! Drop the weapon!"

The flashlight bobbed up and down on Mara's face. The last thing I remembered was a bloody knife in her still-handcuffed left hand, and her voice filling my head as though I were underwater, as though I were falling away from her into a dark and placid lake of unknown depth.

Her black pupils drew me in, even as I felt myself vanishing into the hole, and her muffled voice descended through the darkness. "You told me to kill you, Lucas, if you came back to set me free. You made me promise that I'd kill you."

With that, she lifted the bloodied knife again, and everything went black.

NINE

Mara leads me through the graveyard of our childhood church, to her grandfather's tomb. Everything is just the way I remember it, except Mr. Horace's mausoleum now sits in the middle of an apple orchard. A familiar one. Though I've never seen the orchard in which my mother was killed, I've reconstructed it a million times.

Mara smiles back at me as we walk through the graveyard. She tugs on my hand, pulling me along.

I suddenly notice that at the base of every tree in the orchard, dead girls with bloody letters smeared across their foreheads stare from all sides.

Ahead of me, Mara's hair covers her face. For a moment I'm struck by the sensation that it might not be Mara who leads me by the hand. And I'm terrified by the immovable certainty that my mother's grave site is our new destination in this displaced orchard of dead girls.

"Mara, where are you taking me?"

She turns, hair still covering her face, but a voice other than her own fills my head, tearing me from the dream.

———

"Going somewhere, Madden?"

I struggled to wake up through the gray haze surrounding me. The steady electronic chirp of a monitor slowly ascended into my consciousness, and the odor of a sanitized environment crept through my nostrils.

I opened my eyes to find Alan Parkman's face suspended above the end of the bed. I tried to understand my surroundings, thinking backwards. The dream. Mara. The basement.

Almost on cue an electric spike of pain crackled up my spine and jolted my short-term memory. I recalled the thud of the knife in my back, and how Mara had assured me that I'd somehow told her to kill me.

I looked around. Two chairs and a table were the sole furnishings in a small hospital room. Parkman sat in one of the chairs, twirling the corner of his mustache above a smile. Without a doubt, one of the last people on earth I wanted welcoming me back from the near-afterlife.

"What's going on, Alan?"

He raised his eyebrows in glee. "Well, hell, Lucas, that's what we all want to know."

"Did Mara stab me?"

"Ah, the short-term memory's intact. Yep, that pretty little thing shoved a knife in your back and was about to hack you to little pieces until the local cops showed up." A smirk crawled across his lips before he continued. "Showed up a few seconds too early, if you ask me."

"Where are we?"

"Gulfport. Garden Park Hospital."

"Why the hell are we in Gulfport?"

"You lost a lot of blood. The EMTs had to get you to a town in Mississippi that could accommodate a blood transfusion. Not many down heah 'round dese pahts," he said, in a mocking, slow Southern accent.

"Why are you such an ass?"

"Why did you tie your girlfriend up in that basement?"

"What the hell are you talking about? I don't have time for this." I tried to sit up, but a blinding pain forced me back onto the pillows beneath me.

"Well, you better make time. Your girlfriend Mara says you're the Snow White Killer." Parkman let the words sink in, stood and walked to the hospital room door and opened it, but then looked back at me. "You may want to call any redneck lawyer buddies you might have down here, when you get a chance."

"You're retarded if you think I'm the Snow White Killer. Mara isn't the world's most reliable witness, you jackass."

Parkman laughed. "No, she isn't, I'll give you that. But funny how that suits you in this situation." He paused. "Hey, I'm going down to get some coffee, then maybe you'll open up about this whole thing, Lucas. Better just admit everything up front. How long has this been going on?"

"Fuck off."

"Ah yes, I think you take cream. I'll be right back."

Ten minutes later he returned with a white Styrofoam cup in hand.

"So, you've had a chance to think about it. Got anything you'd like to admit?" He smiled, not genuinely, and swirled the steaming coffee with a flat wooden stirrer. He stopped, licked it, and tossed the stick into a small trash can near the door.

I managed the most remorseful face I could muster. "Well, Parkman," I whispered, "I'm at the end of my rope." I cast my eyes downward. "Yeah," I breathed, "I guess I do have something to tell you."

My change in attitude caught him off guard. "Really?" he whispered from beneath his mustache.

I cleared my throat, drawing out the admission for as long as possible, just to heighten his sense of anticipation. I half-closed my eyes, and lowered my voice. He leaned even closer, "Parkman. I had sex with your mother last night. She was terrific. A little kinky for my tastes, but a fun gal all the same." I lay back in the bed and smiled up at him pleasantly.

He didn't speak for a moment. He held his left fist clenched at his side until he finally found his voice. "You think you're funny, don't you, Madden?"

I nodded and began to accept the accolade, but he cut me off.

"Look, dummy, we know you didn't do this shit. That girlfriend of yours? She's crazier than a poop-house rat and her story's full of holes. But you won't think it's funny if this gets leaked to the press." He looked back at the door, making sure that he wouldn't be heard, then continued. "They'll have a field day with it. Headlines galore. Just think, little tickers at the bottom of CNN and MSNBC. FBI agent a suspect in the Snow White Killer case. Renowned neuroscientist who cloned the ripper gene, foiled by his own genetic code. The author of *The Killing Mind* thinks he can 'beat the system.'" Parkman paused, letting his imaginary tickers run rampant through my mind. He took a sip from his cup. "I'm not only busting your balls, Madden, although it's been fun. Even if it's all bogus, you're still in a precarious situation." He paused, then added, "Not to mention the FBI."

I gazed out the window instead of humoring him with a response.

Parkman continued. "This is serious, Lucas. Your girlfriend is running around telling everyone that you kidnapped her, raped her, then told her that you were coming back to kill her after you had your fun with the other girl."

"What other girl?"

Parkman frowned. "What other girl? The third victim of your Snow White Killer, about a hundred yards from the granny's house, dumbass."

I sat in stunned silence, taking that information in.

"Anyway, here's the kicker. Your girlfriend claims that you *told* her to call you, because it would give you an alibi when you came back—and she says you told her that when you returned the second time you'd be playing the good guy, pretending to rescue her, protect her. That's her story, at least," he said, "and she's sticking to it."

A knock at the door interrupted us.

"What the hell's going on here? Parkman, you—" The hulking form of Big Jim Raritan appeared in the doorway. "What the hell are you doing in here?"

Parkman pointed at me. "We've got problems here, Jim. We've got an eyewitness who puts Madden—"

Jimmy cut him off. "Yeah, I know all about it. What we have is a rape/kidnap victim who doesn't know which day of the week it is. And Madden has dozens of alibis and witnesses along the timeline."

"That's exactly what I was trying to find out!"

"And the last I checked, you weren't Internal Affairs. Get the hell out of here. Now."

I started to make one last smart-ass comment to Parkman, but Jimmy jabbed a thick, meaty finger toward me. "And you shut the hell up, too. Stay put." He stared at me long enough to make me uncomfortable, then followed Parkman out the door.

I lay back on the bed and tried to assimilate everything I'd just learned. Instead of acknowledging I'd rescued her, Mara was telling everyone I was the Snow White Killer? A piercing pain shot through my back and I suddenly wondered just how badly I was hurt.

Minutes or hours later—it was impossible to tell—a familiar voice awoke me. "Madden. Wake up."

I couldn't immediately focus. I could see the vague shape of Raritan on one side and a tall woman on the other.

Raritan spoke again. "I believe you've already met Agent Woodson?"

I sat up, but a dazzling burst of white shooting stars exploded before me. I lay back down slowly, desperate to avoid exacerbating the pounding in my head any further.

"We've appointed Agent Woodson as the profile coordinator in the Mississippi field office. She's going to be taking over the Snow White Killer case from here forward."

"What?"

Raritan leaned forward and spoke more loudly. "The Snow White Killer case. You're in deep shit here."

"Come on, the crap Parkman was talking about? It's bullshit. Everybody knows that."

Raritan nodded, but this time with a sad, repetitive motion. "Yeah, we do know. But we need to cover our asses, too. No matter how tough I sounded with Parkman, things don't look quite as bright as I painted."

I glanced at Woodson, who immediately looked away.

Raritan spoke again. "We have a victim who claims you did some pretty terrible things to her down in that basement. Everyone knows that it's bullshit, but if it gets out, it could look bad for the Bureau. And a lot of people are asking questions. Like what the hell you were doing going into that house alone?"

"My job?"

"Maybe so, but you're off this case, Lucas," he said with finality. "Once you're discharged, you can continue the rest of your casework, but you're off this case."

After that, Raritan droned on about the Bureau's concern for my health, my mental status. How they knew I'd been working overtime, and so on. But I knew what he was really saying.

Ever since the first Behavioral Science Unit had formed in 1972, the FBI had a collectively recurring nightmare: When would one of their own snap and go off the deep end?

After all, I'd authored *The Killing Mind* and had published a controversial article proposing a tenuous link between DNA and serial killers' behavior.

Everyone in the hospital room knew the real reason they'd taken me off the case. It wasn't the PR bullshit. It was because the Bureau didn't trust me with this case, now that Mara was involved. The potential for me to lose my mind or go off my rocker—that was the true subtext.

"Can I at least find out where Mara is?" I asked. "Is she even okay?"

Raritan glanced at Woodson before answering. "She's okay. But she's not around."

"Where is she?"

"She's over in Slidell. Your brother picked her up. He checked her into a mental health facility down there, somewhere she was already being treated on an outpatient basis. She was raped over a dozen times, Lucas. The other girl, the dead girl, wasn't even touched."

"What other girl? I didn't even know anyone else had been found until Parkman told me." But even as I spoke, I vaguely recalled Mara speaking of another woman when she called me on the phone. The woman with the letters on her forehead.

Raritan sighed. "The police didn't just find you and Bliss in the basement. About ninety yards away in the woods the police found Snow White victim number three."

So Parkman hadn't lied, and Mara really had seen a woman with letters smeared onto her forehead. "Who, Jimmy? And what was on her forehead?"

Jimmy stared at me for a moment, glanced at Woodson, then flipped a small pocket notebook open. "Young girl from Lucedale, name of Patricia Swanson. You don't happen to know her, do you?" he asked.

I shook my head before realizing I shouldn't have even dignified him with a response. "What word did you find on her forehead?"

Raritan folded the notepad closed and put it back in his shirt pocket. "*Cat,* Lucas, although I don't know why I'm even telling you, since you're off this case. But it was *cat.* C-A-T."

"A tan cat," I said aloud, enunciating the growing message from the Snow White Killer. But then something else Raritan had said finally registered with me. "Wait a minute—did you say Mara was raped?"

"Yes. Repeatedly."

I thought suddenly not about the Snow White Killer, but of Mara Bliss. The way Mara had been so terrified in the basement. Now I understood. "Did you guys get a rape kit?"

"Of course."

"Have you done the semen analysis yet?"

Raritan glanced at Woodson again but didn't say anything for a moment. "No, the semen analysis hasn't been finished yet. It looks like her abductor used a condom. We don't think a semen analysis will show us anything anyway."

"Any nonself pubic hair?" I felt the sadness giving way to anger as it became more and more impossible to believe that the victim we discussed was my own ex-girlfriend, that I was an unofficial suspect, and that I was hoping a pubic hair test would exonerate me.

Raritan eyed me closely. "The examiners found no evidence of any nonself pubic hair. Like I said, it was a clean sex crime. Like the unsub knew how to clean a crime scene for evidence." He let the statement hang in the air before continuing.

I closed my eyes as he spoke and wondered if my brother would believe Mara's insane story, or if my father or sister knew about the accusations. I could just see them, talking in hushed whispers about the sad spiral of my life as they sat at the little kitchen table in my father's house and spoke over coffee. A kitchen table I hadn't seen for sixteen years.

Some sort of drugs began to kick in, and it suddenly became impossible to keep my eyes open. Eventually I felt a single tear course over my cheek. A moment later, a warm hand touched my shoulder.

As Raritan droned on and on, I managed to open my eyes, look down at the hand, and follow up the arm. Agent Woodson's hand rested on my shoulder. She watched me with her blue-gray eyes as Raritan talked.

I stared at her without words, even as the seams and fabric of my life seemed to be unraveling and falling apart. Her eyes were soothing and her visage was like the glass surface of a calm and windless lake.

Eventually everything faded away. Raritan finished his long-winded spiel, and the utterly silent Woodson removed her comforting hand from my shoulder.

At the door, Raritan said he'd pick me up when the hospital released me the following day.

Too weak to protest, I fell asleep before the door closed behind them.

TEN

"It started in the Garden of Eden." A familiar voice spoke the words into a darkness, and a fragmented, murmured conversation followed.

"A fruit was the first symbol of evil in the Bible."

More hushed whispers. I couldn't unscramble everything, and though I tried with every ounce of will, still couldn't open my eyes.

"This isn't about a serial killer. This is about the devil. It's always been about the devil, and someday Lucas is going to have to accept it."

And all of a sudden I recognized the voice—my father's. It almost sounded like it emanated from a pulpit, but I knew I wasn't in church. I was in a bed—in a hospital.

It all came back to me. Mara, the knife, Raritan, another victim, Woodson, and my dismissal from the Snow White Killer case.

Why was my father talking about the devil?

I managed to pull an eyelid open.

A dim bedside lamp glowed weakly beside me, leaving the rest of the room in a gray haze. Katie sat on the side of the bed and, to my great surprise, both my brother and my father sat in chairs on the opposite wall as well.

It had been a while since I'd seen my brother, Tyler, but he hadn't changed. Longish blond hair and sharp facial features confirmed his status as the middle-child hybrid who shared the high cheeks of our mother along with the square chin of our father. His face carried cold blue eyes and the professional "unshaven" look that approximated eleven o'clock shadow. He sat in the chair uncomfortably, staring at the floor.

"You awake, sweetie?" Katie patted my leg. "How are you feeling?"

My brother and father leaned forward in their chairs, but neither said anything as they waited for me to speak.

"I'm okay. A little sleepy, but okay."

"You in any pain, son?" my father asked.

I hated to admit it, but his simple inquiry sent a chill down my spine—the good kind of chill, one I hadn't felt in years. We'd drifted so far apart after my mother died. . . . Actually, there was no drifting to it; we had fled from each other at full speed. Her murder had somehow strengthened his faith, while utterly destroying mine. We tolerated each other's presence while I finished high school, and after college I never looked back.

Over the years the bitterness toward my father faded, just as the intense grief I'd once felt for the loss of my mother had equally diminished. He and I had spoken a few times after I moved back down South, but it usually ended awkwardly or just plain badly. We quickly discovered that we weren't good at conversation. Religion often crept up, and whenever it did, things just didn't work out between a religious father and a son wholly devoid of faith.

Lost amidst the swirl of memories, I finally answered his question. "No, Dad. No pain."

"Good. That's good, son."

The room fell silent. "So what were you guys talking about?" I asked. "I thought I was dreaming."

"Oh, nothing. Just a sermon I'm working on. You want to hear about it?"

"No thanks," I said quickly.

My father smiled, but a genuine sadness resided behind his eyes.

"You've always blamed God for everything bad in the world, Lucas. I wish you didn't. Ever since your mother died. Someday I hope you understand that there's something else to blame for that, and that God only wants us to—"

"Dad, for the trillionth time. Don't bring her up. Don't bring her up if you're trying to tell me why a God supposedly exists. Believe me, it just doesn't add up."

My father fell silent, then glanced at my sister. "Sorry, Lucas, it's probably best if I just let you rest. I'm sorry to upset you."

"You're not upsetting me," I assured him. "You're just not getting anywhere with me. But you're right—God's not to blame for Mom's death. Just good old-fashioned shithouse luck. Just like what happened to me here. Cosmically pervasive shithouse luck. That's all."

Katie spoke up. "Lucas, when are you supposed to get out? The doctors told us you were lucky."

Her forced cheeriness stood out like a red blanket on a line of white linens. "They haven't said anything yet. Maybe tomorrow."

"Oh, that's good."

The familiar silence returned. Katie, the only person with enough energy to try and keep us functional, spoke again. "Tyler? How's Mara?"

Tyler spoke for the first time. "She's still recovering at Memorial Oaks."

"Is she still saying that I kidnapped her?" I asked.

My younger brother shook his head, but I could see he was lying. I could tell because when he used to lie about stealing candy or breaking a toy, he would frown. "No," he said, with a furrowed forehead. "She's just trying to work things out now. She's confused."

"I'll say."

Tyler stood, anger suddenly contorting his face. "Or maybe she isn't. Who knows? Maybe all this profiling has finally addled your brain. Did you finally lose it? Again?"

"Tyler," Katie said, but I spoke over her.

"Screw you, Tyler. Go tend to your psychotic girlfriend."

"Fuck you, Lucas. I take better care of her than you ever did."

"That's enough. Right now, I mean it." Our father stood between us. Tyler turned and stormed out of the room, and I suddenly felt like a ten-year-old all over again.

My father walked over and laid his hand on my shoulder. "Get some rest, Lucas. I'm sorry if all of this agitated you. We only meant for you to know we're here for you. I'll pray for your recovery. Hang in there, son."

I almost told him not to bother, but finally relented, amazed at how tiring antagonism could be. "Thanks."

He patted my arm, then left the room. Katie, my sole remaining visitor, regarded me with angry, smoldering eyes.

"Hi, little sis."

"Don't try to be cute. I don't know why you just can't make a little effort, Lucas. A modicum of effort. When will you just get over how our father deals with Mom's death, or whether Mara and Tyler are together now? Believe me, you're better off anyway."

Her anger caught me off guard. "You think I'm the one who needs to get over things? I'm the one with a knife in my back here, in case everyone forgot. Don't even start on me with a guilt trip. You heard Tyler, what he said. I honestly think he wishes Mara had been a little more handy with that knife."

"Lucas, I'd slap you right now if I weren't afraid I'd rip out an IV." She blew a strand of hair out of her face. "Why can't you just try?"

"We're just not a *Little House on the Prairie* kind of family, Katie. After all, my brother's girlfriend just tried to kill me."

"Tyler didn't have anything to do with that. He came in and offered an olive branch, and you just threw it right out the window."

I pressed the button on my armrest. "Sorry, Katie," I said, wincing in exaggerated fashion, "but I'm going to need another shot of morphine. Can you come back tomorrow? By yourself?"

She surprised me by grabbing my arm, regardless of the IV. "You think you can always end things on your terms, don't you? You think it makes you tough and powerful, but it's just a weakness, Lucas. Someday you'll realize it."

"I'm not trying to end things on my terms. I'm just tired. All this excitement, you know."

She let go of my arm. "Don't forget who you're talking to here. You may get away with the smart-ass attitude with other people, but not me." She lifted my chin to make me look at her. "I love you, Lucas," she said. "I just wish you were easier to love."

No matter how hard we fought, or how exasperated we made each other, we never left angry. Katie was my last safe haven in the world. "I love you, too, little sis. Tell Grace and Ally I'm still coming to their homecoming football game. Let them know I didn't forget. Go Cougars, all the way."

Katie smiled. "I will. Now go to sleep." She turned and, with a last glance of mock disapproval, dimmed the lights before leaving. In that moment she reminded me so much of our mother. For an instant I could see our mother's shadowy form leaning into the dimly lit bedroom of my childhood, checking on us every night before she went to bed.

"Good night, Katie," I whispered as the door closed, and I found myself alone in the chilly silence of my hospital room once again.

ELEVEN

A knock on the door the next morning woke me as Raritan, Parkman, and Woodson walked into the room. Parkman wore a smirk on his face, as usual, while Raritan looked serious. Woodson wore the only smile.

"What's going on?"

Raritan clapped his hands together. "You're getting out. You're officially off the hook. Your girlfriend—"

"Ex-girlfriend," I said, before having the sense to keep my mouth shut and listen.

"Your girlfriend Mara Bliss has been diagnosed with dissociative identity disorder. Her psychiatrist's current theory is that she's replaced whoever truly did this to her with you, because you're a significant person from her past.

"Her timeline inconsistencies, the various eyewitnesses who saw you before and after her abduction, and her psychiatric evaluation all put you officially off the hook, end of story. Despite what I said yesterday, you're back on the case."

I let out a barely perceptible breath. No longer being the prime suspect in Mara's abduction was good news. Being reassigned to the case was nothing short of a miracle.

"In fact, both the Louisiana and Mississippi field offices are going to work together from here on out, since victims have come from both states. So you and Agent Woodson will be working it together."

"But this was my case."

Raritan's lips tightened. "I've almost been ripped a new asshole because of all this and you're questioning me? Let me repeat myself. You have a partner in this investigation, and you're not working in a vacuum anymore. At all, ever again. The Mississippi and Louisiana field offices will cooperate fully on this one."

I almost threw in a fart joke in reference to his new asshole, but caught myself in the nick of time.

Raritan kept talking. "Anyway, bottom line, you're getting out of here. When you're up to it, you and your new partner here should go over to the morgue and interview the ME regarding the newest victim. Woodson will take you to the morgue then back to your residence, just to make sure you get back in one piece. We already had the towing service transfer your vehicle back to your place, so you need a ride anyway."

"One second," Woodson started to protest, but Raritan smiled curtly toward her.

"All part of being a good partner," he said, turning his attention back to me. "Parkman and I are off to San Diego. They have three missing kids in six weeks out there and it doesn't look good. So you two keep us informed of what goes on down here. We also need an official FBI interview with Mara Bliss. She's the only person to ever see this guy and walk away from it so far. I'll leave it up to you to figure out how to extract any information from our favorite witness. Good luck trying to see her yourself."

I shrugged, but didn't say anything.

"Anyway, work up a profile and set up a debriefing for the locals. We'll videoconference in, probably from Quantico by that time." He glanced at the bandages on my side. "The doctors tell us you're very lucky. The blade penetrated a couple inches deep but somehow missed vitals. You should be fine in no time. You're infection-free and ready to go. Get a shower. They're bringing up your release papers in a half hour. We'll talk to you both once we're settled in San Diego."

They turned to leave. "Jimmy," I called after him. "Thanks."

Raritan paused at the door, but didn't turn around. "By the way, somebody in the police departments down here has a big mouth." As if it was choreographed, Parkman tossed the daily edition of *The Times-Picayune* onto the bed as he walked past. I turned the folded paper around and read a front-page story.

When I looked up again, Raritan and Parkman were gone. Only Woodson stood there, regarding me in silence.

The headline from that day's paper ran in big, black letters:

SNOW WHITE KILLER STRIKES AGAIN

The front-page article included a photo of Donny frowning among a sea of microphones as he addressed the media. It described the identification of a third victim of the so-called Snow White Killer. It read slim on details and I noticed, thankfully, that it mentioned neither my name nor Mara's. Somehow Donny and his boys had managed to keep our incident in the basement under the radar.

Woodson nodded her head toward the doorway. "I'm going down to the cafeteria. You want anything?"

Her words shook me from the newspaper story. "What? Oh, yeah, actually. I'm dying for a cup of coffee. I'm going to have to go into rehab if I don't get some caffeine into my system soon. You mind?"

"Not a problem. Be back in fifteen," she said, and walked out the door.

I swung my legs over the side of the bed. I realized for the first time that my IVs were gone, and I felt good enough to stand. I walked to the bathroom and disrobed.

In the shower stall I tried to prepare myself to step back into the world of the Snow White Killer as the water thudded against my neck. For some reason my mother's face floated into my mind instead, her face still wearing that upside-down smile as she waved nervously to me that night twenty-plus years ago, before she turned to follow that boy into the forest.

My mother's death wasn't the work of a serial killer, all parties had concluded. I'd investigated every piece of information exhaustively with every free moment back when I'd worked in the Behavioral Analysis Unit. And they were right; it didn't look like the work of a serial killer, either. My mother and those boys could have stepped into a drug deal gone sour, an escaped convict, or a cult of Satan worshippers, for all I knew. Impossible to say. But they'd definitely found themselves in the wrong place at the wrong time, and paid the ultimate price. That summed up the long and short of it. End of story. Happened every day, as a matter of fact.

Cosmically pervasive shithouse luck.

The shower suddenly grew colder around me, and I scrambled to turn off the faucet.

I'd just finished changing into my clothes when Woodson materialized in the doorway, two cups of steaming coffee in one hand and a large yellow envelope in the other.

"Here." She held the bulky envelope out toward me.

I took it and peered inside. My badge, my holstered Luger, and my wallet. Tools of the trade.

"Thanks," I said, slipping the wallet into my back pocket. I was still stiff and tried to slip the holster around my chest and shoulder, to no avail. Woodson stepped forward.

"Here. Let me." She slipped the leather loop of the holster strap over my shoulder and I managed to push my arm through. She reached into the bottom of the envelope and held my badge toward me. "Don't forget this."

"Thanks, Woodson."

"Don't mention it."

A nurse opened the doorway behind us and we turned as she spoke. "Dr. Madden? I'm here to take you downstairs. You have to leave in the wheelchair."

I started to protest, but knew it would be futile after seeing the look on the attending nurse's face. I took my seat in the wheelchair, and Woodson led us out of the hospital.

Fifteen minutes later I sat in the passenger seat of Woodson's sleek Audi as she wove her way along Highway 49 and headed north out of Gulfport. "You look pale," Woodson said. "Do you want me to pull over?"

"I'm fine, Agent Woodson."

She glanced over as she slowed down for a red light ahead. "Please, call me Roslyn."

"Hey, if you want me to be informal with you, I'll just call you Woodson. Last names are just my way, if you don't mind."

"Fine, fine *Madden*." She emphasized my last name as she gunned the accelerator. "By the way, *Raritan*," she said, demonstrating her mastery of the new nomenclature, "wants us to go straight to the morgue. So what's the best way?"

"Well, *Woodson*, take Highway 49 north. It's straight up about twenty miles."

She cut in front of a dilapidated pickup truck with an angry honking horn. She shrugged and looked over apologetically. "Sorry. I learned to drive in downtown DC."

I shook my head. "Just remember you're in Mississippi now. Nobody needs to get anywhere fast. Not even us."

"You Southerners are just so laid-back. I don't know how you stand it."

"Y'all Southerners," I corrected her. "And please note that about half of us laid-back Southerners carry loaded guns in the gun racks of our pickup trucks down here. So please try to be considerate, Agent Woodson, as you share the road with us."

I watched out of the corner of my eye as Woodson glanced into the rearview mirror to find out whether there was a gun rack in the truck behind us.

I couldn't help smiling.

A few minutes later I struck up another conversation. "So, Woodson, you know *my* story. But how did *you* wind up in the FBI?"

Woodson shrugged. "To tell the truth, your book *The Killing Mind* had something to do with it, actually."

"Oh stop."

"No, it really did. In fact, I read your book while I was in medical school, of all places."

"Oh yeah, I forgot, Bob mentioned you'd gone to medical school, too. So what inspired you to leave the path of the Hippocratic Oath?" I leaned over as if taking her into confidence. "Our new line of work pays a lot less, by the way."

Woodson smiled, but it was forced. "Why I left the path? During my last year of medical school, my roommate didn't come home from a date one night."

"Uh-oh."

"I figured she decided to stay over at her boyfriend's. The police found her two weeks later, washed up on the banks of the Chattanooga River in a garbage bag. Actually two bags."

"Oh. I see."

She waved me off. "We weren't even that close," she said, "but it affected me. It was something equal parts sorrow and fear, and wouldn't go away. I became obsessed—not with the murder but the murderer. What could drive someone to saw a body in half? What was the rationale, however twisted? How could he be caught?"

"If it's any solace, Woodson, I know what you mean. How did you eventually get connected with the FBI?"

"I called the number," she said, with another forced laugh. "I mean, I went online and called the career opportunities phone number. A month later . . . wait, how did you put it again? I was getting my ass whipped into shape in Hogan's Alley."

In the wake of her unexpected honesty, I considered telling her about my mother and the real reason I'd joined the FBI, but didn't. Instead

I simply nodded along. "A lot of profilers have a story like that. It's just part of who we are, I guess."

She sighed. "I guess so."

We drove on in silence after that, and the red clay hills and groves of skinny pines flew past. After a while I risked another glance over at Agent Woodson, this time noticing the graceful, almost hypnotic curvature of her bare neck.

Two MDs, and not a stethoscope between us.

TWELVE

Half an hour later we arrived at the Stone County morgue.

Donny greeted us at the entrance of the small brick building as we walked up. "Looking pretty good, all things considered."

I shook his extended hand, wincing slightly at the movement. "Wasn't serious, they tell me."

Donny grunted his disbelief. Ordinarily he would have had plenty more to say on the topic of Mara Bliss, had we been alone. Instead, he simply nodded agreeably in Woodson's direction. "Don Noden, Harrison County Sheriff's Department."

"Nice to meet you, Sheriff," Woodson replied, extending her hand. "I'm the profile coordinator for the Jackson field office."

Donny glanced at me as he took her hand, just long enough to betray his surprise. "Nice to meet you, too," he offered amiably, then spat a wad of tobacco juice to the side.

It was his way of letting Woodson know that no matter who might be the newest FBI profile coordinator in Mississippi, he wouldn't be changing his mode of operating one bit. Including spitting at will, whenever he felt like it.

"Well," he said, wiping his lower lip with the back of his hand, "I pulled the evidence documents and crime scene photos." He withdrew a crisp manila folder from his jacket and handed it to me. "They're doing the autopsy now. Y'all ready?"

"After you two," I said, flipping through the charts and walking slowly behind as Donny led us through the front doors of the morgue.

We took an elevator to the bottom floor, where the overpowering pungency of formaldehyde instantly transported me back to classes in gross anatomy.

Donny led us into a small surgical room with a lime-green tiled floor and a copper drain in the middle. An array of empty metal gurneys sat scattered in disorderly fashion about the room. By the time we'd made it halfway across, a jolly little medical examiner stepped away from a body on one of the metal tables in the rear of the room and navigated the empty gurneys towards us.

"Agents Woodson and Madden, pleasure to meet you." He snapped off a rubber latex glove and extended his hand. "I'm Dr. Wilkins. I was just about to get started back there when you called."

Woodson shook his hand. "You mind if we have a look at the body and ask you a few questions before you start your autopsy?"

The coroner looked at Donny, who nodded. "Oh, sure you can. Take photos if you like. Let me know if you have any questions."

We walked through the maze of empty gurneys and surrounded the victim under the lights in the rear of the room. Woodson asked all the right questions, impressing me with her knowledge of procedure and protocol. She clarified the body temp at the time of discovery, the temperature outside, the estimation of time of death prior to the body's discovery, whether he'd found any evidence of entomological activity, and a host of other parameters.

As the ME gave her all the information, I looked down at the girl on the table.

Based on the manila folder, I was staring at Patricia Swanson, a twenty-six-year-old single. She had a closely cropped hairstyle, thick and wavy dark brown hair, and deep brown eyes. Brunette, I noted, which immediately removed a possibility that the SWK was targeting a specific "look." Those kinds of killers are focused in their own right, but for some inexplicable reason I had a feeling that the look for which the SWK searched transcended simple traits like hair color or appearance.

It was evident that Swanson was a victim of SWK, even if I hadn't already seen the telltale photographs of the apple and the extracted razor. The number of cuts on the young girl's body approximated those seen on the other victims, and again, no defense wounds on the wrists, forearms, or hands. Just cuts. Long ones, deep, drawn out, almost in perfect straight lines.

I suddenly realized no bloody lettering remained on Swanson's forehead, even though Jimmy had mentioned they'd found the word *cat* on her forehead when he told me about the victim at the hospital.

"What happened to the word on her forehead?" I asked aloud, with more urgency than I'd intended.

Wilkins looked at me, stopping midsentence with Woodson. "Forehead?"

"Yes. There were letters in blood written on her forehead at the crime scene. Where are they now?"

Wilkins pulled the corners of his mouth down in an exaggerated "whoops" kind of way. "That's why I mentioned I'd just begun the autopsy. We already removed that blood."

"Are you kidding—" I began, but Donny cut me off.

"Don't worry, Lucas," Donny said. "Terry had them swab the letters at the crime scene, long before the body arrived here. He called me as soon as he heard about the third victim and asked me to personally make sure the CSIs took samples."

I exhaled in relief.

"Oh yes, they took several swabs at Sheriff Noden's request," Wilkins added. "But, if you don't mind my asking, what do you expect to find?"

"I don't know. I just want to find out whether it's the victim's blood or someone else's. A quick set of STRs should tell us."

"But whose blood would it be, if not the victim's?"

"Like I said, I don't know. I just have a hunch, that's all." I didn't feel like going into my entire theory.

Wilkins raised his eyebrows. "Maybe the killer's?"

"Maybe," I said, glancing from Donny to Woodson. "Maybe."

We didn't stay around for the rib cage excision and organ weighing and the rest of it. If it turned out like the autopsies of the other two victims, nothing new would be found. Cuts on the body, nearly linear ones, with no defensive hand wounds. Bloody lettering on the forehead, and an apple with a razor in it. That would constitute the extent of the useful physical evidence on the body.

Donny, Woodson, and I reconvened at a small table on the upper floor.

"So, what's the plan of attack?" Donny asked.

I shook my head. "Victim number three and we're already not learning anything new about this killer anymore. He doesn't seem to be evolving. It's like he popped out of the woodwork with the full complement of an organized killer's skills. We'll check ViCAP again, see if he may have moved here from some other area. But it doesn't look promising."

"You think that DNA analysis from the bloody lettering on this girl and the other victims is going to show up as nonself?" Donny asked.

I shrugged. "It's fifty-fifty. But it would be a break for us, in a case where we desperately need one. I'm starting to second-guess myself a little, but we should know one way or another today. If the DNA in the lettering is nonvictim, but matches across the different victims, then we'll know. If that happens," I looked at Woodson, "we'll be able to run a genetic profile on DNA that's likely being left behind by our very own killer."

"You're going to perform that technique you talked about in your lecture, the one that predicts behavior?" Woodson asked.

I nodded. "Yep. And Donny, we're going to hold a debriefing on the three victims when I get settled back down in New Orleans. Unfortunately, you're invited."

Donny's familiar frown came out. "I'd rather sit this one out, if I had my druthers."

"Wouldn't we all," Woodson said simply.

I glanced up, but my new partner was already looking out a window, lost in thought. Usually a new agent would be champing at the bit to get started on a high-profile serial killer investigation. To this point I'd actually considered myself a lone anomaly in the criminal profiling world, with my inherent hesitation to engage in a serial killer case until faced with undeniable facts.

Maybe Woodson and I had more in common than I'd originally suspected.

We talked with Donny for another fifteen minutes, mainly about logistics of the upcoming debriefing—where and when it would be held, who'd be attending. We agreed to wait on it until Woodson and I had a chance to interview Mara to try and discover if she had any descriptions or other insights into the killer, since she was the only victim to have survived an encounter with the Snow White Killer to date. We decided to set up the debriefing at the New Orleans field office in two days' time. All of the local law enforcement in the local counties and parishes where victims had been found would send representatives.

We bade Donny farewell. In the parking lot I climbed, with a good bit of difficulty, into Woodson's car and noticed that the sun was just beginning to dip below the trees.

I faced her as she entered the driver's side. "Listen, Woodson. I know I'm not in very good shape here. But have you had a home-cooked meal since you arrived down South?"

"Nope. After I drop you off tonight I'm driving back up to my hotel in Jackson, then turning around and driving back down tomorrow for our interview in Slidell. Nothing but McDonald's for me tonight."

I shook my head. "Hold on. You're not driving all the way back up to Jackson just to sleep in a hotel room because your name's on the reservation. Cancel it," I said, "and for all the chauffeuring you're doing, I'll cook you my homemade jambalaya. You can stay at my house tonight."

"Thanks but no thanks. It doesn't seem proper. And you need rest. You look like you're stiffening up."

I waved her off. "That's why they gave me painkillers. And don't worry about that, anyway. I have way too many bedrooms in that old house and you can stay in any one that suits you. Honest," I continued, "I'm just trying to do the polite thing here. There really is plenty of room. I mean, as long as you're not allergic to dogs."

"I'm not allergic to dogs, but I don't know. I wouldn't want to impose."

"You wouldn't be imposing. Sorry, Woodson, but it's the least I can do after you've had to cart me around today. I can't let you drive all the way back each way just because Jimmy had you bring me down here. This way, we both get a good night's sleep and a fresh start tomorrow, a whole hell of a lot closer to that mental hospital in Slidell." I paused. "What do you say?"

She cut her eyes to stare at my side, letting several seconds pass before she answered. "You're sure it's not an imposition? And that you're up to it?"

"Sure on both counts."

"Okay," she said, adding, "I have to admit that it'll be nice not to have to drive another three or four hours tonight."

"Would've been closer to five," I said. "Okay then, it's settled." I pointed out my window. "You'll want to take a left out of the parking lot."

Woodson turned the ignition. "You got it."

THIRTEEN

Half an hour later the bright lamps along I-10 gave way to the infrequent mile markers dotting Highway 43 as the gray asphalt disappeared into the black night ahead. I gave Woodson a steady series of directions, taking us farther off the beaten path until she couldn't stand it any longer. "How the hell far out do you live?" she finally asked.

"I told you, I live a little ways out. You can't expect skyscrapers in a place called Bayou La Croix."

"You call this a little ways out?" Woodson swooped her head in a wide arc, as if accusing the entirety of the black forests and swamps surrounding us as she drove.

I shrugged. "I have two dogs and plenty of room for them to run. I have seven wild outdoor cats that consider my porch their home. And I have a red-tailed hawk named Theta who probably can't wait for Ellie to stop feeding her deer meat and for me to take her out hunting in the woods."

"Ellie?

"A veterinarian friend of mine who's taking care of Theta for me. She lives down the road from me, about a mile from where I live."

"And that qualifies as a neighbor?"

"Oh yeah. My closest one, in fact. Like I said, I live a little ways out."

Woodson sighed in false exasperation—she couldn't hide a smile even as she shook her head.

"Okay," I said, "see up ahead, past that oak? My driveway's on the right, just past it."

"Those are quite the directions," she said, turning into the driveway. As she did, the four columns of the old antebellum house appeared in the headlights. We rolled beneath the cypresses on either side and stopped in the U-shaped cobblestone drive in front of the porch.

"Oh my God, Lucas. It's beautiful," Woodson said as we exited the car and walked up the steps.

"I like to think so. Thanks."

A loud series of muffled barks ensued.

"Hush, Watson," I said toward the door as I pushed my key into the lock.

"Your dog's name is Watson?" Woodson asked behind me.

"Yeah. My other dog's name—"

"Don't tell me it's Crick."

"You got it."

"You named your dogs Watson and Crick? After the discoverers of the DNA double helix?"

"Sure," I said, turning the key. "I was a geneticist in a former life. The names sound good together anyway. I always call them both at the same time."

Woodson laughed aloud again. "Oh, I can just hear it now." She cupped a hand to her mouth. "Watson and Crick, come and get it!"

I pushed the front door open tentatively and entered the foyer, but before I could flip the light switch, Watson jumped up and knocked me backwards. An instant later, a thud pounded the floor behind me.

"Ouch! Shit!"

I found the light switch a moment later, only to reveal Woodson sitting awkwardly on the floor, her long legs splayed in the most unprofessional of poses. "Are you okay?" I asked, looking quickly away.

"Yeah, I slipped on something." She picked up a handful of envelopes from the floor. "What's all this stuff? Animal Rescue League, Defenders of Wildlife, SPCA?" She stopped and stared up at me.

I knelt down, Watson nuzzling against me gently as I helped Woodson gather the mailings. "I get a lot of junk mail," I said. "I left a pile of it beside the door to take to recycling. Sorry." I pulled away from Watson as he repeatedly tried to lick my face. "Stop it, Watson," I said, just as he shot a tongue straight into my mouth.

Woodson laughed. "Gross."

I wiped my mouth. "No, no. We're all family here."

Woodson smirked. "Yeah. Except at least one family member here also likes to lick their own ass."

It was my turn to laugh. "You have a point. Not a dog lover, then?" I asked, pulling her up to a standing position again.

"No, no. I like dogs. I just don't let them French me."

At that moment Crick came padding down the hall without so much as a glance in Woodson's direction. Neither of them really met the criteria of a guard dog. Crick, my lazy Irish setter, would probably fall asleep in the middle of a break-in, whereas Watson would only be in danger of trying to *lick* an intruder to death. Crick's boisterous counterpart was still desperately wagging his tail with great fervor as Woodson rubbed beneath Watson's chin.

"Hi there, Crick." I limped over and rubbed the older dog gently, the way he liked to be rubbed under his chin. With Crick receiving all the attention from me, Watson couldn't stand it. He abandoned Woodson and leaped toward me, jumping around and nipping at both Crick and me, growls of excitement emanating from the younger dog's throat. "Settle down, Watson," I said, giving him a final scratch on the head.

I finally looked up at Woodson, who stood silently in the foyer staring at us. I brushed the fur off my clothes and nodded toward the staircase. "Sorry, Woodson. We're not used to having visitors. Where are my manners? Let me show you the guest rooms."

Woodson stepped backwards, eyeing me suspiciously. "One last time—are you sure this isn't too much of an imposition? I could still drive back to Jackson."

"Woodson! I live with two dogs and seven cats. It's impossible for you to 'impose' on someone who has absolutely no life whatsoever. Really. We can trade war stories over dinner. No worries, once and for all."

"Okay. As long as you're sure."

"I'm sure. Come on, and I'll show you where you can wash up." I stepped onto the first step of the old oak staircase and the dogs padded up the stairs expectantly.

With a final sigh, Woodson shook her head and followed.

After a dinner of jambalaya that had sent Woodson into several irrepressible bouts of praise, we retired to the living room. I had told Woodson about some old cases over dinner and was looking forward to continuing our conversation and learning more about her.

I went into the kitchen and grabbed another beer, bringing one back for Woodson. She was sitting on the couch and holding a picture frame. "So when's the last time you saw them?" she asked. "Your parents?"

I looked at Woodson for a moment, then looked away, focusing on an old German cuckoo clock above the mantle. "Well" I said, "my mother died when I was pretty young. After that my father and I sort of . . . drifted apart. I don't see him too much anymore."

Woodson closed her eyes. "Oh, I'm sorry, Lucas. I knew that. I'm stupid. I forgot. Sorry."

"What do you mean?" I asked. "Forgot what?"

"Jimmy had already told me about your mom before he partnered us up. I just forgot."

"Really? And just what did Jimmy tell you?"

"I can't really remem—" she started to say, but I cut her off.

"No, I bet you can remember. Why don't you just tell me what else you know?"

Woodson shifted on the couch. "Nothing else, really. It's not necessary."

"I think it is."

Woodson sighed. "All I know is she died on a Halloween night back in 1983. She and two other boys in the woods were murdered. No suspects ever found."

"Yeah? That's it? Sounds like Raritan gave you the whole story."

"Lucas, I didn't mean to—" Woodson began, but again I cut her off.

"No, you summed it up pretty good," I said. "Pretty lady gets killed, nobody knows why, nobody cares after a while."

"Maybe that's why you're a profiler for the FBI."

"No, that's why I don't trust anybody, ever." I stared at her. "So I bet you heard all about Mara and my brother, too?"

The shift of her body weight told me everything I needed to know. "No."

It wasn't even a good lie. I stood and nodded toward the mantel and the clock above it. "Hey, listen, you know, it's getting pretty late. We've got a big day tomorrow. Probably best if we just turn in."

Woodson shrugged, ill at ease. "Sure. I guess so. So you're finished talking tonight, Madden?"

I patted my leg and Watson jumped down to the floor. "Oh, yeah, can't keep my eyes open for a minute longer. The guest bed is upstairs on the left, all made up. Make yourself at home, like I said. I'll see you in the morning."

I walked up the steps without another word, surprised by what felt like an angry blood flow still pulsing through my fingertips as I gripped the circular banister.

Woodson called from behind. "Good night, Madden."

I pretended not to hear.

FOURTEEN

The next morning I decided it would be a lot easier to deal with my red-tailed hawk than to face Woodson after our unpleasant conversation from the night before.

Watson and Crick accompanied me outside, and we padded silently through the dew-laden grass toward the outdoor shed in the backyard housing the captive bird. My feathered ward watched me warily as I entered the mew, her hungry eyes darting back and forth between my face and the piece of rabbit meat in my gloved hand. After a few more seconds of indecision, she finally flapped twice and landed on my wrist. Once settled on my hand, she tilted her head and stared back at me, waiting for me to open the glove.

I never tired of looking into the wild, golden-flecked eyes of the hawks I rehabilitated. I always found myself wondering what went through their tiny skulls as each bird struggled to assimilate everything—the leather jess around her leg, her strange new environment, the ultralight cast on her broken wing, or the human staring at her only six inches removed from her razor-sharp beak. A human who faithfully fed her, gave her water, and attempted strange-sounding communications while she ate.

Maybe the profiler in me just couldn't resist the desire to try to peer inside a mind, even if it belonged to another species.

After another few moments of the staring contest, I revealed the piece of rabbit meat in my gloved fist. Theta mantled above the snack, spreading her wings to cover her quarry on either side. After a last cock of her ever-suspecting head, she snapped her head toward the meat, using her talons to pin the meat to my glove. As the sharp and shiny black claws tightened into my wrist, I watched as Theta began to use her beak to rip the meat into edible pieces.

"She trusts you, huh?"

The voice startled us both. Theta flapped her wings unsteadily, and we both turned to face Woodson, who peered through the caged front of the mew. I shrugged. "I guess so. Hey, listen, about last night."

Woodson cut me off with a wave of her hand. "Don't mention it, Lucas. You don't need to say anything. I'm sorry it even came up. Not my business."

I started to respond, but let it go. There wasn't much more to say. Instead, I nodded toward Theta, to answer Woodson's question. "You're right, she's pretty trusting. Got her wing clipped on the highway. I've never seen a hawk like this. Doesn't seem afraid of humans at all."

"I wish I could get used to them," she said.

"Red-tailed hawks?"

"No," Woodson said. "Humans."

"Yeah. I know what you mean." I lifted Theta back to the perch. "I'm all finished here. Give me a few seconds to wash up, then we can get going."

"Take your time," she said. "I'm in no rush. C'mon, Watson and Crick," she called, "let's go rustle up some breakfast for everyone."

I stared after her as she walked back with a dog on either side of her, feeling more ashamed than ever. After leaving her last night, I'd quickly realized that I was mainly upset with myself, and maybe Raritan. But not Woodson. I'd had every opportunity to share my own sad story with her back when she'd confided her roommate's story to me, but I'd chosen not to be equally forthcoming. So Raritan had beat me to it instead. It had definitely been a case of shooting the messenger last night, and I'd clearly been in the wrong.

And yet, here this woman was, greeting me and then walking back into my house without the slightest hint of hostility, calling my dogs, preparing to make breakfast for us all.

I left the mew, locked the door behind me, and walked back through the wet grass toward the house. I realized I'd been assigned a solid partner for this investigation, and I had the good sense to know I shouldn't fuck it up for a change.

I opened the back door and called out. "Woodson. I need to talk to you."

The apology went swimmingly, with Woodson reassuring me that none was in order and me overruling her that indeed it was. Afterwards, we sat down and enjoyed a delicious breakfast before preparing ourselves for the day's investigation.

I was desperately relieved to begin the morning on a far better note than the previous night had ended on.

An hour later we were on Highway 90 and headed down to Mara's psychiatrist's office in Slidell. A bit later we passed the gas station where I'd received the eerie phone call from Mara that had set so many events in motion, and I pointed it out to Woodson.

Woodson spoke in a nonchalant tone as the marshy landscape rolled past. "So what's the story with you and Mara Bliss, anyway? All Raritan told me was that she's your ex-girlfriend and now she's with your brother." She looked at me for a second. "Honest."

I smiled. "No worries. Let's see. I met Mara in fourth grade. She and her mother attended my father's church."

"Why do you put it like that? She and her mother? No father?"

"Her father was an atheist." I smiled as I thought of Charlie. "Ironically, despite that, he and my father were best friends back then and are best friends to this very day."

"Really? Your minister father and an atheist? Sounds like it could be a sitcom."

"It is, sometimes. I haven't kept up with him. Mara's father, I mean. But Katie, my sister, sees the two of them from time to time playing chess in the little park in front of the courthouse. They still bicker and argue about religion, but they leave it at that. I guess they find common ground elsewhere."

"So you've known Mara since you were a kid?"

"No. I mean, we knew each other from fourth through eighth grade, but then her dad moved their family and I didn't see her again for almost twenty years."

"How did you run into her again?"

"Sheer chance, right after I transferred to the New Orleans field office. About three months after my relocation I ran into her one night in the Quarter."

"Is that when you two became involved?" Woodson slipped the comment into our conversation without the slightest pause, and I in turn didn't let on that I'd noticed.

"Pretty much. She lived in Biloxi and was a professor at William Carey. She taught classes in the development of the American novel and wrote stories for magazines like *Esquire* and *Story*. I found the adult version of Mara intriguing, and she seemed interested in my profession as well. We started seeing each other."

"Is she still a professor?"

"No, she went full time into art collecting. She started a couple of galleries in New Orleans, which became one of the reasons she'd take off on her frequent trips to the city. I only saw the inside of a few of the art exhibits, but I read all the reviews. They were usually well received. It's what she was doing when we split up, and I don't think it's changed. She met my brother a little while later and they hit it off." I tried to relate the ending of the story with as much nonchalance as Woodson had used to initiate it.

We were silent for several minutes after that, until Woodson spoke up again. "Lucas. I've been wondering something. How do you think the Snow White Killer knew where Mara's grandmother lived?"

"Yeah. Good question," I answered, as we made a left onto a paved driveway leading through a grove of trees to Memorial Oaks. "In fact, it's one of the main questions I intend to ask Mara today."

A few minutes later we were buzzed through monstrous black iron gates and wound our way through a dense enclave of oaks and pines. The paved driveway eventually opened into a small, sparsely populated parking lot in the middle of a shaded grove of trees. Memorial Oaks was a modern-day castle set on rolling hills thick with perfectly manicured, lush green grass.

"Nice," Woodson remarked as we walked to the front entrance. To our left a concrete pavilion housed a series of stone benches encircling a fountain, replete with a sculpted marble deer and fawn drinking lazily from a brook.

"First your house, now this place. No wonder the South holds so many secrets."

"Too many, sometimes," I said as we walked past the fountain and up the steps to the entrance of the main building. The inside foyer bore yet another fountain in the middle of a glossy black marble floor. We signed in with an older security guard behind a maple desk, who directed us to the third floor.

From the elevator we walked down the hallway and made our way to the final door. A brass nameplate reading JAMES A. KINSEY, MD, hung beside it.

I knocked and a deep voice answered. "Come in."

Dr. James Kinsey stood in an outer reception area, waiting for us. He was a tall, well-dressed man about my age, with a head full of prematurely gray hair, thick-rimmed black glasses propped on the bridge of his nose.

"Hello," he said, "and please excuse the appearance around here.

It's my administrative assistant's day off." He nodded toward the empty desk on our right. "But please, come in." He led us from the reception area into his own office, turned, and extended his hand.

Woodson shook it firmly. "Dr. Kinsey. Thank you for meeting us on such short notice."

Kinsey waved her off. "Anything to help Mara."

As he mentioned her by name, the reality hit me that this Kinsey character might also be very well acquainted with our sordid past. The whole world might as well know, I thought sourly, and tried to focus. "Well, I'm sure you know why we're here."

"I do. Please." He gestured to the two leather chairs in front of his maple desk and walked around the corner of the desk to sit in his own high-backed leather chair.

I took a moment to look around his office. Famous reproductions hung between the bookcases. Michelangelo's *The Creation of Adam* hung behind Kinsey's desk, while a *Houses of Parliament* by Monet hung to the left. The glass-paned bookshelves protected rows upon rows of journals: *The American Journal of Psychiatry, Neuron,* and *Journal of Molecular Neuroscience,* the latter two being journals in which I'd actually published during my former life as a neuroscientist.

For a moment I felt like I was peering into what life could have been like for me, had I chosen to live in the sanctuary of a medical profession or an academic career. The serenity of Kinsey's existence almost stupefied me. It seemed so foreign to the violent world of criminal profiling that had become my own way of life.

Stethoscopes and microscopes. I'd traded the pursuit of medicine for the pursuit of madness.

Kinsey's voice pulled me from my thoughts. "Mara's told me a lot about you, Dr. Madden."

I couldn't tell if the smile on his face was intended to challenge me or was an attempt at an icebreaker.

"Anything that's relevant to the investigation can be discussed here."

"Good, good. Well then. Shall we begin?"

Over the next half hour, Kinsey pulled up his notes on the computer and reviewed his sessions with Mara, beginning with their first session from more than two years ago. He'd diagnosed her initially as a schizophrenic, but eventually changed his assessment to dissociative identity disorder.

As he spoke, I found my mind wandering. I hadn't seen any real evidence of her mental instability when we'd dated. Or had I? Suddenly, I wasn't so sure. But I knew from my training that people could hide mental ailments for years or even decades, in some cases. Anything was possible.

"Okay," I said as he concluded his overview. "What's the bottom line, Doc? What's going on with Mara? In layman's terms, if you don't mind."

Kinsey peered at the computer screen. "Her official diagnosis, in my opinion, is atypical dissociative identity disorder. 'Atypical' because she doesn't possess other wholly different personalities. She's not your stereotypical sufferer. You know, Susan, Jane, Jimmy, Little Harry, and Betty all rolled into one. All of Mara's personalities are what I would call 'Maras,' but they're so disparate and unaware of each other that dissociative identity disorder is the only classification that makes any sense in her case. She doesn't, quite simply, know which version of herself she is at any given time."

I pressed him further. "So if that's the case, then how does that explain why she thought I kidnapped and raped her in her grandmother's basement?"

Kinsey sighed. "Well, as you know, Mara's incredibly intelligent and capable of pulling the wool over anyone's eyes. While I can give you my utmost honest opinion, that caveat will always remain. I do sometimes get the feeling that if this is how Mara wanted me to diagnose her, then she could probably pull it off. But in my professional opinion, I don't believe she's malingering here, Dr. Madden."

"But after all the psychoanalysis, you still aren't one hundred percent sure?"

"I'm never one hundred percent sure about anything."

"So you think the dissociative identity disorder is why she can believe that I took her into that basement?"

"No." He leaned back in his chair. "My honest opinion? I think that was simple self-preservation. I think Mara projected you onto the identity of her true abductor in that house in New Hope. Why, you may ask? Because it helped her cope with the rape and the kidnapping that occurred there."

He paused, then ventured the next bit of information cautiously. "Mara actually confided to me in our first interview after this episode that she wasn't even raped. In fact, she insisted that she had simply made love to you during her abduction."

"What?"

"Well, if you think about it, it makes sense. If she reconstructs her ordeal in the basement as a consensual sexual encounter, rather than being forced into an unwanted sex act over and over, then she can convince herself that she never lost control of the situation. Certainly the opposite of what really happened in that basement, a situation in which she became completely powerless at the hand of the perpetrator."

Kinsey's words rang undeniably true, and I finally began to understand one possible explanation for Mara's rationale for claiming I'd abducted her. If there was one thing Mara always wanted, it was to be in control of every situation.

To my side, Woodson spoke up. "Dr. Kinsey, did Mara ever mention anything about what the killer looked like? Anything outstanding about him?"

Kinsey mulled over the question a moment, then flicked away on his keyboard and peered at the computer screen once again. "I don't see anything in my notes, although I'm not sure I would have caught it in our sessions." He looked up. "I don't recall her mentioning anything specific about her abductor, though. From what she's told me, he crept up behind her, knocked her out with something, something a lot more powerful than chloroform, and the next thing she knew she was imprisoned in a basement."

"Does Mara ever speak of her childhood?"

Kinsey seemed slightly surprised at Woodson's question, but nodded. "Yes. Not often, but sometimes." He looked in my direction. "I understand you were in it."

"Small world."

Kinsey eyed me before redirecting his answer to Woodson, as if weighing whether he should say something to us or not. "Funny you ask, actually. I do think there's something in her childhood that haunts her, but I haven't been able to broach it with her yet. She has a curious love–hate relationship with her father. When her guard is down, she speaks of him fondly. But when different masks are on, she despises him. Something happened in her past that I haven't been able to uncover. She swears up and down that her father wasn't abusive, so I'm at a loss until Mara decides to elaborate." He stopped, then seemed to have a sudden idea. "Do you happen to know of anything, Dr. Madden?"

"Sorry. No clue."

Kinsey shrugged. "Then maybe it really isn't anything important. But Mara certainly hasn't been willing to revisit her childhood with me in any great detail yet, that's for certain."

I nodded and thought for a moment of Mara's father, Charlie, and wondered if Kinsey might be right. Maybe Charlie could shed additional light on Mara's current fragile state in adulthood. I glanced at Kinsey, who in turn looked at the clock. He was clearly ready to get on with his day.

"Well, Dr. Kinsey. Thank you for meeting with us. Do you think we can meet with Mara now?"

"We can try." Kinsey stood and walked to his office door, then turned back to us before opening it. "I'll check with her now. Again, if she's ready to talk to you, I'll allow you to see her. Under supervision. If not, I'm afraid you can't interview her just yet. It's completely up to her."

"Understood."

With that he nodded politely and left, closing the door. I leaned toward Woodson, still keeping my voice low. "Let's hope Mara is up to this. If not, we're at a dead end."

Woodson looked toward the office door. "So what do you think of the good doctor?"

I shrugged. "He seems okay. He seems to be concerned for Mara. He has a pretty solid bullshit meter, too. I like that in a person."

Woodson smiled. "You know what they say. Can't bullshit a bullshitter, right? I'm surprised he's letting you anywhere near her at this point, though."

"Me too."

"Just better make sure she doesn't have a knife on her when he brings her up," Woodson said.

The icy finger of fear suddenly stabbing my chest surprised me, as I recalled my last interaction with Mara in her grandmother's basement.

When I looked up at Woodson she was still smiling at her joke. The cold-dread sensation vanished almost as quickly as it had appeared.

A few moments later the door to the office opened and Kinsey walked in. "Good news. Mara agrees to see you. She assures me that she understands that you weren't her abductor, and she's expressed a great deal of remorse for the incident, in fact. Given these developments in her psychological state, I'm comfortable allowing her to speak with you, as long as you both promise to simply ask questions related to your investigation."

"You have our word, Doctor."

"Good, then. Follow me."

Woodson and I followed Kinsey and an accompanying orderly down the hallway and through a twisting series of wings and stairwells. I couldn't believe that I was getting a chance to interview Mara. We finally arrived at a nondescript door. "This is the interview room," Kinsey said. "Go inside with Martin here, and I'll bring Mara into the other side. If everything goes well, I'll step away and leave you to your interview. Martin will be in the room at all times. And I'll be watching everything from behind the one-way mirror."

"That's fine, Dr. Kinsey. Much appreciated."

Kinsey put forth his hand. A Rolex watch slipped out from beneath a shirt cuff held together by an expensive monogrammed cuff link, everything a reminder of how drastically our respective chosen career paths had diverged after medical school. I shook his hand and looked up from his wrist quickly as he spoke.

"It was nice meeting you both. Good luck in your investigation." With that Kinsey excused himself, and told us he'd return momentarily with our interviewee.

We bade him farewell, and I tried mightily to prepare myself to come face-to-face with Mara Bliss for the first time since she'd tried to kill me.

FIFTEEN

The small interview room reminded me of a prison visitation area. Woodson and I sat in folding metal chairs and waited while staring through a glass partition into the opposite room.

The silent orderly, Martin, stood in a corner of the white room across from us, waiting patiently.

I wondered what Mara's reaction would be. The last time I'd seen her, she'd compressed herself into the corner of a basement and filled my head with a scream that I'd never forget—then plunged a knife into my back in a premeditated attempt to kill me.

A small door in the opposite room opened, and Mara followed Kinsey inside. He escorted her to a seat on the other side of the partition, bent down, and whispered a few words of apparent comfort.

She wore a white terry cloth robe over a white T-shirt and white flannel pajama pants. The familiar black curls of hair spilling over her shoulders and surrounding her pale face provided the only real contrast in the white room. For a strange moment it almost seemed that her disembodied head floated in a background of clouds all around.

Kinsey spoke into the circular phonelike opening in the middle of the glass. "Mara's ready to speak with you. Just tap on the door behind you when you're finished."

Mara touched his hand, and Kinsey bent down to listen as she whispered. When he looked up, he spoke in an apologetic tone. "I'm sorry, but Mara will only speak with you, Dr. Madden."

"What?" Woodson asked, preparing to protest.

At the sound of Woodson's voice, Mara stood defiantly and began to back toward the door.

"Mara, wait," I called after her, just before I glared and whispered behind me in a hushed tone. "She doesn't know you, Woodson. She won't trust you. Let me talk to her. Leave with Kinsey and watch the interview through the one-way mirror in the side room. You won't miss a thing."

Despite her disappointment, Woodson shrugged indifferently and stood to go. "Okay."

"Thanks." I said simply, turning back to the glass partition. Mara stayed near the exit until Woodson left. Once the door closed, she slowly made her way back to Kinsey.

He nodded to her, as if to confirm that the crisis was past. He patted Mara on the arm and left us, with only a glass pane between us, for the first time since the basement.

"How are you holding up, Mara?"

She looked behind her to make sure Kinsey was gone, then pulled out a pack of cigarettes. She tapped one out, lit it, and inhaled deeply. "You want one, Lucas?" she let the smoke pour out of her mouth as she spoke. "I bet you do."

I'd expected contrition, or even profuse apologies, but not this. I tried to reel her back into reality. "Are you okay, Mara?"

She blew another lazy ring of cigarette smoke from her lips. "Thank you for asking, Lucas. Always the gentleman. But I'm fine. Fully recovered. Really."

Her newfound flippancy about the entire ordeal threw me completely off guard. "Dr. Kinsey says you're doing better. I'm glad to hear it."

Mara slowly shifted her weight, arching her back as her voice dropped to a smoky growl of an aging cabaret dancer. "So you didn't die in Nana's basement?"

With a slight ache in my suddenly dry throat, I shook my head. "Nope. Here I am." I didn't know what else to say, and didn't want to admit the degree of hurt that her simple comment caused.

Mara studied me for a moment, then a deep expression of wonderment crossed her features. "Oh, Lucas, you'd love the new one I'm working on, by the way. I just know you would. I remember all the nights you'd sit with me while I read my chapters to you. God, those were nice nights."

My brain scrambled to catch up. I realized that she must be talking about a new novel. Her mind was jumping like hypertext, and I was reminded of Kinsey's diagnosis of dissociative identity disorder. "Mara, that's great. But I need to ask you some questions."

She leaned forward and crushed her cigarette into a tin ashtray, never moving her eyes off me. "Don't you miss me?" Her mouth opened slightly at the end of the question, as though she wanted to kiss me through the glass.

The idea of an interview began to seem like a much worse idea than I'd originally suspected. I ignored her advances. "What's the last thing you remember, Mara, before you were abducted?"

She leaned back in her chair and closed her eyes. "It's hard to remember. Everything is so fuzzy. I went to the store. Tyler had already left for his conference, and I just wanted to pick up some food for the next couple of nights."

"What store?" I scribbled the notes in my notepad without looking up.

"Acme," Mara said. "The one off Waveland."

"Then what?"

"Then I woke up in a basement. Getting raped."

Her words slammed into me like a wrecking ball. I thought I'd sympathized with her, but I hadn't. I tried a new line of questioning, in a gentler tone. "Mara. Why in the world did you think I was your attacker? I would never . . ." I started to say, but didn't finish.

"You said . . . I mean, *he* said that he was you." She leaned forward and whispered. "I honestly thought it was you, Lucas. I swear to God, he sounded just like you."

"So this person spoke to you?"

"No. He only whispered."

"I see. So he whispered to you. And that whisper sounded like me?"

She nodded.

"So when the man spoke to you, did he tell you where he wanted to take you?"

She shook her head in confusion. "No. You said . . . I mean, he said that he wanted to take me somewhere where no one could find us."

"What happened next?"

"So I told him about my grandmother's house." Mara smiled, but I could see tears in her eyes. "I thought it was you, Lucas. I wanted to go there and be with you. Alone. I was excited. I thought you were tricking me or something. That you wanted to come back to me."

I exhaled as the answer to our main question—namely, how the SWK had known how to take Mara to her grandmother's house—was finally revealed. Mara had directed him there herself.

I sighed. "Okay. But this guy surely didn't look like me?"

She shook her head back and forth, this time choosing to elaborate. "No. I mean, I couldn't tell. He didn't let me see his face. I felt so fuzzy, Lucas. He blindfolded me after we went down into the basement. But he had a gentle touch, Lucas. And he whispered to me, told me he was you. He even told me that he'd come back to save me, but that later you'd pretend that you were never there."

I noticed she was switching the pronouns *he* and *you* more frequently as she spoke. Despite her sessions with Kinsey in recent days, deep down she apparently still wasn't sure about her kidnapper's identity.

"Mara," I asked. "You know it wasn't me. Right?"

"But he was *you*, Lucas. And now you say he wasn't you. And the police say it wasn't you. And Dr. Kinsey says it wasn't you. Everybody says there's all this goddamned proof." Her eyes gleamed with tears. "I don't know what to believe anymore."

I looked at her through the partition, overcome with pity. Maybe she had problems, issues I didn't understand, and while I was perhaps not quite ready to fully buy into Kinsey's dissociative identity disorder once and for all, I knew one thing: Mara was, if nothing else, extremely frightened and confused.

She leaned forward, stopping only a few inches from the glass again. "It had to be you," she whispered. "I've felt it before, I know I have. We made love. It wasn't like rape at all."

Suddenly Kinsey's diagnosis sounded more and more correct, that Mara had made peace with what had happened in that basement through sheer, unadulterated repression and fantasy. Just as he'd claimed, she'd distorted the rape into an act of consensual intimacy. She whispered the disturbing falsehood again. "We made love, Lucas."

"Mara," I said, slowly shaking my head. "I swear to you that it wasn't me. And what happened to you wasn't love."

"How can you be so sure?" She pulled away from the partition and spoke more loudly. "Why is everyone so fucking sure that it wasn't you? Except me?"

I didn't have any answers for her as she looked away and wiped her cheeks in anger. I'd abandoned her after her affair with Tyler and never looked back, because no woman made a fool out of Lucas Madden. Now, for the first time, I seriously considered the possibility that I shared some of the blame for her present condition. How could I have not seen this?

Suddenly our past, the hurt we'd caused each other, the confusion Mara now felt, the unresolved nature of our own dissolution . . . it all crashed into me like an angry wave of regret.

"Mara," I said. "I have one last question for you. It's about something you said to me that day on the phone."

"Yes?"

"You mentioned a girl with writing on her forehead. Did you actually see the girl with writing on her forehead?"

She thought for a moment, but then shook her head. "No. I mean, I can't remember. I'm sorry; everything's so fuzzy. I think so? But I'm not sure. Maybe he just mentioned her?"

I smiled in a genuine attempt to put her at ease. "Okay." I stood and pushed my chair back. "That's everything, then. You should rest now. Can you think of anything else before I go?"

Mara leaned closer and motioned me toward her. She dropped her voice so that only I could possibly hear her, as if she knew we'd been observed through the one-way mirror all along. "Lucas," she said, "I dream of all those girls before they die."

"What's that again?"

"Dead girls, sleeping, looking up at me through closed eyes. Their eyeballs move underneath their eyelids, but they can't wake up because they're dead. And then cuts appear on their bodies and they still don't wake up. They just bleed and bleed and bleed. And their faces contort in pain, but they still don't wake up. They can't." She took a deep breath, forcing herself to continue. "Then they die, and I watch the letters appear on their foreheads."

"When do you dream them, Mara?"

"All the time."

"Who are they?"

"Anna Cross, Jessica Harrison, and that girl in the basement with me."

I stayed silent, scanning her face for any sign that she was either lying or toying with me. But I saw nothing.

Mara pushed her forehead against the window like a child, but her eyes fixed me with an adult intensity. "*He* talks to me, too," she said, opening her eyes to emphasize it. "*He* tells me how he does it."

My pulse quickened. "Who talks to you, Mara? The killer?" I heard my words and understood how foolish I sounded, but for some reason, even if I didn't believe her, I wanted to hear her answer. Time had run out on the interview, and I had nothing. I'd take a chance on anything if it would help link Mara to the murderer and help us gain any tiny bit of better understanding about the Snow White Killer.

She bit her lip and shook her head, smiling, but on the verge of tears—as though smiling were her only option in the face of absurdity.

I leaned closer to the partition and pressed her for the answer. "Who do you see in your dreams, Mara? Who's killing these women?"

She looked up at me, her eyes still rimmed with tears. "I never see his face, Lucas," she whispered, the words finally spilling out of her mouth like water falling over the edge of a cliff. "But he tells me he'll kill me if I ever tell anyone what he says. And he sounds just like you."

She began to cry uncontrollably, then signaled to the exit door on her side of the partition.

At that moment Kinsey opened the door behind. I watched as Martin the orderly led her away. At the door, Mara looked back at me with a faint smile.

I realized I'd been so angry with her until that very moment. The ridiculous accusations, everything. And then in a moment, it was all gone. I only felt sorry for her and wished I could have seen it sooner or helped. Or even that my brother still could, possibly.

I stood up and left the room in which I'd interviewed Mara Bliss— my former lover, my brother's companion, my recent assailant, and a near-victim of the Snow White Killer.

I suddenly appreciated Mara's need to smile in the face of a universe gone otherwise completely mad.

SIXTEEN

"So, Madden." Woodson pushed open the front doors of Memorial Oaks and waited for me to exit. "What do you think?"

"Not sure," I said, as we walked down the steps toward the parking lot, hoping she was asking for a professional, rather than personal, opinion. "It sounds like she was drugged. She can't remember anything. Do you think there's any chance we missed something in the tox screen?"

"Anything's possible," Woodson said, adding, "I could review the toxicology reports with your man Terry, if you want."

"Sure," I said, as we arrived at the SUV.

Woodson stopped on the passenger's side and looked over the roof at me. "Your friend certainly seemed convinced that you're the Snow White Killer," she said.

"So do *you* think I'm the Snow White Killer, Woodson?"

She shook her head, smiling at the inflection in my question. "No, Madden, I don't. But it's pretty strange that Mara Bliss does. I wonder if that's more significant than the psychobabble we were fed in there."

I shrugged. "Maybe Kinsey is right. Maybe Mara just projected me onto the identity of her abductor to cope with a traumatic experience.

Just compensation on her part. Maybe it has nothing to do with the Snow White Killer."

I unlocked the doors and we started to get into the car, but Woodson spoke again. "Honestly, Lucas? Some people might say it's not you she's describing, but your brother."

"Are you shitting me?"

Woodson held up a hand. "I'm not saying it *is* him, Lucas, but think about it for a second. If you didn't know Mara, wouldn't you at least wonder whether she was talking about a companion? The killer talks to her in her sleep? Threatens to kill her if she says anything? Sounds like a lot of husbands or boyfriends to me."

I realized Woodson and Kinsey must have heard Mara's whispered conversation with me at the end of our interview. "Mara's not reliable, Woodson. The person she describes doesn't sound like my brother. It sounds more like Freddy fucking Krueger."

"So if you're sure about that, then why not interview him?"

"Who?"

"Your brother," Woodson answered.

"Are you nuts? You want me to interview my own brother and ask him if he's the Snow White Killer?"

Woodson leaned farther over the roof. "Yes," she said, "and if you were thinking objectively, you'd agree. You better turn over every stone here or Jimmy is going to take you off this case. For good."

I stared at Woodson as she spoke, unable to dismiss the soundness of her logic. She was right. I needed a paper trail to prove I'd treated this case objectively. Otherwise, Jimmy Raritan had all the ammunition he needed to remove me. If there was one thing I wanted, it was to stay on the SWK investigation. And if there was one thing Jimmy wanted, it was probably one good reason to take me off it.

I opened the driver's side door. "So I guess we have to drive all the way up to Hattiesburg and talk to my brother, just to put a checkmark in the box and take it off the list of Things I Need to Do to Stay Off Jimmy's Shit List. Right?"

Woodson opened her door as well. "Hey, it may not seem like it, but I really am just trying to look out for you."

I climbed inside, started the engine without responding. Woodson shrugged her shoulders as she settled in the passenger seat. Hattiesburg was a good two hours away. Even though I suspected Woodson really was looking out for my best interests, I couldn't bring myself to thank her for suggesting that I interrogate my brother as a suspect in the Snow White Killer case just to maintain my appearance as an objective agent of the FBI.

Even if she was right.

Two and a half hours later we arrived in the reception area of yet another doctor's office, this time at my brother's. I'd never been to his new office in the renovated medical wing at the University of Southern Mississippi. Except for our recent run-in at the hospital, it had been two years since he and I had spoken, and even longer since I'd visited him at work.

His assistant brought us into his office and assured us that he was on his way, encouraging us to make ourselves comfortable. Woodson took a seat in one of the three chairs facing my brother's large desk, massaging her neck in silence. I stood to the side and looked around at the various scientific magazines and journals stacked in piles. Unlike the neuroscience theme in Kinsey's office, all of the journals in Tyler's office were related to reproduction and women's health. *Reproductive Sciences, Molecular Reproduction and Development,* and other journals lay in ordered piles on his desk. In contrast to Kinsey's office, the spaces on Tyler's wall were taken up not with serene paintings but with anatomical charts, reproduction pathways, and other scientific wall hangings.

I walked around his desk and looked at the picture frames staring back at me. A large picture of Mara and Tyler sat in the center in a golden frame, both of them smiling, at some black-tie affair, laughing in mid dance. The other pictures were of Katie and the girls, and of my father fishing.

The absence of my own image on his desk wasn't lost on me, but it wasn't surprising, either. It wasn't as if I had any pictures of Tyler displayed at home, except for one along my stairwell containing a framed picture of the two of us in elementary school, standing at the end of our parents' driveway, waiting on a school bus with our backs toward the picture-taker, our mother. Tyler was in first grade and I was a fourth grader. That morning I'd held my arm around his shoulders to comfort him as he prepared for his first day of school.

"What are you doing here?"

I turned to face my brother, the memory swept away in a moment. "We just need to ask you a few questions, Tyler, to wrap up the inquiry about Mara's disappearance."

"Like what?"

I sighed. "Like whatever the hell we need to ask you. Don't get defensive. I promise this is just to make sure we don't leave any loose ends. We have to interview all the relevant witnesses. The sooner we get finished, the sooner we don't have to deal with each other anymore."

Tyler looked at me for a moment longer, the way someone sizes up a person they're considering sucker punching, then abruptly extended his hand toward Woodson. "Hello."

"Hello, Dr. Madden. Special Agent Woodson. I'm working with your brother on this case. Thank you for seeing us on such short notice."

Tyler nodded pleasantly enough, but stiffened when Woodson referred to me as his brother. He leaned back against his office desk. "Well, let's get on with it. I have ten minutes at most before my next appointment."

I looked at Woodson. "Please. Feel free to start the interview at any time."

The scowl on Woodson's face confirmed her displeasure, but I didn't care. After all, she'd been the one to push so hard to speak with Tyler. It was only fitting that she conduct the bogus interview.

She recovered quickly enough. "So, Dr. Madden," she began, "you were out of town when Mara was initially noted as missing, presumably abducted?"

"Yes. I already told you people this. And she wasn't *presumably* abducted. She *was* abducted."

Woodson cleared her throat. "Right. I meant to establish that you were out of town at the time when she *claims* to have been abducted. Her abduction isn't in doubt, but her timeline is pretty fuzzy."

Tyler sighed. "All I can say for certain is that Mara was at home when I left for a conference in Mobile on Friday. When I returned on Sunday, she was gone. So *presumably*," at this point he paused for emphasis, "she was abducted between two P.M. on Friday and six P.M. on Sunday."

Woodson smiled a forced smile, while I smiled a genuine one. I didn't know from whom we'd received it, but Tyler and I had inherited the same gift of sarcasm from one of our parents. I suspected our mother.

"Great," Woodson said, flipping her pad closed. "Okay, I think at this point Lucas wants to review the results of his interview with Mara from earlier today."

She looked up at me with what appeared to be a polite, professional smile. It took a moment to realize she'd just victimized me as efficiently as when I'd surprised her with an invitation to begin the interview.

Tyler stood, stepping away from desk. "What? You talked to Mara today?" His voice rose with each successive syllable.

I remained seated. "Yes, Tyler. With both her doctor's and her approval. I didn't interrogate her, I just asked if she could remember anything from her ordeal."

Tyler looked at me with an incredulity that distorted his face. "So does she still claim that *you* were the one who kidnapped and raped her?"

"No. She seems to have made good progress with her psychiatrist and seems pretty convinced now that it wasn't me. But she didn't remember much of anything else."

"What else could she remember? The only thing she kept saying over and over was that you did it, Lucas." Tyler hesitated and looked at Woodson, but then looked back at me. "What did you do to her? What terrible thing did you ever do to her in the past that would make her think that?"

"I didn't do anything to her, Tyler. And you're the one being questioned here, not me. I'll ask the questions." I waited for a response, but received none. Tyler just stood there seething, so I continued. "She also mentioned something else that we found rather strange. She claimed that the killer talks to her in her dreams. While she sleeps."

Tyler raised his eyebrows. "So?"

"She said the killer talks to her in her sleep, Tyler."

"And again, I repeat, so what?"

"I guess I have to spell it out for you. You sleep with Mara. She says the killer talks to her in her sleep. Can you shed any light on this?"

Tyler laughed so loudly that I jumped. "You've got to be kidding me." He glanced at Woodson. "You're both serious?"

Neither of us replied.

He leaned forward and spoke directly to me as if Woodson wasn't there. "I don't know anything about that, Lucas. Are you that screwed up over the idea of me and Mara together?"

"Don't kid yourself."

He balled his hands into fists, but left them on his desk. "What kind of a hit did your ego take, Lucas? Was it bad enough for you to try to accuse me of being your killer?" He shook his head. "Get the hell out of my office. I'm not saying another word to either of you." He picked up his telephone, but kept his eyes on us. "Janie? Get security on the phone."

I stood. "There's no need for that. We'll go." I saw Woodson begin to protest, but spoke over her. "We're leaving."

Woodson shot me an angry glare as she passed through the door. Without another word I turned and walked in silence down the hospital hallway behind her.

————

Woodson didn't speak to me until we got in the car. As I turned the key, she faced me. "What happened in there?"

"I just needed to avoid an embarrassing situation, for one. For God's sake, he's my brother."

"Then maybe Jimmy's right. Maybe you *are* too close to this case."

"That's for Jimmy to decide. Not you."

"He could be persuaded. There's a reason he assigned me to this case."

"Look, Woodson. I realize he's placed you in a watchdog role here. It's painfully evident. But just think about it. How did you think my brother would react? Just because Mara said that she's dreamed about these women getting killed and she thinks the killer spoke to her, so what? She has a professionally documented mental disorder. And let's not forget that she believed I was her abductor, not Tyler. She even admitted in her interview today that she never even saw her kidnapper. Based on all of that, do you really think that interrogating my brother was the most important lead we could follow in this case?"

Woodson shifted in her seat and looked away, out the window. "No, I don't. But you have to trust me. You needed to interview your brother in order to stay on this case."

"And only time will tell whether it was worth it or not. But for now, I'd rather get back to the crime lab and find out whether Terry's pulled any trace evidence that can actually help us identify the real killer. Maybe some DNA evidence, I don't know, or a fingerprint. Something."

"You get no arguments from me."

"Great." I started the car but didn't put it in reverse. "Woodson. I want to catch this guy as bad as anyone. But if I don't have to further destroy the remnants of my relationship with my brother in the process, I'd prefer to avoid doing so. Okay?"

"Okay, Madden. I really am looking out for you. We had to interview your brother today, after what Mara said in the interview. Jimmy would have pounced on you otherwise."

"I get it. So, are we back in business?"

"We're back in business."

———————

We didn't get back to my place until seven o'clock. I confirmed with Woodson that I'd see her at the New Orleans field office the next morning, where she, Terry, and I would organize the debriefing for local law enforcement that afternoon. After a cordial and brief exchange of good-nights, she ducked into her car and left.

Back inside I lay down on the couch, pushing Watson gently aside to make room. Sleep was coming on, but it seemed like such a terrible luxury.

I stared at the picture of Tyler and me waiting on that school bus, my arm protectively around his tiny shoulders. I realized that when I'd stepped into Tyler's office today I'd crossed a bridge and burned it, probably never to return. I hadn't realized how much I'd hoped we'd still be able to get back to those days somehow.

Sometimes I had bad ideas in life, and followed through with them anyway. I was fairly certain that interviewing my brother about Mara's disappearance had been one of those bad ideas. I worried that the price for that mistake might well turn out to be immeasurable.

It was my last thought before I finally succumbed to sleep.

SEVENTEEN

The next morning I walked into the New Orleans field office and ran a gauntlet of agents welcoming me back with nervous greetings and awkward pauses. St. Clair and Harmon, older agents, winked at me in an almost conspiratorial fashion. Faraday and Tucker, the newest agents in the department, shook hands with me gently and patted my back softly. Everyone, veterans and rookies alike, acted slightly out of sorts, not quite themselves. My return from a near-fatal knifing served as a grim reminder of the ever-present potential for disaster in our chosen line of work.

On the way I saw Woodson's silhouette through the thin curtain of the "hot office" reserved for visiting agents. I thought about dropping by and saying hello as the rest of the agents filtered back to their offices, but there were far too many eavesdropping ears around.

Instead, I walked down the hall to my own office. I sent an e-mail to Terry and Woodson about the upcoming debriefing. I asked Woodson to prepare an overview of the victimology—who was killed and any common links between them—and asked Terry to provide an overview of the forensics.

I set about organizing the entire session, from the geography of the kill sites to possible symbolism in the modus operandi. I called Shelly

Vondifer, a linguistics expert in the Jackson field office, to find out if she could offer any insight into the word pattern we'd observed to date—"a tan cat." If there were any literary references out there, Shelly could find them. But she didn't sound enthusiastic.

"I haven't found anything yet, Lucas. This just isn't enough to go on. You can't even breach copyright with three words."

"There's no mention of a tan cat, not anywhere?"

"Honestly, you name it, we've looked. From Egypt to T. S. Eliot to Andrew Lloyd Webber. Nothing sticks out about a tan cat."

"Sounds like you turned over every stone you could."

"Lucas, as sick as this sounds, you're going to need more to go on if we're going to get anywhere with this message. I hope other leads pan out for you before linguistics is able to help."

I thanked her and hung up, disappointed. The only way Shelly was going to figure out the message was if we had more bodies. There had to be another way.

At that moment Terry poked his face through my doorway. "Got a minute?"

"For you, always." I waved him in.

He sat in the chair opposite my desk. "Good news for a change. We looked at the short tandem repeats in the DNA from the blood samples taken from the victims' foreheads. Those messages on the foreheads aren't drawn with the victims' own blood. Just like you thought."

I whistled. "No shit?"

"No shit," he confirmed. "But, get this. The DNA in the blood left on each of the victims' foreheads? It's not from the victims, but it's all from the same source. In other words, the blood left on each of the victims is coming from the same person."

"Then the blood left on the victims' foreheads probably comes from our killer, right?"

"Hey. Anything's possible. But if I had to bet on it, I'd say yes." Terry paused, then added, "Of course, that's assuming our guy is as screwed up as they usually are."

I leaned forward with a sudden thought. "Did you search that DNA against CODIS?"

"Yeah, I checked the combined DNA indexing system. But no hits there, either, unfortunately. Whoever owns that DNA hasn't spent time in our judicial system. Not yet, at least."

I waved it away. "Not surprising, actually. If I had to bet, I would have guessed our killer's never been incarcerated anyway."

"Why do you say that?"

"I'm getting the sense of a perfectionist here. No trace evidence, no witnesses. And did you see how straight the letters are on the victims' foreheads? It's like he uses a ruler. The guy may be sick, but he's anally retentive, too."

"I agree with that."

"Some people think an offender only gains that sort of expertise by learning from past mistakes, but I think some of them, at least the superintelligent ones, just start out like this when they finally snap. No previous record; they just wake up one morning and start killing, completely in control of their faculties. I think that's who we're dealing with here," I said. "A superintelligent, obsessive-compulsive psychotic who just snapped."

Terry raised his eyebrows. "Wow. Sounds like someone I work for. Are you the Snow White Killer?"

"Very funny. Everyone seems to be asking that question lately."

"Hey, at least I'm only kidding."

"I know. So anyway, if we think the blood left on the foreheads may come from our killer . . ."

Terry nodded before I finished the thought. "I already know what you're thinking."

"Then we should run those samples through the Damnation Algorithm. If SWK really is leaving behind those messages on their foreheads with his own blood, then analyzing that DNA sample might give us a lot of insight into the Snow White Killer."

"I'm already on it." Terry stood. "I'll get the lab moving on it, and I'll still see you at the debriefing later."

As the door closed behind him I could barely contain my excitement. The opportunity for a real-life test of the Damnation Algorithm was finally at hand.

Terry stuck his head back in the door. "By the way."

"Yes?"

"I forgot to mention. Your buddy Agent Woodson has been down on the mass spec all morning. She's driving the techs crazy."

"What the hell's she doing down on the mass spec? Running samples herself?"

"No. She's using the software to screen toxicology databases. She thinks she might have found something in one of the victim's blood samples. From the tox reports. Something they might have missed."

"Really?"

"That's what she said, but wouldn't tell me any more. She jumps in with both feet, you know? I like it. I told the techs to calm down and let her do her thing." Terry shrugged. "Who knows, maybe she's on to something. Anyway, see you around."

"Sounds good."

Terry closed the door, and I returned to the slide presentation on my desktop: "FBI Field Office Debriefing for Local Jurisdictions: Serial Killer Patterns in Three Deaths in the Mississippi Delta."

We had a lot of ground to cover.

Four hours later I stood in the middle of our main conference room as about a dozen attendees filed inside and took their seats around an oval-shaped mahogany conference table.

Woodson sat on the opposite end of the table, and Terry sat beside her. Several other agents sat in chairs, holding cups of coffee, quietly whispering. I noticed Shelly, our linguistics expert, had shown up in person.

The two young guys, Faraday and Tucker, came in late and took their places, opened their legal pads, and poised their ballpoint pens for notes. I noticed Harmon nudge St. Clair and gesture toward the rookies in a "get a load of this" fashion.

The remaining individuals around the table weren't from the Bureau, and included my old buddy Sheriff Pratt, the Elvis impersonator from the first crime scene, and several other uniformed state and local law enforcement officers from Mississippi and Louisiana who I didn't recognize. At the last second, Donny slipped through the door and winked a silent hello before sitting down in a final empty chair on the far end.

Woodson flicked on the videoconference monitor with a remote, and the images of Raritan and Parkman shimmered into view at the end of a nondescript table from some conference room in Quantico.

"Hello, guys."

They nodded. "Lucas," Raritan spoke my name simply, as a salutation.

"Okay, folks," I said, turning back to the gathered group, "everyone's here, so let's get started. As you know this is a debriefing regarding the investigation of three murders in the state of Mississippi attributed to the unsub currently referred to in the media as the Snow White Killer."

I clicked the remote, and the first slide of the presentation appeared, depicting a map of the western Mississippi–eastern Louisiana border. Three yellow stars dotted Mississippi towns in an area delineated by the Mississippi River on the west and by Highway 49 on the east.

"First, the kill sites. To date we have three victims, each with residences within a forty-mile radius spanning the various dump sites."

"So it's a local killer?" one of the sheriffs from Louisiana asked.

"Looks like it," I answered, "but not much else to say about that for now. Geography assessments are just difficult when there are only three sites, but Terry's nevertheless going to work up a jeopardy surface map as soon as he can. Once he finishes it, we'll distribute it so you all can see areas with predicted higher probability for future abductions. It may help, it may not. Any questions?"

After a moment of silence, I continued. "Okay, next is victimology.

What did the victims share in common, what did the killings have in common? Any leads there? Agent Woodson?"

Woodson took over. "All the victims have been in their late twenties or early thirties, all white." She flicked to a slide of their faces, pulled from their driver's licenses. "There are no obvious links among the three victims to date, although we're cross-referencing the credit card receipts of each as far back as three years. Beyond all three sharing Caucasian origin, there are no demographic commonalities of note. One victim was married, the other two were single. Two blondes, one brunette. One girl had a tattoo, the others didn't. A Virgo, a Sagittarius, and a Libra."

At this St. Clair and Harmon chuckled. "Not leaving any stones unturned, huh?" Harmon asked.

Woodson shrugged. "We're covering every commonality angle we can dream up right now, beyond the standard ones. Doesn't look like they share a single common link at this point. I could go through the laundry list, but won't. There haven't been any hits yet. We'll keep the team updated as data become available. That's all we've got for now." She sat back down.

"Okay then," I said, "if there are no questions, let's move on to how they were killed. Terry?"

Terry flicked to the next slide, a close-up photograph of one of the knife marks discovered on the bodies. He also fanned a photocopied stack of micrographs around the table. "The weapon of choice is a knife," he said, "and these are some close-ups of one of the knife wounds. Notice the jagged and imperfect serrated edge that leaves this sort of a pattern, a tick-tick-tick-tack-tick sort of repeat." Terry highlighted each of five jagged marks with a laser pointer. "This pattern was found on the body of the first victim."

He clicked to the next slide, a side-by-side comparison of two separate knife wounds, blown up to about twentyfold magnification. "That same tick-tick-tick-tack-tick pattern shows up on knife marks on the other two bodies as well. We're pretty certain the same knife did this. We're matching fractal edges right now by electron microscopy, just to put a statistical certainty to it, but we're already in the ninety-nine percent likely range, by eye. The computer will take that likelihood even higher." He paused before adding, "Trust us, the same knife did this, and the same killer is responsible for all three victims so far."

He flicked to the next slide, a photocopied report form. "We've also run a preliminary scan of the weapons database in Quantico and reconstructed the blade that most likely caused the slash marks on the victims. It suggests that the cutting blade is from a Khyber knife series, a heavy-duty knife with a ten-inch blade and a locking mechanism." Terry paused. "Suggesting our killer had a rural upbringing."

"Why do you say that?"

"Khybers are hunting knives, and the broken edges imply it's seen better days, so to speak." Terry shrugged. "He may not be a mountain man. It may just possess some sort of special meaning to him, since he's clearly committed himself to using this rather imperfect weapon on his victims rather than a sharper blade."

I thought of the jackknife my own father had given me, which I'd carried in my pocket every day for the last twenty years. If nothing else, Terry's hypothesis was worth keeping in the back of our minds. "Okay. Anything else?"

"All of the victims' cars have been found at places of business, abandoned. A strip mall, a bar, and a boutique. These victims were followed, then abducted while conducting their day-to-day activities. We're definitely not dealing with a simpleminded, opportunistic killer. We have an organized killer here, in case that's not apparent to anyone."

"Thanks, Terry." I waited a moment but still no one spoke, so I continued. "Okay. Next topic of interest, we know the cuts are premortem, because there's plenty of blood loss from the wounds." I highlighted the close-up cut marks still on the screen. "Although the serrated edge is imperfect, Terry's photos just reinforced how straight these cuts are when they're made. And yet these victims were alive. We don't understand how the killer is able to make such straight lines on still-living victims."

"The victims make no movement at all in response?" one officer asked.

I nodded. "For some reason, the victims are unable to resist."

"But how could that be?" a different officer asked.

"The victims are either forcefully restrained or hypnotized or numbed or drugged or something. That's the only way those slash marks could stay so linear but still cause active bleeding. And there's no evidence the victims were restrained physically because we've got no ligature marks or bruises. So that leaves us with victims who were hypnotized, drugged, or otherwise incapacitated."

"What about the toxicology reports?" someone asked.

"Good question," I said, "but they showed us nothing initially." I refocused on Woodson. "Do you have any updates based on the re-analysis you've been doing lately?"

"An update maybe, but not a lead. Not yet." Everyone turned in unison to hear what she had to say next. "Even though the initial tox screens came back normal for all three victims, I did notice that all three victims had extremely high levels of caffeine in their system. I had hoped this might suggest a commonality of a coffeehouse used by the killer to identify and select his victims. But it's an unlikely lead at best."

"So tox is a dead end?" Raritan spoke up from Quantico for the first time, over the videoconference monitor.

Woodson swung her eyes to him. "For now, yes, but I want to take a more in-depth look at the raw data. There's something strange about the caffeine peaks from the original mass spec traces, but I can't put my finger on it just yet. We'll look into it."

I waited, but Woodson was finished. "So," I said, "all in all, the relatively sparse physical data, the victimology, and the MO give us an initial profile that suggests we have a mobile killer with a car, someone who's local, likely a Caucasian male due to the victimology, who may be using some sort of nonphysical restraint while he slashes his victims, after they're abducted, while they're still alive. Victims are abducted in daylight from out-of-the-way locations. In short, we appear to have an organized, non-opportunistic killer on our hands."

I clicked to the next slide. "Now for the crime scene profile. The SWK takes his time here, folks. He takes at least enough time at the crime scene to position the victim's body. He dresses her up, but spread-eagles her legs. It's sexually evocative posturing without a hint of sexual gratification for the killer. He's obviously not trying to elicit excitement in the body positioning; he's just positioning the victim for discovery. He's banking on its shock value once the person who finds the apparently living body realizes that the victim is dead."

Raritan spoke up again from the monitor. "This is the strangest aspect of the entire case, in my estimation. Why does he cover them up if he goes through all the effort to position the women sexually? What do you make of it, Lucas?"

"Not sure. Most of the so-called lust murderers position bodies sexually, but the bodies are always naked, scantily clad, or even left mid-violation with a foreign object. I honestly don't have a clue why the SWK would pose his victims in sexually suggestive positions but fully clothed. That one's open to interpretation all day long. No precedent, as far as I know."

Raritan nodded on the screen.

"Any trace evidence?" asked one of the locals.

I glanced at Terry and shook my head imperceptibly before answering. "Nope, nothing so far. No saliva, no semen, no skin under the victims' fingernails. Nada." I looked around the rest of the room and shrugged. "We just have to believe we'll come across some physical evidence eventually, if we keep looking."

Terry stared at me, but didn't object. I knew he didn't understand why I wouldn't at least mention our pet theory about the bloody lettering on the victims' foreheads possibly coming from our killer. But he'd seen the slight shake of my head and had trusted my instincts. Although an exciting possibility, the idea that our killer might *intentionally* be leaving his own blood behind was just too speculative for this forum. Terry and I would need more evidence before I was willing to float that idea in front of Raritan.

"So what about the signature, Lucas?" Parkman asked over the video monitor. "Any ideas there?"

Due to a slight delay in the video feed, Parkman moved his lips about a half second ahead of each word. Despite the seemingly earnest question, a smug smile appeared on Parkman's face before the question ended over the audio conference speakers.

I knew his game. He was hoping to bait me into a premature interpretation, just like the Alvarez case. He'd get no such pleasure from me. "No ideas of my own," I answered pleasantly, "but we could discuss the killer's signature as a group if that would be worthwhile." I looked around the room with an earnest expression that surpassed Parkman's. "I mean, as long as we're finished reviewing all the other evidence here first?" I kept my tone as similar to a second-grade teacher's as possible, and watched in silent glee as Parkman's body language stiffened to an almost comical extent on the other end of the video monitor.

Everyone stayed silent. A discussion of the signature was probably just what they were waiting for, and probably the main reason they'd come.

"Okay then," I said, "let's talk about the Snow White Killer's signature, at least to this point in time."

I flicked to the next slide and the words "A TAN CAT" shone in big red letters on the projection screen. "It's a complex signature, for certain, and it's composed of two distinct components. First, there's the deliberate message left on the foreheads of the victims."

"What the hell does that mean, 'a tan cat'?" one of the sheriffs from Mississippi asked.

"Honestly? At this point, your guess is as good as mine. It's not much to go on, but we've turned it over to our linguistics colleagues in the Jackson field office nonetheless." I raised my eyebrows in Shelly's direction. "Do you want to mention anything at this juncture?"

Shelly stood and addressed the group. "Well, our group typically assesses verbal or written tendencies in kidnapping and ransom cases.

But from time to time we also work with cryptographers and code breakers in the Bureau on cases like this."

"So y'all think them words are a code of some sort?" asked one of the officers from Saint Tammany Parish.

"It's possible, but we're only dealing with three words so far. We've exhausted references to tan cats in English and American literature and found nothing to date. Given its brevity, it's likely that we've only found a portion of what is intended to become a much longer message from the Snow White Killer at this point."

"Reminds me of a child's story, or some sort of a fairy tale or something," Donny said, from the back of the room. "A tan cat," he repeated softly.

"It reminded us of that, too, Donny," Shelly said. "But we've not found any references to a tan cat specifically in any fairy tales or children's stories so far. 'Puss in Boots,' the Cheshire cat from *Alice in Wonderland,* you name it. None of them are tan, per se."

She shrugged with a look of genuine disappointment. "We wish we could help more, but we just don't have enough to go on for now, Lucas. That's all we've got. For now."

"Thanks, Shell," I said, and looked around the table. "Any more questions?"

The room stayed silent, so I continued. "Then let's consider the final aspect of the Snow White Killer's modus operandi." I flicked to the last slide depicting a photograph of an apple, sliced in half, with a razor embedded inside. "Here's the second part of the signature. We just discussed the dangers of trying to prematurely interpret the brief message our killer is leaving behind. It's safe to say it's probably too early to conjecture on the meaning of the razored apples he leaves behind as well."

"This guy is leaving apples with razors inside?"

"That's right," I said, looking at each of the officers around the table. "So for those of you who don't know, our killer has left each of his victims holding an apple with a razor inside, every time. Maybe the razors inside the apples symbolize Halloween, or maybe it symbolizes some sick attempt to bring an urban legend to life. We really don't know."

"So why show us at all, if you don't know what it means?" A younger cop in the front row asked, leaning back.

"Well," I answered, "mainly so you guys can figure out if you're dealing with the true Snow White Killer or not, at your next copycat confession from the next schizophrenic that walks through your doors." I let the simple explanation hang in the silent room for several seconds before continuing. "We need to keep this peculiar aspect of the signature to ourselves," I said, "at least for now, if we want to leverage it for verifying or nullifying confessions down the road. The only people that know the killer is leaving behind a razor in his apples are the officials on this conference call and the killer himself. Let's keep it that way."

For the last five minutes of the videoconference, I summarized the relevant facts and reviewed the assignments of the various agents. Shelly would continue to coordinate linguistics and code deciphering, while Faraday and Tucker would interview neighbors and families. St. Clair and Harmon would review the data and items recovered from the searches of the victims' houses. Last, Woodson and I were going to function as rovers. Wherever we were needed, we'd go. We were the points of contact for all the local departments.

The session adjourned and officers and agents filed out of the room. Donny waited around and shook my hand after the rest of the locals left.

"Don't be a stranger," he said, with a tired smile. "I sure as shit hope I don't need to call you anytime soon."

"I sure as shit hope you don't, either."

Donny nodded somberly. Once to me, once to Woodson, and then he left.

EIGHTEEN

After everyone cleared out, Woodson and I sat back down at the conference table and looked up at the video screen, where Raritan and Parkman still waited. Parkman spoke first, in a tone that almost sounded reconciliatory. "Nice debriefing."

"Thanks. Lot of information to cover in an hour."

Raritan's face on the grainy monitor didn't let on whether he agreed or not. "Listen, Lucas," he said, "now that the papers have picked up on the so-called Snow White Killer, this case has skyrocketed onto the Bureau's radar screen. The director just wants to make sure everything moves along before the national press blows it all out of proportion."

"I understand."

"So is there anything else going on that you didn't divulge in the debriefing today?"

I momentarily debated the wisdom of withholding the genetic angle Terry and I were working on, but then recalled the last time I'd lied to Jim Raritan, and quickly decided to come clean. "The only thing I left out today is that Terry's going to screen the DNA from the blood samples on the victims' foreheads. From the last two victims, at least."

"Why?"

"Because the bloody messages being left on the victims' foreheads aren't from the victims' own blood."

The video monitor was silent as Raritan and Parkman both digested this.

"You're sure?"

"Yes, we've checked and rechecked. The DNA from each victim's forehead never matches that victim's own DNA, in either case."

"But if those messages aren't being left with their blood, then whose is it?"

"Well," I said, "in addition to showing that the DNA isn't coming from the victim in either case, Terry's also shown that the forehead-swabbed DNA is nonetheless identical *between* the two victims."

More silence greeted me over the video monitor, so I continued. "In other words, the blood being used to write the message on each victim's forehead is coming from the same source."

"How do you know?"

"Terry already ran the thirteen STRs on blood samples from the words *tan* and *cat,* and they match each other, they just don't match the victims' DNA."

"I see."

"So we're also going ahead and testing the damnation signature on the forehead-swabbed DNA samples as well."

Raritan stayed silent on the other end, and this time I did too. I saw him glance at Parkman and heard a whisper, but I couldn't make it out. Finally he asked, "So you think the messages left on the victims is coming from the killer's own blood?"

"Yes. Exactly. So we want to—" I started to say, but Jimmy silenced me.

"Why the hell do you think it's the killer's blood? It could be any-one's."

"Like I said, it's a hunch."

"Beware this guy's hunches," Parkman said in the background.

"Fuck you, Parkman."

"Hey, hey." Parkman held up his hands on the monitor, smiling. "Settle down there, Lucas. Didn't mean to touch a nerve."

"Both of you, knock it off. Lucas, I don't know about a hunch. I don't like it. But I can't deny that it's significant that the DNA in the bloody letters is coming from the same source. I'm willing to throw you a bone and let you keep working on this angle. But it's low priority. Understood?"

"Absolutely."

Raritan added, "And let me know what you guys find." He changed the subject. "Speaking of topics you failed to cover during the briefing, didn't you interview Mara Bliss yet?"

"Yes. Yesterday."

"And?"

"And nothing."

"Nothing?" Raritan asked.

"Yeah, nothing." I glanced at Woodson but she stayed silent as I continued. "Mara has dissociative identity disorder. You can't make any sense out of anything she says. She's useless as a material witness right now, unless her doctor makes some tremendous breakthroughs with her real soon. And even then it's highly doubtful that she'll be able to give us any important information."

Raritan looked at Parkman without speaking, then back at the camera. "Okay then, Lucas, let me just go straight to the point. How in the bloody blue hell did the Snow White Killer himself know where Mara Bliss's grandmother used to live? Miss Bliss is a critical link in this case, Lucas. SWK must have known Mara personally. And I'm worried—"

I cut him off, seeing where he was headed. "Woodson had asked the same question, so I asked Mara when I interviewed her. She said the guy who kidnapped her told her he needed to take her someplace where no one could find her. He literally asked her where he should take her. It was Mara who actually suggested her grandmother's house. At least that's what she claims. So even though we all had similar concerns about how the hell Mara and SWK ended up at her grandmother's house, I'm now convinced that this guy had no previous connection with Mara beforehand. He just wound up following her directions after he abducted her."

Jimmy paused on the videoconference, then leaned back in his chair and sighed aloud. "Who the fuck tells an abductor where to take her?"

"Honestly, I don't know what to think either, but for that matter, neither does her psychiatrist. But that's her story. There's no way to confirm it." I paused, then added, "And she gave me that explanation without a split-second hesitation when I asked her out of the blue. I don't think she's lying in this case."

"Shit," Jimmy said from the video monitor. "I thought we really had a lead there. Okay. So you and Woodson need to keep working on this, I guess. But I want an executive summary of your interview with Mara Bliss and her psychiatrist on my desk tomorrow morning. Don't leave anything out. Got it?"

"Got it. I mean, aye aye, Captain," I added.

"Yeah, yeah. All right, we're signing off. Let us know if anything breaks. Woodson, keep this guy on a short leash."

"Aye aye, Captain," Woodson said, and I had to stifle a laugh.

"I see our favorite black sheep in the Bureau is rubbing off unfavorably on our recent graduate," Raritan said, shaking his head on the monitor.

"And she was such a nice girl, too," Parkman added.

"Okay, okay. We'll call if anything happens." I waved the remote toward them.

"Stay in line down there, Woodson," Raritan stated a final warning, "and you, too, Lucas."

"Aye aye, Captain," we both said in unison, and I clicked the remote before Raritan could hear or see us break out into laughter together.

Woodson and I were walking back to our offices when my cell phone rang and Donny's number glowed on its face. "Donny," I answered, "I didn't expect you so soon! What's up?"

"You know the drill, Lucas. Get over to Willow Grove. I just received a call from a deputy. He's standing over the body of another girl. Our third in ten days, Lucas. Fourth overall."

"Goddamn it," I said, and Woodson's face filled with concern. "Yes, we can get there. We'll be there."

Donny hung up without speaking further, perfectly accentuating the tension that was growing steadily between us, the longer the Snow White Killer stayed at large and wreaked havoc in his home county. Woodson looked at me, but I could tell she already knew, so I didn't even bother saying anything. Every time we gained an inch of ground, we found another body and slid back a hundred feet. The SWK was striking with a frequency that I'd never before witnessed in a newly emerged killer. He certainly wasn't waiting on a lunar cycle.

"Another body?" Woodson finally made the perfunctory inquiry.

"Yes," I said simply. "Your car or mine?"

NINETEEN

An hour later we followed a deputy through knee-high grass and into a stretch of woods off Highway 63. As we approached, Donny stepped away from a group of half a dozen law enforcement officers standing around a prominent tree lit by high-powered lamps.

Woodson and I ducked under a ribbon of yellow tape. "Did the coroner estimate the time of death yet?" I asked.

Donny nodded. "He just took a core temp, thinks we're looking at around ten o'clock this morning." He circled around the tree to the victim, who sat propped against it. "I'm getting real tired of this shit, Lucas."

"I know," I said, unable to look him in the eyes. "We are, too. Can we check her out?"

"Yep. The CSIs already got their photos."

Donny stepped back and Woodson and I knelt on either side of the victim. The next installment of the killer's cryptic message, left upon her forehead and partially visible beneath her bangs, was the word *CANT*.

As usual, the girl had been leaned against a tree, her legs spread-eagled as if inviting copulation, yet fully clothed in her original garb. Just like the other victims. An apple lay on the ground beside her.

"He's nothing if not consistent," Woodson muttered as she snapped gloves around her wrists.

I crouched on the other side of the girl, using a pointer to draw her bangs back and better observe the word *CANT* stretched across her forehead. Something bothered me, but I couldn't put my finger on it.

"Any ID, Donny?" I finally asked over my shoulder.

Donny walked to Woodson's side and pulled a small notepad from his breast pocket, flipping it open. "Yep. Penny Hughes. Twenty-three years old, single, no kids. Her next of kin, her mother, has been notified. The girl was from Brandon, but had just moved down to Biloxi a few weeks ago."

I grimaced. "Any idea where she was abducted?"

"Not yet. We're working on it. Her car wasn't at her place, though, so we already have an APB out for her plates on the radio—we'll find it soon."

I looked back down. Like the other victims, the girl named Penny Hughes had been attractive. Her asymmetrically bobbed haircut gleamed with maroon strands, the false color that dark-haired women sometimes wear. Her eyes were thick with mascara, and glitter covered her cheeks. She wore a black turtleneck sweater tucked into a red-and-green plaid skirt clasped with an oversize safety pin. Her legs were covered with black stockings. In short, she was a Goth.

I could see the cuts on her legs through the sheer netting.

"Same modus operandi, looks like," Donny said.

I nodded. "Rural dump site, young white woman, cut up, reclothed in a sexually evocative position, yet another nonsensical word on a forehead, the razored apple, no trace of the perp. It's the same old story, and believe me, he's telling one." I sighed. "This guy's a perfectionist."

"Not quite," Woodson said.

"What do you mean?"

She pointed to the victim's head. "If he's so perfect, why didn't he include an apostrophe?"

I looked at the word *CANT* lined along the girl's forehead and finally realized what had initially struck me as strange. "I knew there was something odd about the way the letters looked, but I couldn't put my finger on it. You're right."

Donny cleared his throat behind us. "All this discussion just because the fucker has bad grammar habits? Maybe he was just in a hurry, for shit's sake."

"Or maybe he just doesn't use them," Woodson said. "You know, when he writes." She rose to her feet. "Maybe it doesn't mean anything."

"Maybe," I said, neither convinced nor unconvinced, as Woodson resumed her examination of the body. She used a clipboard and carefully copied the position of each cut onto the front and back body outlines of an autopsy report form.

We found nothing more illuminating at the crime scene. I instructed the ME to send blood samples swabbed from the word *CANT* to Terry's attention in the FBI laboratory for immediate DNA analysis, while Woodson took some final photos. A bit later she spoke in my direction. "Hey, Lucas, come look at this."

I walked over. "What is it?"

Woodson aimed the narrow beam of a penlight down to illuminate the victim's hand. "Look at her index finger."

The flashlight illuminated a tiny circular marking on the tip of the victim's finger. "What's that?" I asked. "Blood spatter? Nonvictim blood?"

"Neither," Woodson said. "I think it's a pinprick."

I squinted. "You may be right. Like the kind you get at a doctor's office, right?"

"That's what I was thinking. Did any of the other victims have pinpricks?"

"Not that I recall," I answered. "But that doesn't mean we looked carefully enough at the bodies to notice."

Donny walked back over. "We're just about done here. Anything else before we let the coroner take her away?"

"No, no." I said. "We're done here, too. For now, at least."

"Okay." Donny opened his mouth but then closed it, as if trying to decide whether to speak or not. After another moment, he spoke. "Hey, Lucas, can I talk to you for a second?"

"Sure."

Donny glanced at Woodson, then motioned with his head toward the perimeter of the crime scene. "Come on over for a second."

I frowned but Woodson gave a disaffected shrug. I followed Donny into the darkness outside the yellow taped area. "What's going on?"

Donny spit to the side, wiped his lip, and then looked over my shoulder before answering. "Look. I didn't want to say anything in front of your partner. But you ought to know, in case you haven't already realized."

"What?"

"You're standing on land owned by somebody you know."

"Who?"

"Charlie Bliss."

I glanced around, as if looking about in the dark woods might help me verify or refute the statement. "Mara's father? Are you sure?"

"Yep. I'm sure. And I hate to say this, but that's just fucking weird, man. And I thought you should know. First Mara and that victim are found at her grandmother's house . . . the house that Charlie grew up in when you stop to think about it. And now this? Something ain't adding up here, Lucas."

A cold dread settled in my chest. After all the convoluted logic we'd used to convince ourselves that Mara's abduction was just coincidence. Was it possible, after everything, that this really was still about Mara? Or her father?

I thought of what Mara's psychiatrist had said, about how something might have transpired in her childhood that even Kinsey hadn't been able to broach with her. Donny's voice pulled me back to the present. "I can't ignore this, man. I've got to bring him in for questions."

"Wait." I placed my hand on his shoulder. "Let me talk to him first. Please."

He shrugged out from under my hand. "Lucas, you're too close to all this shit. You should have pulled out of this whole investigation as soon as you found Mara in that basement." He spat again on the ground. "Hell, you know that."

My closest friend had come to sound just like Raritan, but I ignored it. "Just let me talk to him, Donny. You know I want to find the killer just as bad as you do."

Instead of answering, Donny just stared at me. Into me. The look on his face was accusatory, but uncertain, too. I could tell he was weighing in his mind whether I'd keep tracking down the Snow White Killer if the tracks led to Charlie Bliss. After another moment, his eyebrows unknotted and his face relaxed. "Okay, Lucas. But what are you going to say to him?"

"I don't know. I guess I'm going to start with whether he knows why the hell two of the four victims of the Snow White Killer have been discovered on his property. That's as good a place to start as any."

"Well, hell, if you want to take the direct route, I guess. You may want to ease into it, though."

At that moment he looked over my left shoulder. "You may want to keep this on the down-low, too, if you know what I mean. Here comes your partner."

Woodson walked up and greeted us with a forced smile. "Are we all set? I need to get back." She looked at Donny. "Unless I'm interrupting something here?"

"Oh no, not at all," Donny said with an equally forced smile. "We're all finished up here. Y'all have a good night," he said, tipping the brim of his sheriff's hat. "Talk to you tomorrow, Lucas," he added.

"Until then, Donny."

Woodson and I watched him stoop beneath the yellow tape and amble back toward the crime scene. In the background the coroner's van backed up to the body. "So. You ready?" she asked.

"Yes. I'll just—"

Woodson put her hand out to stop me. "Listen. I don't know whether what you two were just talking about really was private, or if it was about this case, but if it's about this investigation, then I hope you plan on filling me in."

"Don't worry. I will. I promise." I looked around to make sure Donny wasn't in hearing range. He was already engaged in a conversation with the coroner in the distance. I turned back to Woodson. "Come with me to the car, and I'll get you up to speed," I said. "I promise."

Once in the car, I wasted no time relaying to Woodson the link to Charlie's property that Donny had divulged.

"What do you make of it?" Woodson finally asked.

"Honestly? I don't know. I'd like to chalk it up to coincidence, but I can't. First Mara in her grandmother's basement, now this link to Charlie's property? I don't know what to think."

Woodson nodded thoughtfully and waited for several more miles before speaking again. "You have any idea why, you know, Mara's father might, you know, be involved?"

"He's not involved necessarily," I said, surprised by my own defensiveness. "We should just drive out to talk to him tomorrow and find out what he says."

Woodson didn't say anything in response, and we rode in silence after that. As we drove I found my mind swirling with an increasing number of questions, but the one that remained at the forefront of my mind didn't involve anyone by the last name of Bliss.

I couldn't shake from my mind the bloody word *CANT* smeared across the latest girl's forehead.

And instead of questions about Mara, her father, or anyone else, a singular question seemed to hold the entire key to this investigation: What the hell did the SWK think a tan cat couldn't do?

TWENTY

The next morning Terry walked into my office and closed the door behind him. "You're not going to believe this," he said.

"What is it?"

"We just finished analyzing the DNA patterns from the blood left on the victims' foreheads with our algorithm. You want to see how the DNA of your unsub compares to DNA profiles of the most infamous serial killers of all time?"

"You really need to ask?"

"Check this out." He tossed a stack of papers on my desk. "Look at page two."

Page two of the report contained an upside-down tree-shaped graph showing the individual branches of serial killers clustered into different subgroups. The familiar cluster of Bundy/Green River Killer/Son of Sam sat on the leftmost cluster. Another familiar cluster bore Brady, Gacy, and Dahmer. I scanned the rest of the DNA similarity clusters and finally found our newest blood sample in the collection, SWK, on the far right edge of the two-dimensional dendrogram.

Terry pointed. "We have a new cluster." He tapped the page as my eyes tracked to the labels in an all-new grouping of DNA profiles on the far right: BTK, Zodiac, and SWK.

"Holy shit."

Our algorithm was designed to recluster all the serial killer DNA samples whenever a new DNA sample was added. When the DNA profiles of the fifty-two original serial killers in our database were clustered, they gave seven subgroups. BTK and Zodiac had always resided in separate clusters. Now, after Terry had added the SWK's genetic profile to the mix, the algorithm identified eight subgroups. The three DNA samples from BTK, Zodiac, and SWK now formed a new category unto themselves.

"You know," Terry observed, "it took twenty-plus years to catch BTK, and Zodiac was never caught."

I stared at the results tree and focused on the names in the cluster. BTK–Zodiac–SWK.

I finally spoke. "Maybe it all fits, you know? SWK's crime scenes are spotless. And he's obviously on a mission . . . exactly what kind, we don't know yet."

"God complex?"

"God, messiah, something. Just like Zodiac and BTK. But one thing doesn't fit."

"What's that?" Terry asked.

"BTK and Zodiac both mocked the police, almost to an absurd extent. They were big-time taunters, as if in the end they killed less for the thrill of it and more just to be able to continue their one-sided rapport with law enforcement."

"But our guy isn't like that," Terry said. "At least not yet. I mean, unless the message SWK's been leaving on the foreheads of his victims *is* the taunt."

I weighed the possibility. "You may be on to something there. Maybe. But I still would have expected him to communicate with law enforcement more directly. That kind of guy just can't stand it if he's being misinterpreted, or worse, ignored."

"Hey, he's still out there. He may communicate with us still."

I shrugged, about to speak, but at that moment a knock sounded on Terry's door.

"Come in," he said.

Woodson appeared in a navy blue skirt, white blouse, and navy coat. "Ready to go visit your friend Charlie?"

I shook my head and motioned toward Terry's screen instead. "Come on in," I said. "You've got to see this first. You're not going to believe it."

After Terry and I explained to Woodson that the DNA profile of SWK was more similar to BTK and Zodiac than any of the other serial killers we'd profiled, the three of us plotted our next courses of action.

Terry would go back to constructing a jeopardy map based on the four body dump sites to try and come up with the jeopardy surface we'd promised at the debriefing. The end result would be a three-dimensional, contoured map of probabilities indicating likely spots where the killer might live, as well as places where the killer might strike again.

Woodson went back to reanalyze the toxicology data, while I was going to screen the original autopsy reports to check whether any of the other victims had pinpricks on their fingers.

We decided we'd try to get all of this done before Woodson and I paid a visit to Charlie Bliss in the afternoon.

At three o'clock I stood from my desk, stretched, and felt the slightly painful pull in my back where Mara's stab wound continued to heal. I hadn't found anything indicating pinpricks in the autopsy reports and hadn't reached any of the MEs, for that matter, either. Regardless, Woodson and I needed to get on the road.

Woodson sat in her office, typing on the computer, when I walked in. "You ready?" she asked.

"No, but no time like the present," I said. "I guess it's time we go talk to Charles Bliss. Hey, by the way, I was able to find out that the other two victims weren't dropped on land that Charlie owns. So maybe this is just another bogus coincidence."

"You trying to get out of this?" Woodson squinted her eyes as she asked the question.

"No, not in the least," I answered. "Let's just get this over with."

"You got it," Woodson said, sliding her laptop into her briefcase and standing. "Let's go."

An hour later I watched in my rearview mirror as Woodson drove behind and followed me onto Highway 26. A gas station with old pumps shimmered into view in the distance on my right, the West Poplarville Gas and Oil Mart.

Soon the Bliss residence came into view in the middle of a clearing on the right, an old antebellum farmhouse, yellowed white, with two stories and a screened-in porch. As I pulled in to the gravel driveway I caught sight of an old bloodhound lying on the sidewalk in front of the steps. Charlie had gotten a new dog.

Woodson and I walked side by side through the ankle-deep grass of the front yard. The dog opened one of its eyes, witnessed us, then closed its eye and immediately went back to sleep.

On the screened porch, rusty metal chairs sat next to a huge, overturned wooden spool, the kind used for rolling up telephone cables. A deck of playing cards sat scattered about the top of it in a half-finished game of solitaire.

I opened the screen door and we stepped into the shade of the porch. I pressed the yellow doorbell and waited.

"I'm coming, I'm coming," a muffled voice called from inside, over the chimes.

A second later Charlie Bliss's dark face came in to full view. "Well, I'll be damned," he said.

"How you been, Mr. Bliss?" I immediately fell into the old comfortable parlance, despite my strongest inner desire to stay professional.

He was dressed like a Southern gentleman, crisp tan pants and an aqua-blue shirt. He leaned pleasantly upon a polished wooden cane, but his smile vanished as he noticed Woodson standing behind me, and his eyes narrowed. "Can I help you?"

"Yes, in fact," Woodson answered. "We were hoping to talk to you for a bit."

The older man looked from my partner to me. "I suppose so, come on in." He held the door open as we walked inside. It took a few seconds for my eyes to adjust to the dark interior. Charlie's shadowy form moved down the dimly lit hallway. As he tilted unsteadily with each step, I wondered why he now had a limp.

Dark rectangles on the walls revealed themselves to be framed pictures. And suddenly the beautiful, mesmerizing eyes of Mara Bliss stared at me from all directions.

I did a double take when I spied a picture of Mara and myself among them. "Where was this photo?" I pointed and asked, but Charlie cut me off.

"I don't know. I just always liked that picture of you two." Without waiting to continue any further chitchat, he opened a swinging door on the left and ushered us into a small dining room just off the kitchen and sat down.

"Is this about what happened to my little girl? And you?" Charlie asked as he took a seat across from us, with a break in his voice. "My little Mara," he said simply, then added, "you know she's not well, Lucas."

I glanced at Woodson before I spoke. "I know, Charlie. I know that now."

"Didn't always used to be like that." Charlie stood, walked over to a small triangular table in the corner, and picked up a small picture frame. He brought it over and set it on the table between us. Woodson picked it up.

"It's a nice picture," Woodson said, handing it to me.

It was a picture of Mara and her mother and father, taken a good twenty years ago, during what had been a terrible summer. My mother had died the year before, then Mara and her family disappeared. I only saw Mara a few times that summer, and whenever I did, she seemed sullen and distant, incredibly different from the girl who'd led me into the graveyard the first night we ever met, to give me my first kiss. That summer, she and her ever-faithful mother eventually stopped coming to church.

That same summer my father kept specifically alluding to racism in every sermon. If Christ had shared the good news with a Samaritan woman, he'd ask, then how could we foster such prejudice in our enlightened day and age? Even at the age of thirteen, I somehow knew my father was referring to Mara's father as he admonished the congregation. It seemed in every sermon he repeated the old saying, "Evil is what happens when good men sit by and do nothing," or something to that effect. I just never knew why. I handed the picture frame back to Charlie. "Nice."

"She won't talk to me anymore, Lucas. Not about what happened down in her Nana's basement, not about anything. She doesn't even let me visit her anymore."

"She's been under a lot of stress lately."

"Oh yeah? Well then, why don't you fill me in? I still don't know what happened. Why her?"

"We were hoping you could tell us."

A brittle laugh from his lungs held no solace whatsoever. "You're barking up the wrong tree. I don't know any more about Mara than a person on the street, nowadays."

I pressed further. "Mara's psychiatrist says there may have been a traumatic event in her childhood. We'd like to know about it. Anything in her childhood we should know about?"

Charlie leaned back, and an empty smile holding no true emotion creased his lips. "Everybody thinks all the problems go back to childhood. It's not the person's fault. It's their momma's or daddy's fault." He snorted in derision, but then his face grew instantly wary. "Why are you asking me? You think I did something to my little girl?"

"No, Charlie," I said. "I don't think anything right now. I'm just asking you if anything happened in her childhood."

"But I still have to tell you officially that I didn't do anything to her, right?" He glared at me. "For your goddamned record."

"You know what, Charlie? And I shouldn't even have to tell you this. But yes, you need to tell me and Agent Woodson whether you know if anyone sexually abused her—you or anybody else. For the goddamned record, as you put it."

The anger pulsed through the small capillaries in his eyes, but he bit it back. In a strained voice he replied, "I never laid a hand on my daughter that way. No one ever did."

"Thank you. Now we have one more question for you."

"Go ahead, Agent Madden."

I ignored his new, more formal appellation for me. "Do you know why some of the victims of the Snow White Killer are winding up on property that you own?"

"What? Oh, you mean Mara and that girl found with her at her Nana's?"

"Not just them. Plus another victim from last night found in one of your fields."

"What victim last night? Where?"

Woodson cut her eyes toward me, but I kept talking. "Another victim showed up last night on some hunting acreage you own over near Willow Grove. You know anything about that?"

"Well, hell no, I don't know anything about that," he answered. "I didn't even know until you just asked me! I can't control where this guy is dumping these poor girls."

"So you'd claim that it's just coincidence that two of the four victims have wound up on your property so far?"

"I don't claim shit. I state it. Of course it's just coincidence. What? Do you think I'm the Snow White Killer?" He laughed, somehow with more derision than he'd used previously.

I looked at Woodson with a shrug. "Do you have any questions?"

Woodson smiled politely, and her next question caught me completely unaware. "Just one. Can you fill us in on your former arrest and status as a convicted rapist?"

At a loss for words, I looked back at Charlie, intent on apologizing for the error that must have occurred. "Charlie," I began to say, but he shook his head and raised a hand to silence me.

"So that whole business has finally come up again, after all these years? I'll be damned."

"What are you talking about?" I asked, then rotated to face Woodson. "And what the hell are *you* talking about?"

Woodson regarded me with a stare that was equal parts apologetic and resolute. She didn't answer and instead waited for Charlie to speak. I turned back to face him.

"You don't know about all that mess, Lucas?" Charlie asked. "Your daddy never told you?"

"Told me what?"

"You still don't know why we left town back in eighty-two?"

"You took another job at a different college. Mara told me once she and I met up again in New Orleans."

He laughed, self-deprecatingly. "Well, yes, eventually I did find a new job. But that's not why we left in the first place.

"Long story short, while I was a professor at Ole Miss, a couple of girls in one of my classes were failing, and once they figured out they really were going to fail, they went to school administrators and claimed I'd raped them in my office. That I made them both have sex with me right there in my office and told them I'd kill them if they ever told anybody."

"Charlie. For God's sake. I never had any idea."

Charlie laughed again, this time bitterly. "Weren't no 'God' to it," he said. "I told my side of the story, which didn't do me any good. Your daddy came down, the only one of my supposed friends who even bothered. He helped me find as good a lawyer as he and I could afford."

And in a crystal clear moment of clarity, I suddenly understood the unspoken topic of my father's sermons for that entire summer.

Charlie continued. "Didn't matter, though. They found me guilty within thirty minutes after the jury closed the doors. In fact, the judge advised everyone to stay after the closing arguments and the jury adjourned. I guess he knew as well as I did that it wasn't going to take long for them to reach a guilty verdict."

"But it was a lie, right?"

"Of course it was a lie."

"So what evidence did they have? How the hell did they ever build a case against you?"

"They didn't have all the fancy DNA techniques worked out back then, Lucas. All they had were my words against those two white girls. It didn't take long."

"I never knew," I mumbled, before falling silent again.

"I was in jail for a while, but then your daddy found another lawyer who filed an appeal, literally a god-awful man, someone of whom the whole Mississippi judiciary system was terrified. And we were going to take it public, and it was going to be big news, none of this small town cover-up business. Back then it was still real en vogue to liberate unjustly accused black men, Medgar Evers, all that. So the odds were suddenly in my favor, despite the initial miscarriage of justice. So when those girls and their families found out about the appeal, they gave me a plea bargain—that if I left the state of Mississippi, they'd drop all charges and I could have my life back."

"God," I said.

Charlie raised his eyebrows. "Like I said. Weren't no 'God' to it. They made me sign a statement that I'd done what they said, but that I hadn't used a weapon and that they were just scared, so perhaps I'd thought it consensual. I can't remember the exact wording. It must have embarrassed the person who wrote it, much less me, who had to read it and sign it."

Charlie stood and placed both hands on the table. "Yep. I signed my life away on that dotted line. And forever, whether I'm the only one who believes it or not, I'll go down in history as a rapist. So that's who I am, Agent Woodson, at least when it comes to your goddamned record. Anything else before you leave?"

It was silent for several seconds as I struggled to assimilate his story.

Woodson finally broke the silence. "So do you have an alibi for your whereabouts between the hours of two and eight P.M. two nights ago?"

"Me?" He focused on me with an anger he couldn't disguise. Suddenly his face broke into a wide grin as he recalled something. "Matter of fact, I do, Agent Woodson. In fact," he gestured toward me, "I caught a movie with this man's father that afternoon, then he and I parted ways and I went and played poker until midnight over at Bill Carlisle's place." He smiled. "Sorry to disappoint you."

"Charlie," I said, "it's not like that."

"Oh yeah? Then what the hell is it like? You came over here to find out whether I was your Snow White Killer. Whether, I presume, I had kidnapped and raped my own daughter?" He cleared his throat. "You can go fuck yourself, Lucas."

"This wasn't Lucas's idea, Mr. Bliss. The FBI made him come." Woodson spoke the words in a steady tone, without hesitation.

Charlie peered at me as he spoke to her. "Well, that may be so, young lady. Whatever the case, now you both know what happened. And for your record you can still both go fuck yourselves."

It was silent for a moment, then Charlie looked at a clock on the wall. "So, is there anything else? I need to get some errands done today."

Woodson and I both shook our heads in the negative, consumed by silence, and Charlie bade us farewell.

The interview was over.

At the door I turned and tried to use a conciliatory tone for one last question down the hall. "Charlie. What ever happened to those girls, the ones who lied about you in school?"

I couldn't see him in the darkness of the house, but his voice answered from the hallway. "Well, you Christian folk, y'all might see it as divine providence. Or your buddy John Lennon might say it was instant karma. But I say it's the way the ball bounces." An orange glow appeared in the hallway, and then a whiff of smoke passed through the doorway. He'd lit a cigar. "Those two girls died in a car accident about two years later over in Atlanta, I heard. And that's the last time I've given them a second thought in a long time."

I waited, trying to think of something else to say, but it was obvious he didn't want to continue the conversation. I nodded and followed Woodson down the porch. We stepped around the hound dog, still lounging in the same position from before. I heard the screen door bang shut behind us with a finality that seemed to perfectly punctuate the day's proceedings.

I knew in that moment that my relationship with Charles Bliss had come to an end, forever.

TWENTY-ONE

In the wake of all the stunning revelations, I had momentarily forgotten how angry I was with Woodson in the first place. At our first opportunity I pulled over at a small gas station on Highway 26 to fill up.

Woodson began filling her tank, too, on the other side of the island. "So why the hell didn't you tell me about the rape charge you dug up?" I finally asked, then changed to a sarcastic tone. "I thought we were in the circle of trust now."

Woodson held up her hands. "I'm sorry, Lucas. I came across it last night and didn't know what to do. The only thing I knew was I couldn't tell you beforehand."

"Why not?"

"Because you'd ruin it by talking with him on your own first."

"Well, great idea. The way it played out, I'm pretty sure I just lost a friend forever today."

"I'm sorry about that, Lucas. I really am."

"Well, that remorse you're feeling plus a dollar buys you a cup of coffee at McDonald's."

She started to speak but I didn't let her. "What's done is done. Or should I say what's fucked is fucked. But from now on this . . ." I waved my hand back and forth in the air between us, "this is a two-way street. Just the other day you were giving me shit when Donny told me about the link to Charlie's property, and I came clean to you from the get-go. But now I don't get the same treatment in return."

Woodson opened her mouth to protest, but closed it just as quickly. She nodded instead.

"From now on, no more secrets," I said. "None. Or one of us is going to have to go. I don't so much care who at this point, anymore. But we can't be partners like this. We either trust each other the rest of the way, or we don't. What's it going to be?"

Woodson looked up at me, and I could see genuine regret in her eyes as she spoke. "Okay, Lucas. I'm sorry. No more secrets. I promise."

I clicked the last bit of gas into my tank, replaced the nozzle, and stepped across to Woodson's side as she finished up as well. "One last thing," I said.

"Yeah?"

"I just wanted to tell you that I do appreciate what you did back there," I said.

"I'm not following you."

"At the end, I mean. How you tried to protect me in front of Charlie by blaming yourself and the Bureau for the interrogation."

Woodson nodded and smiled slightly. "Oh, that. I know you do. You don't have to say it."

"But I'm saying it anyway. Thanks, Woodson. It means a lot, actually. Really."

She eyed me, but didn't say anything, and just continued to look at me.

I found myself staring at her as well. And suddenly realized I needed to say something—if I didn't, I was afraid of what might happen. I suddenly couldn't shake the idea of trying to kiss her.

I clapped my hands together hard, much more intensely than I'd intended. "So," I said. "How about comparing notes?"

Woodson looked at me a moment longer, and then smiled. "Okay," she said, simply.

––––––

We sat in her car and reviewed everything, but the conversation really boiled down to two main facts. First, the rape charge against Charlie was a case of false accusation and not necessarily significant to the search for SWK. Secondly, and more importantly, Charlie had an alibi for his whereabouts the previous night, which we could also check.

The stirring of feelings I'd felt toward Woodson at the gas pump had eventually died down, at least to some extent. I still wasn't sure what to make of them and was worried that it would become a distraction if we kept working together that night.

Rather than suggesting another late night, I instead bade her farewell and advised her to go home and get some much-needed rest. She agreed without any argument, and we made plans to meet the next morning in the New Orleans field office and come up with next steps.

On my way home I tried to assimilate everything we'd learned in the last few days, from Charlie's past, to the pinprick on the fourth victim's finger, to the SWK/BTK/Zodiac results in the Damnation Algorithm, to the huge caffeine levels Woodson had discovered in the victims' systems, to the ever-extending message left on the foreheads, to the lack of an apostrophe in CANT.

Everything.

And nothing added up.

So many observations, so few leads. Nothing tying everything together.

At the next intersection leading back to the interstate I pulled to a stop behind Woodson. She proceeded, and I found myself staring at a rectangular green sign indicating Crossroads, only three miles away to the left. After another moment's hesitation, I decided.

I needed to meet with one more person, without Woodson in tow. I needed to confirm Charlie's alibi about his whereabouts last night.

Instead of going back to the interstate, I turned to the left just as Woodson's taillights disappeared over a hill in the distance.

Ten minutes later I pulled into my father's church parking lot and realized a prayer service was just letting out. No one in the emerging congregation paid me much attention as they exited the doors and broke off into smaller groups. Older farmers lit up pipes, ladies laughed over an infomercial or gossip, and kids threw a football in the grass.

A few middle-aged couples conversed with my father at the top of the steps, laughing as each took a turn relaying some story.

I walked up the steps toward him, suddenly doubting my decision to come here, feeling as though I were caught in some genetic tractor beam, unable to avoid my father any longer.

None of the congregation members recognized me. My father had changed churches several times since I left for college, and I hadn't been to any of his churches for even longer than that, ever since my mother's death.

But the members suddenly went quiet as they glanced from me and back to my father, recognizing the off-kilter similarities in our faces. My own features like a genetic peek-a-boo into the way my father once looked long ago. The laughter in my father's face vanished, and his own expression went indecipherable.

As I made my way up the last few steps, he bade farewell to the group. They parted for me, the women cutting their eyes at me ominously, the men ignoring eye contact altogether.

Behind me, one of the men turned and called up. "Pastor Madden? You want one of us to help you lock up?"

"No thank you, John. You all have a good night, and I'll see you Sunday." He raised his eyebrows and smiled as I reached the top step. "How are you, son?"

"Good, good. Just dropping by for a visit, if you have a second."

He touched my shoulder. "Of course. Is everything okay? How's your back doing?"

I realized I didn't have any idea how to talk to my father on my own. The only times I'd interacted with him for the last fifteen years had been in the presence of Katie, who was always trying to bring us together and constantly played the mediator. "It's okay, Dad. Just working on this case and wanted to stop by. Was up by Charlie Bliss's a little while ago."

My father's face relaxed into a smile. "Good old Charlie," he said, and laughed. "God-fearing Charlie, I call him. He hates it when I call him that, atheist that he is!"

He opened the door to the church. "Come inside with me. I need to turn down the church."

I caught the glass door behind him and was instantly transported back to my childhood. Time to turn out the lights, shut down the air-conditioning, and lock the doors to the church, just like we'd done so many times before.

I followed him through the vestibule and into the sanctuary but my eyes couldn't adjust to the change in light. I blinked and kept them closed for a second, but when I looked up I couldn't see my father anywhere in the grayness.

"What brings you here, son?"

Vision slowly returned, revealing the pews on either side, the long carpeted walkway to the front of the church, and my father in his white robe, behind the formidable pulpit of magnificently carved wood. "I stopped to talk to Charlie about the Snow White Killer investigation."

My father's voice echoed from behind the pulpit as he bent down to flick a variety of switches. "I read about it in the papers, and Katie's filled me in since the hospital." He dusted off his hands as he rose to his full height again behind the pulpit. "This killer of yours leaves apples in these young women's hands? Blasphemy on top of everything else he's doing?"

"Blasphemy? Why do you say that?"

"Seems to me he's recreating the Garden of Eden, you know, Eve holding the apple, don't you think?"

"Oh," I said, finally understanding his logic, "who knows? We're not sure about the meaning yet." I changed the subject back to Charlie. "We had to question Charlie because two of the four victims have wound up on property he owns, so far."

My father stopped what he was doing. "Why did you have to go talk to Charlie?"

"We found out about the old rape charges. We had to follow up on them."

My father descended the steps and walked rapidly back toward me. "Did Charlie tell you all about that so-called rape charge? Did he set you straight?" There was an unsettling anger in his voice that I'd seldom heard.

"Well, actually, yes he did," I said. "He told us all about it. Sounds like he was royally screwed. Sounds like he might still be in jail if you hadn't helped him."

"It was a shame I had to help him at all. Terrible, what happened to him. Still makes me angry."

"I can see that."

My comment seemed to snap him back to the present. "And it concerns me when my own flesh and blood goes over and questions him as to whether he was involved with something as sick and twisted as this Snow White Killer case of yours."

"It wasn't like that," I said. "We just had to talk to him, that's all. We couldn't ignore it, not after two of the victims showed up on his property."

"What, did you ask if he had an alibi or something?" My father asked the question as though it were the most outlandish suggestion in the world.

"Yes, in fact, we did. And he said he was with you initially, then played poker at some fellow's place. I'm assuming that's correct?"

"Of course it's correct. Is that why you're here? To check his alibi? Hasn't the poor man been through enough?"

"Hold on," I said. "For one thing, until a few hours ago, I had no idea he'd ever 'been through' anything at all. Second, you do your job and I'll do mine. Of course I had to follow up on it. It's what I do."

An uncomfortable silence ensued, until my father spoke again, with a softer tone. "I'm sorry. You're right. It's what you do. I should know that by now. But this whole Snow White Killer case. It worries me."

"Why? If your Garden of Eden theory is correct, maybe the guy has issues with religion."

"Who doesn't anymore, Lucas?" My father held up his hands and gestured as though to a crowd of spectators. "These halls? They used to be filled with people. Now, half full. On a good day."

"Dad, don't take it personally. People are just, they're just—"

"What, Lucas? They're just uninterested? Or busy? Well, you're right about that. I don't understand it. God showed us the way and now nobody's listening. It's the end days, Lucas. Surely you can see that. The devil's stronger than ever."

"The devil?" I tried, but failed, to filter out the disbelief in my tone.

"Yes, the devil. I know, you're smart, Lucas. Much smarter than me or anyone else. There's no devil. The devil doesn't exist, does he?"

"Well—"

"Let me ask you something, Lucas. Indulge me. What brought you here again?"

"I'm not following—"

"Didn't you say you came here to investigate your case?"

"Well, yes, but—"

"So what does that killer do to these poor young women he kills?" My father peered at me in the dark.

"We're not making that public, Dad."

"I'm only asking in general terms. I bet you have a term for it."

"What?"

"Overkill? Isn't that the name you give it?"

"I guess."

My father continued. "Then who is that, who pushes the knife into those poor girls even as they beg for mercy, and there's none to be given? Who is using that knife, Lucas?"

"A sick and disturbed killer dubbed—"

"No. That's just the human who lifts the knife. I could kill somebody. I have an arm, I own knives. Big long ones. But I don't. I don't go around killing people. No, it's something inside that person that drives the person to do it himself. And you know who it is as well as I do. You can't deny it. It's the devil, Lucas. Satan. The dragon. Whatever you want to call him. Leviathan. Prince of Darkness. Oh, I see it in your rolling eyes. You still pretend like you're too smart to believe in a spiritual world. Go on then, Lucas, look at those bodies, measure the knife marks, look for fingerprints. Check the DNA, get a match. Go ahead. And when you're done, what do you have?"

"Hopefully, the killer."

"Maybe. You'll have the who. But you won't have the why."

"The why being the devil?"

"Exactly."

"Dad, I hate to break it to you. There is no devil. And these killers I chase? They aren't the devil's handiwork. You know what the real problem is?"

"Enlighten me."

"It's their brains. They can't think right. They carry a mutated gene in a tiny part of their brain called—"

"The amygdala. Yes, Lucas. I've heard it before. Show them a picture of a bunny, then a picture of a dead person, and oh no! Their blood flow doesn't increase. They have *ripper* mutations."

Genuine surprise gripped me as I realized that my father must have kept up with my research. I tried not to show it. "Exactly."

"But some people carry ripper mutations and never hurt a soul, right?"

"Yes, but—"

"But what?"

"I never said that ripper was the *only* determinant of serial killer behavior. Just that it predisposes people to serial killer tendencies. If you must pursue this, it's likely a multigenic trait, in which multiple genes are probably mutated and culminate in such a personality disorder."

My father shook his head and walked back up the steps, past the pulpit. He stopped on the far side of the podium by the choir loft and turned around. "And you think I'm stupid for having faith in an all-powerful, omnipotent creator? At least I put my faith in an infinite concept. You put your faith in something as finite as the human genome." He paused. "Good luck when you get to the end of it, Lucas, and find that no matter how many experiments you run, no matter how many hypotheses you generate, no matter how many genes you think are the answer . . . you'll never get to the end, either."

"Dad."

"You know, Lucas, there's not much difference between you and me. We both have faith. I know that I'll never know for sure until I die. And I'm happy with the faith that I have. But you don't even understand that you'll never know. You keep expecting the answer to be right around the next corner, or the next. And you aren't happy with what you believe, either, Lucas. I can tell it. Do you really, truly believe a couple of scrambled genes in the brain are the entire reason they're killers? Because if it is, then these serial killers, they're just biological aberrations. And what they do shouldn't offend a society, because it's just . . ." at this point he made imaginary quotation marks, "it's just Darwin's random chance, probability, that's all, and they simply sit on the tails of the normal distribution." He leaned forward. "And yet, son, I can see that it bothers you. It repulses you on some other level. If you were a true biologist, you'd find their behavior no different than that of any other animal on the planet. But it bothers you, because you have a conscience. And you need to think about where that comes from."

I wasn't really listening and was instead stunned that my father had actually kept up with my research. And I was trying, with all my might, to block out his words. He'd always been able to leave me confused and doubtful, even when he tried to explain what he believed as truth.

At that moment the entire sanctuary plunged into total darkness as my father flipped the last panel of light switches. "A long time ago, Lucas, back when you were a little boy," my father's disembodied voice suddenly emerged from the dark silence, "I came into the church to pray one night. Times were tough then. Your mother was having a difficult pregnancy with Katie, you and Tyler were both sick, deathly sick with flu, and we had no money. The church wasn't able to pay us, so I'd started working at a gas station for your lunch money and our rent. And I asked God, I asked him to please help us through this."

I tried to speak but couldn't find my voice. I strained to see some shape in the darkness as the voice grew nearer, but couldn't.

My father's voice continued. "And he did. But that night, while I prayed in the dark, I heard the door creak open in that little country church. I lay on the altar, praying with all my heart, 'God please help me do your will.' And in the middle of that prayer I heard boards creaking and swore I heard the devil whisper behind me *Madden, you don't believe.* But I kept praying. Told myself it was a test, and that if I turned around, I wouldn't have the right kind of faith. So I kept praying, ignoring the voice that kept whispering in my mind, and the hairs on the back of my neck prickled. I kept praying and then—all of the sudden—it stopped.

"I finished praying, walked back through the dark church, walked back across the gravel road and back into our house. When I got there you and Tyler were sleeping. Your little bodies were soaking wet with sweat because both your fevers had finally broken. And your mother? She was comfortable for the first time in months, smiling away while she waited on me in the living room. And the next day Broadman published my devotional book, and we had enough money to get through."

A hand touched my arm in the dark and I jumped. "Who's there?"

"It's just me, son."

There was a brief pause, a beat of silence. I could smell my father's scent, a mixture of aftershave and soap, one that I hadn't smelled in years. My father leaned in close. I couldn't recall the name of the cologne.

"Just think on it, Lucas. Why would serial killers repulse you so? Come on and follow me out of here." He took my arm and led me through the dark sanctuary toward the exits in the rear of the church. "I didn't mean to start another argument with you. You're a grown man, you're entitled to your own beliefs."

I took a deep breath and tried to discern his shape in the darkness as we walked. I could almost make out his face within the shadows. "Dad, I didn't come here to fight, either. I honestly just wanted to stop by, check on Charlie's alibi."

He pushed open the door to the vestibule in front of us and the moonlight streamed through the glass entrance doors. I was able to once again see my father, who turned to face me with a smile. "I know, Lucas. It's what you do. And I'm proud of you. Just be careful as you search out these wicked devils. Just be careful." He paused but then spoke again. "Why don't you come by again tomorrow? I'm heading over to the cemetery to visit your mother. Why don't you come with me? She'd like it."

He always had to bring her up. Our long-dead mother. A bag of bones. And talk about her like she still walked the earth. "Dad, I'm not going over there."

He stopped just short of the vestibule and tilted his head in the moonlight, a quizzical look on his face. "Why not?"

I sighed. "Because she's dead. She died a long time ago, in a shitty little stretch of woods in a shitty little town because some piece of shit killed her."

"Lucas."

"And you act like nothing ever happened. Like she's still waltzing around cooking dinner or drawing a bath. She's dead." The anger suddenly overwhelmed me, and I didn't even know why. "Your bountiful God let her die. Don't you remember?"

My father's eyes tightened as though a tangible pain shot through his body.

"Good old God," I said. "Really looking out for the Madden clan, right?" I stared up into the rafters and then raised my hands. "Hey, God! Thanks, but no thanks!" I yelled the mocking appreciation out loud, and my voice traveled through the vestibule to echo in the sanctuary. "Please. Focus your tender mercies elsewhere for a while. Please! Give us Maddens a break down here!"

When I looked down again I saw that my father had taken several steps backwards, distancing himself from my tirade. He leaned upon a wall. "Lucas," he began, but I cut him off.

"Just forget it," I said. "It doesn't matter anymore anyway."

My father put his hand to his forehead. "Okay, Lucas. You best get on your way, then. I'm sorry I mentioned her."

I suddenly realized he was kicking me out of his church—politely, but kicking me out just the same. And that was fine by me. "Hey Dad, I can take a hint. See you around then. Tell Mom hello. And throw in a prayer for me."

I whirled around and walked toward the exit doors, but heard him murmur something behind me. "What was that?" I asked, whirling around angrily.

My father only stared at me. "I said, 'I do every night,' Lucas."

I frowned. "Do what?"

My father shook his head. "Never mind, Lucas. Just try to be—" he started to say, but I didn't hear him finish.

I'd already walked out of the church as fast as I could.

TWENTY-TWO

The next morning Woodson and Terry were already in the field office when I arrived. I knew I needed to hide the bad mood plaguing me.

"What's up, boss?" Terry asked. He and Woodson were leaning against a table, cups of steaming coffee in their hands.

"Plenty. We have a lot of territory to cover today. Let's meet this afternoon and compare notes."

"Sounds good."

"Come prepared," I said. "Then this afternoon Woodson and I will start hitting the bricks with an actual purpose in mind, for a change."

Woodson glanced up at me, but didn't challenge the statement. After going home last night in a sour mood following the conversation with my father, I'd realized that for the last two days I had been running around interviewing people just to cover my ass and prove to Raritan that I could still stay assigned to the case. I'd talked to Mara, her shrink, my brother, Mara's father, Charlie, and my own father as well.

I'd decided that the rest of this investigation wasn't going to center around the people of my past anymore. We needed to start funneling our energies into the search for the *actual* Snow White Killer, immediately. This new, almost angry sense of resolve had solidified my commitment to the case even further.

Terry spoke up. "The jeopardy surface should be ready by then."

"Good. What are you up to this morning, Woodson?"

"Going back through the drug screens to see if anything else pops up. I still believe he's drugging the victims before he starts in on them."

I nodded. "Sounds good. Let's plan on reconvening at two in the conference room."

We parted ways, each heading off to work our respective angles.

Back in my office I sat at my desk and listed as many salient observations as I could.

Mara—dissociative, no recollection of SWK—dead end

Tyler—alibi at scientific conference—(and superpissed)

Charlie—solid alibis—rape charge from past—effect on Mara?

The next two facing pages, far more relevant in my opinion, contained the main list of all the salient crime scene observations to date.

Elevated caffeine in tox reports—any commonalities between victims, coffeehouses, etc.?

Pinpricks on finger of fourth victim—commonality or coincidence? Recent physical or physician visits? (Need to follow up with the other three victims/autopsy reports/MEs)

Linear slashes on still-living victims—implies restraint (no ligature bruises) or drugs (likely but none detected in tox screens)—Woodson reexamining the raw data

Razored apples—Gillette razors are dead end—apples are Ein Shemers (local?)—freshly picked each time before a murder. Symbolizes? Garden of Eden re-creation? Halloween urban legend? Death in the fruit? Danger in the fruit?

Message—a tan cat can't—check with Shelly about any literary references now that it refers to something a tan cat can't do—a tan cat can't what?

Any significance regarding lack of an apostrophe in CANT on fourth victim's forehead? Consider anagrams.

Body posturing—sexual but fully reclothed—killer uncomfortable around naked female victims? Homosexual-oriented predator who kills women? Highly unusual (no rapes in other cases, except Mara)—possibly an impotent heterosexual predator? Remorse for victims?

Crime scene locations—two of four—just coincidence with Charlie's property?

UNSUB DNA—28 SNPs in the damnation signature—implies the killer uses own blood for the messages—no hits in CODIS, no previous incarcerations

Finally I turned to the last page I'd recorded in the notebook, entitled "Damnation Signature."

UNSUB DNA clustering result—SWK clusters with BTK and Zodiac (check p-values)

Predicted behavioral characteristics if DNA similarity results are significant—BTK and Zodiac taunted media and/or authority figures (no communications from SWK yet); Zodiac sent cryptograms/BTK alluded to the X factor (again, no communications from SWK); both capable of long periods of inactivity (opposed to the frenetic pace of SWK to date)

I sighed, pushing backwards in the chair. We had a lot to think about. And figuring out where to start seemed most important at this point. I glanced up at the clock above my office door. It was already nine thirty. I hoped Woodson or Terry was going to make a breakthrough. One of us needed to have one.

A little after two o'clock I made my way to the conference room where Woodson and Terry were waiting. "Let's get to it."

Terry tapped a button on his laptop and the projector sprang to life, illuminating the far wall of the conference room. "Okay," he said, "so I've calculated a jeopardy surface based on the drop sites of the victims." As he spoke, the blurry image on the screen began to resolve, pixel by pixel clicking into focus.

"The downloading graphic is a jeopardy map. To generate it, I input all the data about the victims' abduction sites and body drop sites into a computer algorithm which outputs the data into the form of a contoured geographical map."

Woodson stared intently at the image coming into focus. "We studied these in the academy, but I've never seen one before. How does it work?"

Terry pointed to a series of raised areas on the map. "It combines positions of the original crime scenes and all known routes to those crime scenes to yield a jeopardy surface."

Woodson said, "Jeopardy surface. Areas of risk?"

"Yes, but more. It calculates both where the predator may live as well as where the predator may strike again." Terry looked down at the laptop for a moment. "The blue contours indicate potential residences, while the red indicate potential predatory activity."

I stared at the map with dismay as the data simply reinforced that our killer was both organized and mobile. Usually, jeopardy surfaces were calculated in a single city, but this killer's range encompassed the entire southeastern corner of Mississippi and even parts of Louisiana, forming a triangle that spread from Bogalusa to Gulfport to Slidell and everything in between. It was so expansive that even a small town in my area, like Bay Saint Louis, rose as a minor peak of potential predatory activity. Peering more intently, I saw that a moderate peak swelled near Picayune as well. Katie's and the girls' hometown.

I had to remind myself that it was just statistics, just like the algorithms we used with DNA and behavior prediction. But the glowing jeopardy surface served as a sobering reminder that the SWK still roamed free out there, nonetheless.

"Look," Woodson said to me, "it's even picking your hometown as a possible place the killer might strike next. Better lock your doors," she cautioned.

"Yeah, I noticed. But it's just statistics. These algorithms are usually far more informative concerning the killer's residence than predicting future crime scene locations."

Terry nodded. "And jeopardy surfaces are far more effective for predicting movements of serial rapists than serial killers. Serial rapists tend to be opportunistic and stalk within a fairly defined radius, and once a pattern of victim selection is observed, jeopardy maps can provide valuable information. The jury's still out on their effectiveness for wide-ranging serial killers, but we went ahead and ran a similar simulation for the Snow White Killer using our four abduction sites, just in case."

Woodson squinted as she looked at the map. "So where does your simulation say the killer most likely lives?"

Terry pointed to areas on the blue contour map with the highest elevation. "Well, based on centrality to the crime scene locations, it's a four-way toss-up among areas south of Wiggins, an area north of Slidell, an area north of Gulfport, and an area east of Bogalusa."

"Again," I added, "it's all just probabilities. If you notice, those four areas also form the four corners of a box bounded by three highways and Interstate 10."

Terry looked back and forth between us, but we had no more questions. "That's all I've got," he said, sitting back down.

"Thanks, Terry. I'm hoping we can use the jeopardy map along with everything else we've learned to date to better pinpoint these locations."

Woodson frowned. "How do you propose to do that?"

"Well," I said, "when we first came across our killer I asked Terry to dig up all the information he could find on Ein Shemer apple orchards in Mississippi. Recall that the apples left with the victims appear to be freshly picked from a tree, not store-bought. There are a limited number of these kinds of orchards in Mississippi, but still quite a few, around three or four hundred big ones. Based on where they're primarily cultivated, in the richer soil near the Mississippi Delta, it

makes it more likely that the killer probably resides in the western locations of the jeopardy surface, rather than the locations distal to the
Mississippi River, like Gulfport or Wiggins."

"Aha."

"Anyway, we'll see. There are other parameters we can couple to
the map and hopefully narrow our area of focus down even further.
But before that, what about this caffeine observation of yours, Woodson? Any updates?"

"You could say that," she said, plugging her laptop into the projector and displaying a chromatogram on the far wall. I recognized the
series of peaks as a chromatographic separation of a standard panel
of narcotics typically analyzed in postmortem blood samples—
amphetamines, barbiturates, benzodiazepines, cannabinoids, cocaine,
methadone, opiates, PCP; all the usual suspects.

"Here," Woodson shined a laser pointer on one of the peaks, "is
caffeine."

"But we already knew from the toxicology reports that caffeine
levels were high," Terry said.

"Right, but look closely at your caffeine peak." She flipped to another slide, which zoomed in on the very top of the caffeine peak.

I followed the laser pointer to the top of the peak and suddenly understood Woodson's interest. The top of the caffeine peak wasn't a single peak but rather a doublet, indicating there was a second chemical
in the victims' blood that had been mistaken for caffeine. But the toxicology analysis had only detected caffeine, not the mystery compound,
when the samples were analyzed.

"So we finally understand why these victims all appeared to have
high levels of caffeine," I said. "Not because they had high caffeine,
but because they had high levels of something very similar to caffeine
in their blood?"

"Exactly," Woodson said, circling the top of the peak with the laser
pointer. "But we don't know what it is."

"This could be huge," I said, looking at Terry.

Terry nodded, already anticipating my next question. "I'm already on it. I'll order several different chromatography columns for overnight delivery. We'll get the caffeine and our mystery chemical separated as fast as we can, put it on our mass spec, and should figure out what else is in their blood in a matter of a few days."

"This could be the break we've needed. If it's some sort of sedative, maybe we can trace it to our killer. Nice, Woodson."

"It may bring a lot into focus," she said. "If it turns out to be a sedative, it could explain a lot. The pinpricks on the fingers, the lack of struggle from the victims, the lack of physical restraint."

"Absolutely, which is why it will be critical for Terry here to start screening every database we can think of once he solves the pattern of our mystery peak."

"I'll place a call to Linda Warren over at the National Institutes of Health and ask her for access to the mass spec library for all FDA-approved drugs," Woodson said. "If we're lucky, and it is a drug, we should find our mystery peak in there."

"Sounds good," I said. "Anything else?"

"That's all I've got for now."

"Okay then, next items." I glanced at the list. "The ever-elongating message on the foreheads. Any new ideas?"

Woodson spoke up. "I did a little digging yesterday after you guys showed me the DNA analysis that clustered SWK with BTK and Zodiac. I looked back through the original BTK and Zodiac communications to the police. Maybe it's coincidence, but those guys were poor spellers and had even poorer grammar. Maybe the lack of an apostrophe in the word *can't* isn't so unusual."

"And he really may be communicating with authority figures here," Terry said. "He's just not using a pen and paper. He's using his own blood smeared on the foreheads of his victims."

"Perhaps," I said, and looked at Woodson. "Did you find any other similarities—or differences—between our guy and BTK or Zodiac?"

"There seem to be only differences after that. Both BTK and Zodiac went for long periods of inactivity, whereas our guy apparently can't."

"Perhaps he's just started up again after a long period of inactivity," Terry suggested.

"But we've looked at ViCAP and haven't found any similar kills anywhere in the United States, going back as far as a decade," Woodson said.

"Well, maybe a dead end. Let's leave it for now, come back to it if it can help us down the road. Terry, how long before we have anything from the mass spec?"

"I'll be spending the entire weekend setting everything up. We should have something by end of next week."

"Great. But don't burn out. I don't want any of us getting sick or immunocompromised or anything. Take a break, okay?"

"Sure thing, Dad," Terry said, and Woodson and he both laughed. I laughed, too, but I'd also seen what could happen when you immersed yourself too deeply into a case. I'd come out on the wrong end of a nervous breakdown during the Richmond Slasher case.

I turned to the still chuckling Woodson. "Same for you. No weekend-long study sessions. Get outside, get some air, do whatever reminds you to enjoy being alive. I'm serious."

"Same to you, Dr. Madden."

"Well, all right, now that that's settled, what are your next steps?"

Woodson blew a strand of hair from her face. "We still need to go back to the medical examiner reports for the first three victims and find out about the pinpricks. Also St. Clair and Harmon should go over their receipts, interview family members, whatever it takes to identify any common link between the victims that hasn't surfaced yet."

"We can start on Monday and I'll help you. For now I'll phone Shelly and find out if she has any ideas about what a tan cat can or can't do. Whether it's a message or a code or a quote, if she can break that, we'll be in a lot better shape."

I glanced at the clock: it was almost three thirty. "Okay. We all have some things to do before end of business today, so try and get the hell out of here by five or six. Have nice weekends, and I'll see you both on Monday."

Terry said good-bye and went back down to the labs, leaving Woodson and me to gather our things. I opened the door for her as she walked out. "And nice work again, by the way, Woodson. We're finally making some headway here. We're going to nail this guy."

Woodson smiled and winked as she walked past me. "You're damn right we are." She headed down the hallway, but then stopped and looked back. "And I really did mean what I said, too. *You* make sure that *you* have a nice and relaxing weekend, too, Madden."

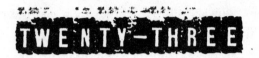

TWENTY-THREE

At five thirty, Woodson stopped by my office before leaving. "So Madden, what are your big plans for your mandatory, glorious weekend, anyway?"

I leaned forward in my chair and shut down my laptop. "Have a seat for a second, I'm closing down myself. What am I doing? I'm heading to a high school football game with my sister and nieces tonight."

Woodson's face broke into a smile. "Oh my god, I haven't gone to a high school football game in years. Not since I was a senior in high school, at least."

"So. What are you doing tonight?"

Woodson shrugged. "Me? Oh, I don't know. I was thinking about wandering in the French Quarter for a bit, then calling it a night."

"Well," I said, "instead of wandering around the Quarter all by yourself, like a big loser, why don't you come to the game with us? You'll get a kick out of it: popcorn, cotton candy, hot dogs, screaming kids, and good football. If that's your thing, I mean."

Woodson tilted her head, with an odd expression that seemed halfway between a smile and a frown. "I don't know. Maybe. But only if," she added, "you let me stop by my place so I can change."

I looked at the clock. It would be tight, but we'd make it. "Deal. I'll meet you in five minutes downstairs."

We pulled into the gravel parking lot of the Picayune Cougars' football stadium an hour later. I found a space to park out near some old giant cypress tree, and we walked through rows and rows of tightly packed cars toward the thundering stadium in the distance.

Woodson spoke as we walked. "So. High school football is a big deal down here, huh?"

I laughed. "Understatement of the year."

The ticket taker for the Cougars games was Bill Kimball, a tenth-grade history teacher at Grace and Ally's school. He grinned as we approached. "Well how you doin', Dr. Madden?" he asked, leaning over the small ticket stand next to the stadium opening.

"Fine, just fine, Bill. Hey, how are *we* doing?" The crowd cheered anew and the band began to play a fight song with vigor.

"Oh, I don't know. I don't get a chance to check the score until the second half, once we stop taking tickets." He accepted my six dollars and handed me two pink tickets. "Oh, I almost forgot. Principal Smith wanted me to give you this." He reached into the booth and withdrew a small manila envelope. "Somebody asked him to give this to you tonight when you got to the game."

"Who's it from?"

Bill shrugged. "No idea. Smith said it just showed up on his desk. A letter wrapped around the envelope said it was from an old friend hoping to catch up with you." He grinned. "Maybe an old girlfriend, eh? No offense, miss."

Woodson waved her hand. "Believe me, none taken."

"Highly unlikely, Bill." I waved the envelope. "If it was from an old girlfriend, it would have been in a box, ticking."

"Ha! You got that right!" Bill laughed until he coughed, then pointed toward the gate to his left. "Okay, y'all have a nice evening, now. See you around, Dr. Madden!"

With that, Woodson and I pushed through the turnstile and entered a darkened area underneath the stadium bleachers. The single entrance funneled all game-goers under the stadium, past the various, delicious-smelling food concessions, then back up sloped walkways to the open air, through a series of exits into the bleacher sections along the football field, much like a college stadium. The smell of hot dogs, pretzels, and popcorn filled the air, and the sound of trumpets and drums pounding out marching band tunes echoed all around. A cheer went up from the crowd above and an auditory cascade of feet stamping on aluminum bleachers descended upon us.

While Woodson waited on popcorn, I opened the envelope and unfolded the letter.

"What does it say?" Woodson asked over her shoulder, just as another roar went up from the crowd above. The sound was deafening.

As my eyes adjusted to the dim light underneath the stadium, two short sentences appeared centered in the middle of the white page in block letters:

A TAN CAT CANT WHAT, MADDEN?
GO COUGARS!

I stared at the page for a second without speaking. A moment after that, the "GO COUGARS!" at the bottom of the message registered in my mind as well.

In the seconds that followed, my pulse pounded, and the sound of blood rushing through my head filled my ears and drowned out the crowd above. I should have known, I told myself, as soon as SWK went after Mara. I'd bent over backwards to convince everyone that the details of this case were just coincidence. But all along it hadn't been about Mara; it had been about me.

There were no such things as coincidences.

Woodson shook me by the arm. "What's going on?"

I ran away without speaking, up the concrete ramp leading into the open air and the bleachers and crowd above. I could hear Woodson pounding up the pavement behind me.

"What's going on?" she yelled again.

We burst through the bleacher opening, immediately awash in a sea of people screaming and making noise on all sides. I ran down the remainder of the bleachers, taking two at a time toward the field below, just as a football player tumbled out of bounds and sent the cheerleaders on the ground scattering in a flash of pom-poms, megaphones, and high-pitched screams.

I leaned over the railing at the bottom and searched frantically for Ally in that chaotic scene on the field, desperate to see her long brown locks. But she wasn't among the cheerleaders who'd been spilled.

Finally I spotted her, another fifteen yards away, as a gush of relief washed through my body and flowed along my spine. Ally was okay. She stood suspended in midair, held up by a boy cheerleader, and she led the fans in a cheer. Standing atop his hands, she exhorted the crowd to build itself into an even greater frenzy, her blue-and-gold pom-poms flashing furiously above her like screaming heads.

I turned around to find her mother and sister in the stands behind me, but quickly realized the futility of trying to find Kate and Grace in the bleachers from my position. I could see better from the field.

I leaped over the railing down onto the field, still without having uttered a word to Woodson, just as she called behind me to wait. A chain-link fence separated the field of play from the stands, and I ran full tilt toward it, grabbing the smooth circular railing along the top as I jumped. I landed awkwardly on the turf, but stayed upright, and in the next moment began making my way toward Ally and the boy at full speed, surprised by the intensity of the floodlights shining down on the field. To my left, a man dressed in a brown windbreaker and a cap that read "Security" crossed quickly into my path. I didn't even bother pulling my badge.

I knew he was just trying to do his job, but I had to get to Ally. He stopped ten feet ahead of me and held up his arms. "Stop, sir!"

I kept going, driving my fist into his solar plexus just as he prepared to tackle me. Not as hard as I could, but hard enough to paralyze him for a good five seconds while his brain tried to figure out where all the oxygen had suddenly gone.

I skirted around him as he sank to his knees behind me, and kept running.

By this time Ally and the boy had seen me coming, and she jumped from his shoulders to the ground. "Uncle Lucas, what's the matter?"

I put both hands on her shoulders and leaned against her, gasping for air. "Ally," I said, pointing to the crowd. "Where are your mother and sister? Where are they?"

"What's the matter, Uncle Lucas?"

I faced her and shouted above the noise of the crowd, shaking her shoulders. "Ally. I don't have fucking time for this! Where are they? Now!"

She blinked back tears, lifted her finger, and pointed. "They're up there, in the high school section."

"Come on." I grasped her hand in mine and we ran back across the field toward the fence. I realized I'd lost Woodson when I left the bleachers. Once Ally and I made it back to the fence, I lifted her over by the waist and quickly scrambled over behind her, scanning the crowd.

"Which way, Ally?"

"This way. Follow me."

I followed her through another chain-link fence and up some side steps leading back to the stadium bleachers from the left. I tried to assimilate the faces flying past on every row, but it was impossible. I had to trust Ally, trust that she would take me to Katie and Grace. Our shoes clanged against the metallic steps.

"Kate! Grace!" I screamed their names. Ahead of me, Ally looked back at me once, her face twisted in fear and questioning. But she continued up the steps.

"They're up here, Uncle Lucas. I saw them earlier."

I looked up and down the rows as we ran. Women, children, and men stood all around, but there was no sign of my sister or niece. "Kate! Grace!" I jerked around as a tremendous gunshot rumbled through the air. I caught sight of a large plume of gray smoke rising from the end zone. A cannon had fired. The home team had scored.

And then the crowd rose to its feet all around us, clanging cowbells, cheering, whistling, and screaming.

I yelled at the top of my voice, "Ally! Do you see them?"

"No!"

I started to wade into the crowd when Ally pulled me back. "Wait, there she is! There's Mom!"

I followed Ally's finger. Sure enough, there stood Kate, laughing and talking with another lady her age, clapping along with the rest of the crowd, which seemed far too enrapt with the game on the field to have even noticed my on-field antics yet.

"Come on!" I clambered up the remaining steps, taking Ally by the hand before I called to her mother again. "Katie!"

Finally she heard us above the noise of the crowd and turned her head. She waved, and her face broke into a smile that lasted only a second before dissolving into a look of sheer terror. She pushed her way through the crowd and met us on the stairs. "What's wrong?"

"Where's Gracie, Katie?"

"She went to get sodas and popcorn, downstairs. What's wrong, Lucas?" She repeated the question and gripped me by the lapels of my jacket as I turned. "What's wrong, goddamn it?"

"I just have to make sure she's safe right now. Come with us." I turned to Ally. "Take us down to the concessions."

The three of us ran back down the bleachers as the radio announcer declared that the score was home team 14, visitors 7. The crowd once again roared around us. At the bottom of the stands I searched for Woodson for a split second, but she was nowhere to be found. After another moment, I turned and followed Katie and Ally into the darkness beneath the bleachers.

Underneath the stadium a few dozen people milled around the dimly lit concession stands. The single bulbs hanging intermittently from the ceiling shimmered in unison with the vibrations in the bleachers above.

The three of us ran along the dusty concrete floor. The bleachers pounded above us as another chant rose from the crowd outside.

"There she is," Katie said and pointed. There Grace stood, a few dozen feet away, safe and sound, waiting in line with a group of two other girls and three boys. She lazily tore off a piece of pink cotton candy and poked it into her mouth, laughing at something one of the boys said.

The last reserve of adrenaline released inside me as I realized all three of them were safe. I started to run toward Grace just as a man wearing a black beret and black overcoat appeared under the stands from a different stadium entrance, approaching Grace and her friends in the distance. Something about him set off my creep meter and I knew what it was: the way he walked quickly, with purpose.

"Gracie! Gracie!" I screamed her name and broke into a full-fledged sprint. Katie and Ally ran behind me, too, frantically yelling for Grace along with me, but without knowing why.

Grace looked up as she heard us. Just like her mother, she smiled at first, surprised to see me. But her smile dissolved just as quickly as she watched me continue to run recklessly toward her and scream her name over and over.

I watched as the man in black continued to approach her, and pulled out my Luger and held it up, aiming. "Stop!" I screamed.

The man kept walking, and reached into his coat.

At that moment I stopped running and lined up the beaded sights of the Luger on the man's head. As Grace and her group of friends finally saw what was happening, they screamed and fell sprawling to the floor.

If I had to do it, I was going to shoot him in front of a hundred witnesses. I steadied the gun and kept the front sight bead focused just above his ear as he continued to walk. "Stop walking immediately, and put your hands on your head!" I yelled at the top of my voice, one last time, to no avail. The man kept walking. I thumbed the safety off.

I began to squeeze when at the last second he veered away from

Grace and her friends and disappeared behind a crush of people pouring down the bleachers—the first half of the game had just ended and a crowd began to pour through the opening.

I stopped walking, lifted the Luger into the air, and flicked the safety back on. Katie and Ally rushed around me and scrambled to Grace on the floor ahead of me. I was torn: follow the man or stay with the girls and keep them safe? Though I desperately wanted this guy, I had to make sure they were okay first.

Katie looked up from the ground as she clutched Grace in her arms. Several of the girls were crying, and the rest were looking up at me in stunned fascination. I started to tell them that everything was all right, but Katie spoke, or rather, screamed first. "What the fuck, Lucas?" she yelled at the top of her voice. "What were you doing?"

I saw the girls look at each other in surprise through tearstained faces as they heard Gracie's mother's angry words.

"Kate. The killer. He left a message."

"What?"

I held up my hands in a lame attempt to calm her. "The Snow White Killer. He left a message for me here, at the game tonight, which made me think you might . . ." I stopped before finishing the sentence. "I just had to find all three of you, make sure you were safe."

At that moment a pair of hands grasped my shoulders and I spun around, only to look into the eyes of Woodson. "What the hell, Madden? What's going on?"

"Woodson! SWK—he's here."

"What? Are you sh—" Woodson started to say, but at that moment a woman's scream split the growing conversational roar surrounding us, echoing off the rafters above our heads for what felt like an eternity. It came from the opposite direction, behind us.

"Come on," I said to Woodson, and we turned toward the source of the scream.

Either someone had found SWK, or SWK had found them.

TWENTY-FOUR

As we turned toward the scream, I saw a deputy approaching in the crowd and I flashed my badge toward him. "You! Come here."

He ran over as a second long wail echoed down the halls.

"What's going on? We better—"

"We're with the FBI," I explained. "I need you to stay here and protect that group of women, got it? You're not to take your eyes off these three women. Do you understand me?"

The young deputy glanced at the badge, then toward Katie and the girls, then back to me. "Yes, sir."

"Draw your gun, and take it off the safety. This is serious. Don't let anyone fucking near them. Anyone. You follow?"

"Yes, sir. I won't let them out of my sight."

I next spoke to Katie, addressing her the way an older brother needs to address a younger sister when he's not telling her, not asking her, but simply begging her to do something. "Kate. You and the girls have to stay here with the officer until I get back. Please, Kate. Promise me."

She nodded wordlessly. The look of true fright on her face told me that, for once, she was going to listen to her big brother.

Having confirmed their cooperation with the deputy, we finally left and made our way through the crowd toward the source of the screams. I noticed with chagrin that they'd come from the opposite direction in which the SWK, or the black-clad person I believed to be the SWK, had just fled. Another howl filled the air as Woodson and I weaved through the growing crowd. I pulled my badge and held it above my head as we maneuvered, telling people to clear a path.

The screams originated from the very end of the stadium. Woodson and I finally broke free of the crowd and ran along the dusty concrete floor, unimpeded the rest of the way. There were no concessions underneath this portion of the stadium, and the lights strung up on the ceiling were fewer and farther between. Only old football equipment—a couple of old blocking sleds, a stack of tractor tires, some folded-up green padded mats, and a pile of old cleats—even inhabited this area under the stadium anymore. The half-inch layer of dust cloaking the equipment suggested no one had been in this part of the stadium for months, until tonight. I looked back down the length of the stadium and could just make out Katie and the girls standing next to the deputy in the distance.

Another scream echoed up the walls. "Help! Somebody, help!"

Woodson and I ran the last twenty yards and nearly crashed into a pair of kids sitting on the dirt floor near the very back corner of the home team's side of the old stadium.

"What's the matter?" Woodson asked them.

The huddled-together couple pointed wordlessly to their right, and Woodson and I followed their fingers into the gloomy corner of the stadium's underbelly. As my eyes adjusted I saw exactly what I had known we'd find, ever since I'd read that letter at the ticket booth. I just hadn't known where, or who, or when.

Another dead girl sat in the corner, staring out at us with open eyes. Her knees were propped up and she was fully clothed, only partially lit by an old overhead lamp swinging above us, shaking in time with the concrete stadium above. She offered a green apple into the air and bore the bloody craftsmanship of the SWK on her forehead.

Morbidly, I paused to take it in. Across the poor girl's forehead was smeared the single word to which the Snow White Killer had referred in his earlier message.

ATTACK.

And like the rest of the words smeared onto the foreheads of all the other unfortunate victims, it meant absolutely nothing to me. A tan cat can't attack.

I turned to face the teens. "Stay here until the police get here. Don't move."

They nodded in fearful, silent agreement.

I walked toward the body and spoke to Woodson over my shoulder. "Come on, let's get this crime scene secured before we have a carnival down here."

Less than an hour later, yellow tape reading POLICE LINE—DO NOT CROSS surrounded the final section underneath the stadium. Although Woodson took control of the crime scene and allowed me to look around the rest of the grounds, I had no luck tracking the man who'd approached Gracie and her friends earlier in the evening. Officials from the high school conferred with us and agreed to stop the game. All exiting fans were searched and questioned. The local police officers did a good job of keeping all the curious onlookers and media vultures at bay.

After the crowds cleared out, Woodson and I spoke with the local medical examiner, explaining what the FBI would need from the autopsy. The body hadn't been removed from her sitting position yet, since the locals were still documenting the crime scene. Flashbulbs popped in the interim. After the CSI paparazzi were finished, Woodson moved in closer to examine the body directly.

Donny showed up a little later, ducking under the tape and walking directly toward me. "Where are Katie and the girls?" he asked.

"Over there," I told him, looking over my shoulder toward the concession stands, but seeing no one. "Wait a minute." I pushed past him, the familiar frantic clutch in my chest. Just as I started to yell their names, the girls popped into view on my left. They stood only a few yards away, and the deputy I'd assigned to their safekeeping was still keeping them faithfully in sight. The girls were straining to look around the corner and catch a glimpse of the crime scene. I looked around to find Katie and yell at her, but finally found her on the perimeter sharing a comforting embrace with, of all people, our brother.

It bothered me to see her talking intimately with Tyler.

I knew that they'd remained close all these years. Tyler and I were the ones who'd grown apart over the Mara incident. It hadn't affected Katie and Tyler, just as it hadn't affected Katie and me. And yet I felt that I should be the one consoling her, not him. That I deserved her love and attention. After all, wasn't I the one who'd rescued her and the girls?

As soon as I had the thought, I realized it was a sad state of affairs when I felt myself growing jealous over which brother deserved to protect his sister and her children from a serial killer loose in the Mississippi Delta.

Donny's voice behind me brought my attention back to the crime scene. "What's on this one's forehead? I can't see."

I turned to Donny. "Attack," I said. "She has the word *attack* written on her forehead."

Woodson overheard us and stood up from where she'd been kneeling beside the body, shaking her head. "Not quite, Lucas. Her hair was covering her forehead. Look again. Our killer forgot to write the *K*." She pulled out a pointer and lifted a lock of hair from the victim's forehead.

Donny and I walked over. As Woodson lifted the hair, I could see that she was right—there was no *K*. Only ATTAC had been inscribed on the victim's forehead. Not ATTACK.

"Bad speller," Donny grunted.

"No way," I said. "With this level of complexity in the modus operandi, our guy knows how to spell."

"Maybe he was interrupted."

I looked at the girl's forehead again. "Maybe," I offered in weak agreement with Woodson, despite a nagging feeling that this wasn't the case, either.

Woodson spoke. "She died about eighteen to twenty-four hours ago. But judging from the immature state of several faint hematomas on her body, I believe she was postured only recently, probably only a few hours before the game started."

"Well, maybe somebody saw him do it this time. Interrupted him or something. I'll have the sheriff set up interviews," Donny said.

"You know," I said to Woodson, "he's finally communicated with authorities, just like the algorithm suggested he would."

Donny frowned. "What algorithm?"

"The Damnation Algorithm Terry and I developed."

"Not following you."

"We used the blood sample from SWK as our first true test case, Donny. The blood samples from the bloody letters on the victims all match, and they all carry a ton of mutations in the damnation signature. We're almost certain the messages are left with the killer's own blood."

"I see . . ."

"And the SWK's DNA clusters most closely to the DNA profiles of BTK and Zodiac."

"Jesus," Donny laughed, but with a bitter tone. "Can't say I like the company he keeps. Genetically speaking, at least. So you think he's leaving those messages with his own blood?"

"Ninety-nine percent sure at this point."

I flinched as the vision of the stranger approaching Grace and her friends suddenly flashed through my mind. "By the way, Donny. I think he was at the game tonight."

"Who?" Donny asked.

"SWK himself."

"Are you shitting me?"

"No, I saw a guy—a suspicious guy—walking toward Grace and her friends down near the concession stands. Right before those kids found the body here underneath the stadium."

"You really aren't shitting me?" Donny asked.

"No, honestly. I even drew my weapon on him. He didn't flinch when I tried to call him down. I was seconds from blowing him to kingdom come before he disappeared into a crowd."

Woodson's face gave a look of disapproval not entirely dissimilar to the one I'd received from Raritan on many occasions. "What made him look so suspicious?" she asked.

"I'm not sure."

"There had to be something. What was it?"

"I don't know, Woodson. The way he walked? Or maybe it was just the way he didn't respond when I first called out for him to stop. He didn't move a muscle even though by that point I'm certain he'd heard me. He was the only person in the crowd who didn't respond to my voice."

"Really?"

"Yes. And I was so worried for Grace, Kate, and Ally that I stayed with them a few seconds, and then this girl was discovered. I should have gone after him."

"Hold on there," Woodson said. "For all you know this was somebody's out-of-town uncle who happens to also be hard of hearing. Don't go jumping to conclusions. You did the right thing. You had to take care of Kate and your nieces first."

Donny nodded in agreement just as a CSI requested Woodson's assistance, and she walked away. Donny lowered his voice once they were out of hearing range. "She's right. But I'll be honest, Lucas. That story scares the living piss out of me," he whispered, locking onto me with his steel gray eyes. "Scares me for you."

"I'm telling you, Donny, it was *him*."

"Maybe it was, maybe it wasn't. But that kind of shit is why you're going to get pulled from this case. You've got to calm everything down here."

"He walked straight toward Gracie! He'd just left me a message that asked what I thought a tan cat can't do, and then wrote 'Go Cougars' at the bottom. What the hell was I supposed to do?"

"I'm not saying I don't sympathize. I'm just saying that it looks bad. Hell, I probably would have done the same thing if I were in your shoes. But you have to be more careful, Lucas. You can't have any mistakes in this case. That's all I'm saying."

I let it go at that, just as Woodson reappeared and knelt back down beside the victim. I was growing tired of all my colleagues telling me to be careful.

I looked down. "Anything else, Woodson?" I asked.

She shook her head. "The CSIs did a good job. No footprints, no latent fingerprints anywhere. Again, typical SWK. We're essentially finished here, until the autopsy. The important thing with this victim is going to be the need for extensive interviews, to see if anyone saw the guy when he deposited the body in the stadium. I think he's getting careless as he ups the ante with us."

"Agreed," I said, addressing both Donny and Woodson at the same time, "but I have to take my sister and her girls home tonight. They're pretty shaken up."

They both nodded, and Woodson turned back to focus further on the body. She smoothed the protective plastic already wrapped around the victim's hands by the CSIs and lifted it. "Before you guys go. Check this out."

Donny and I stepped over and bent down for a closer look.

On the tip of the girl's ring finger sat a tiny red dot, in the same location as the pinprick on the previous victim.

"Well, well," I said to Woodson. "Two pinpricks in a row? What are the chances of that? You may finally have found a common physical link between our victims that can connect them to a common activity or place." Then added, "If we're lucky, that is."

"Hey, sometimes it's the little things that matter," Woodson said simply, looking up and smiling at me for what seemed the first time that night.

I nodded and looked from Woodson to Donny. "Let's hope so in this case, guys. Let's hope so."

Although Woodson's discovery of a second pinprick in a row was exciting, unfortunately, that red dot also turned out to be just about the only piece of physical evidence of merit from the crime scene. The CSIs vacuumed as a matter of course, but they were most likely just vacuuming up bags full of forensic disappointment. To no one's surprise there was no skin remaining beneath the victim's fingernails. Multiple linear slash wounds covered her body, all caused by the increasingly dull serrated edge of the now well-known knife, the tick-tick-tack signature that Terry had identified on the other victims. The apple held in her hand, as expected, contained a razor.

I looked around. Tyler was nowhere to be seen. Katie and the girls were now sitting with the younger FBI agents who'd driven up from New Orleans at my request, Greg Tucker and Dave Faraday. They were on call, and I'd given them a new assignment. Effective immediately, they would shadow my sister and nieces all day, every day, until the SWK investigation concluded. During school hours Greg would stake out the high school the girls attended, while Dave would cover the elementary school where Katie worked. They would accompany them home at night and stay inside the house, taking shifts during the evening to make sure Katie and the girls stayed safe.

It was an admittedly severe response, but I wasn't taking any more chances. I'd deal with the inevitable questions from the Bureau later, but I was reasonably sure I possessed a piece of paper that would justify the delegation of these two agents to surveillance. I'd already dropped it into a chain-of-custody mailer and personally delivered it to Harmon and St. Clair to take back to the New Orleans office. Terry, our resident document examiner, would give the note from the SWK a thorough examination before sending it on to Quantico.

Just as our DNA algorithm had predicted—just like BTK and Zodiac—the SWK had finally communicated with authorities as well. And he'd done so via a letter addressed to me.

TWENTY-FIVE

An hour later I stood with Katie and the girls in the foyer of their house, peering at the three frightened faces looking back at me. "Let's wait down here while Faraday and Tucker check the place out."

All three of them nodded silently in unison. I saw their collective fear, the familiar terror of potential victims reflected in their eyes. I wasn't accustomed to seeing that kind of fear in the faces of my own family.

The seconds ticked by awkwardly. I tried to think of something, anything to say. "Hey, girls," I finally said, putting on a mischievous smirk and gesturing upstairs with my thumb. "Faraday and Tucker, Faraday and Tucker, Faraday and Tucker. Try saying that over and over again as fast as you can ten times in a row."

After a couple seconds both girls smiled, and a few seconds later they both laughed aloud as they realized the potential for a vulgar transposition between the two last names.

"Oh, don't encourage them," Katie said disapprovingly, which made them laugh even louder.

A few minutes later the boys had finished sweeping the house. "Okay, all clear, boss," Tucker hollered down the stairs.

"You're sure?" I called back up to the younger agent, almost unable to bring myself to trust him and let the girls back into their house.

"Yes, sir."

I started up the stairs. "Okay, girls. Follow me upstairs, then we'll get settled into your beds."

"Uncle Lucas. I don't want to go up there."

I looked back at Grace. Thirteen, almost fourteen—just old enough to begin feeling like a young woman, but still young enough to react to certain frightening situations with a childlike fear. I walked back down the carpeted steps.

"Come on, Gracie. I know you've seen some pretty scary things to-night." This time it was my chance to cast a disapproving stare Katie's way, as I was still perturbed that she'd allowed the girls to get so close to the crime scene before an officer shooed them away. Now both Ally and Grace would forever have that dead girl's body etched in their mind. Maybe their mother shouldn't have been so busy talking with good old Uncle Tyler.

I refocused and smiled down at Grace again, pushing the chaotic train of thought out of my mind. "But this is what I do for a living. I chase these bad guys and stop them. So we're going to catch this guy and stop him, too." I fixed her with my most confident gaze, one that had won over the families of countless victims, one that had reassured whole cities watching press conferences as we pursued a killer in their midst. "I promise, honey."

Gracie kept looking at me for a second, then looked away. She, for one, didn't believe a word Uncle Lucas had just said, and there was nothing in the world I could do or say to change it.

Eventually I convinced the three of them to walk through the house with me. A strange silence accompanied us as we peered into closets, opened cabinets, withdrew shower curtains, and bolted down windows. Afterwards neither of the girls was ready to sleep in her own bedroom, so we all went back downstairs. Tucker and Faraday had already taken up their positions: Faraday sat in a chair at a computer desk in the corner of the den, and Tucker was stationed outside in the car, watching the only entrance to the house. Thankfully, Katie lived on a corner lot nestled against a steep natural hill, beyond which lay miles of swampy marsh. The only way to get to her house was from the front.

Downstairs, Katie and I pulled out the foldout couch in the living room, and the girls clambered under the covers. We tucked them in, and Katie kissed them on their foreheads. I switched on the TV with the remote and handed it to Ally.

"Your mom and I are going to be in the kitchen. You need anything, just call. Okay?"

"Okay, Uncle Lucas."

In the kitchen Katie brought over two cups of coffee and sat across from me at the small circular wooden table in the breakfast nook. Outside, the wind picked up and rain began to pelt against the bay windows surrounding us.

Katie took a long, drawn-out sip of the steaming coffee, grimaced momentarily as it scorched her tongue, then leaned back. "Thanks for staying here tonight, big brother."

"Don't mention it, little sis. Are you going to be okay?" I gestured into the living room where Faraday now sat on the recliner. "With these guys around?"

"Yeah. We'll be all right. We'll adjust."

"Kate. I'm so sorry this is happening."

"You don't have to apologize, Lucas. We're tough. We've made it this far together, the girls and I. We'll make it through this, too."

"I know."

Katie stayed silent for a while, and the sounds of an old *Saturday Night Live* rerun echoed into the kitchen from the living room. "Don't Fear the Reaper" played for a moment, then the TV switched off . . . exhaustion had finally caught up with the girls.

"Why is this guy so fixated with you?" Katie finally asked.

Her question caught me by surprise. "I—I don't know, Kate. I wish I did."

"What do you know about him? Does he know you personally? Or do you think he just knows you because of what you do? Maybe he's read your books?"

I nodded, even though I wasn't so sure. "I think that's more likely. This guy doesn't know me personally. It's some insecure little fucker, some little shmuck who realizes he's gone too far and figures he might as well play it out. And what better way to play out the ending than to confront the FBI? That's all I probably am to him. A symbol of law enforcement. Nothing more."

Katie smiled and took another sip. "You know, Lucas. You used to be able to get away with that shit when I was younger."

"Kate, I honestly—"

"Save it, Lucas. For some reason I know you believe this is personal, too. I don't know why, and I don't even care." She cut her eyes into the living room. "Just find him, Lucas. Find him and stop him. Before he has a chance to come near the girls, ever again."

I followed her gaze. Ally and Grace had fallen asleep peacefully under the covers of the pullout couch. Ally's slender arm rested along the top of the pillow over Grace's head.

"I will, Katie. I swear it."

Eventually Katie went into the living room, too, and lay down beside the girls on the pullout sofa. I helped her into bed. She nestled beside Grace, got comfortable, then rolled over and stared up at me in the dark, the light from the street lamp outside spilling through the blinds, across her face. The effect made her look like our mother more than ever before.

"Everything's going to be fine, Kate," I whispered down to her. "I promise."

Katie closed her eyes, yawned, and put her arm around Grace, pulling her head into her shoulder. "I believe you, Lucas. Good night."

I kissed all three of them on the forehead before sitting in a recliner and staring at them for what seemed like hours, before finally succumbing to sleep.

TWENTY-SIX

The next morning I woke up in a recliner, not a bed, and didn't recognize my surroundings. My legs throbbed from a lack of circulation the night before, but I sat bolt upright in a panic nevertheless as the tingling peaked and finally subsided.

When I saw Faraday typing on his laptop in Katie's kitchen, everything came back in a rush.

Katie and the girls still slumbered under quilts on the sofa bed. I tiptoed into the kitchen and proceeded to recap responsibilities with Faraday. They were to call me twice a day and give me a brief report. At no time could Katie, Grace, or Ally leave their sight. The FBI would alert the Picayune High School principal's office and Katie's elementary school about the surveillances.

I peeked in on the girls one last time. An unprecedented urgency swelled inside me as I regarded their sleeping faces. Then I forced myself to walk out the front door and back into the world of the SWK, as a strange concoction of anger, fear, and resolve percolated inside my veins.

I drove straight from Katie's house into New Orleans and encountered almost no traffic at that time on a Saturday morning. Once at the field office, I sat down and spread five manila folders across my desk. As I slowly opened each, photographs of the five victims stared up at me in turn. Each of the various crime scene photographers had taken photos of the women from a short distance away, at eye level. Each girl sat with legs propped up, forearms resting on knees. Sexual, but fully clothed. The significance continued to elude me.

I walked to my office bookshelf and withdrew a textbook that I hadn't read for a long, long time.

Three hours later I closed my own book, *The Killing Mind,* and reviewed the main points I'd noted in the chapter entitled "Tableau Killers." Namely, how tableau killers represented the most difficult type of serial killer to catch, while being the most intelligent and usually the most deranged of all. Characterized by heightened boldness and a desire to leave a mythical mark on history, the Snow White Killer seemed to be shaping up into a perfect example of this type of killer.

Alone in the silence of my office for a few hours, I also had time to think back through the SWK's signature. The razored apple, the enigmatic message on the victims' foreheads, the sexual posturing of the bodies. All were bread crumbs leading straight to the dark source of a serial killer's motive.

The message continued to confound us: "a tan cat can't attack." Shelly's group over in Jackson still hadn't come up with anything related to such a statement in the comprehensive literary searches she'd run so far. No luck anywhere with cryptology, either.

My mind turned to the apple and the razor. In my estimation this most likely reflected the Halloween urban legend, just a way for SWK to say to the world, "I'm the guy your mother warned you about." But tableau killers usually used more intricate symbolism, so it was possible that the Snow White Killer was saying more than just "I told you so" with his razored apples.

I decided if I was going to get anywhere with an interpretation that might help us catch this killer, I needed to deconstruct the signature and consider each symbol separately.

First, there was the razor. Razor, a sharp instrument for cutting, an inspiration of terror, a symbol of pain, a path to suicide.

Then there were the apples. The forbidden fruit, the womb, a symbol of renewal.

I tried to link them together. Were these victims a forbidden fruit that caused him terror? Possibly. Were they women's wombs with a symbolic razor inside them? Perhaps an unwanted child? Possibly again, but none of the victims had been pregnant.

The general direction felt right to me, a worldview where women are seen as fruit, carrying around hidden razors as some sort of indicator of death. But it only felt lukewarm at best.

I moved on to the posturing, the third main element of the signature. The women were postured sexually, propped on their backs, legs open suggestively, but with clothes on. An atypical signature, to be sure.

The reclothing phenomenon specific to this case suggested to me that the postures weren't meant to be sexual. As I stared at some of the full-body shots from the crime scenes, taken head-on, it struck me. These women, propped up on their haunches, legs spread open and doubled up.

They weren't arranged in a sexually inviting pose. They seemed more as if they were frozen in the act of childbirth.

A voice in my head started saying, *Warmer . . . Warmer . . . Warmer.*

But why the razor? And what about the tan cat?

It was noon, and I'd been working for four hours in an empty office. I heard a door close down the hall and decided to check it out.

When I walked up behind him, Terry turned and did a double take. "What are you doing in here on a Saturday morning? Don't you have a hawk to feed or squirrels to eat or some crazy shit like that?"

"I do, but couldn't stay away. What are you doing here?"

"I went ahead and checked out your note from the game last night. It's on the document examiner downstairs. You want to see what I've found so far?"

It took a moment to follow what he was talking about, but then it dawned on me: the letter left for me at the stadium's ticket window. Oh, I was definitely interested in anything he'd found on that note.

"Lead the way, man."

Down on the lower level of our office building, I followed Terry into a small, dimly lit room. A tiny area had been set aside for document examination. Terry had taken a monthlong training course in Quantico, and he was our point person for the small number of ransom letter and fraudulent deeds we dealt with over the course of any given year in New Orleans.

A lighted box in the corner illuminated the now-familiar letter from the Snow White Killer on its top. Terry moved a separately mounted lens piece slightly downward, and peered through it. "I think we have a lead here."

He scooted back in his stool and invited me to look.

"Is that a watermark?" I asked.

"Yes, and I've never seen anything like it before."

"Really?" I scooted back on my stool and waited for him to explain.

"Yeah. For one thing, it's a lot smaller than most other watermarks. And it reads T-A-K. I looked online today and couldn't find any TAK presses, so I think there's a chance that it's a unique watermark from an extremely small paper producer or printing press."

"Nice, Terry. Sometimes it's the littlest thing. What's next?"

"I'm sending it up to the department in Quantico. They'll run it against our watermark database. If one exists, there's a good chance they'll come up with a hit."

I glanced back down at the message. "A TAN CAT CANT WHAT, MADDEN?" challenged me to decipher its meaning. "Fantastic, Terry.

Let me know what happens. I'm going to head back upstairs and try to research this message a bit more."

"Will do," Terry called after me.

Back upstairs in my office I walked over to the whiteboard and uncapped a red Magic Marker from the eraser tray.

I wrote out the message left on the foreheads of the five victims, in all caps, in the order they'd been killed, just as the SWK had listed them in his letter.

A TAN CAT CAN'T ATTACK

I studied several of the most recent victims' autopsy photos. I recalled that CAN'T hadn't included an apostrophe on the body, and also remembered that ATTACK hadn't included a *K*. Rather, ATTAC had actually sat perfectly centered on her forehead, just like every other message left behind on the victims' foreheads. I was also struck by how straight the bloody lines of the letters were on each victim. That symmetry convinced me that this perfectionist killer had wanted to write five letters—ATTAC—and not ATTACK, at all. I rewrote it more faithfully to the killer's original messages.

A TAN CAT CANT ATTAC

If CANT didn't merit an apostrophe and the perfectly centered ATTAC hadn't been the word *attack* in the first place, then perhaps these weren't words at all. Perhaps they were simply letters. I next considered this possibility and performed the simple experiment of running the letters together. I erased the board again and rewrote the message anew.

ATANCATCANTATTAC

I sat back down at my desk as an idea slammed into me like a rogue wave. It didn't seem possible, and yet, perhaps this was the key.

I typed the address for the NCBI—the National Center for Biotechnological Information—with trembling fingers and found the website.

Once there, I selected the hyperlink to the Basic Local Alignment Search Tool, entered the string of letters from the victims' foreheads carefully into BLAST, and pressed Enter.

And in the next few moments, I couldn't believe my eyes.

TWENTY-SEVEN

This kind of breakthrough needed an audience, so I went to find Terry and invite him to my own private exhibition, much the same as he'd done with his watermark breakthrough for me a few hours before.

He wasn't downstairs or in his office. I found him in Woodson's office, where they were discussing the watermark. She'd come in on a Saturday, too.

Woodson smiled as I entered. "Nice lead this watermark, huh? What do you think?" she asked.

They both regarded me strangely and I realized I must have had quite the silly smirk on my face. I didn't care. "I think," I began, pausing for dramatic effect, "that both of you might want to come down to my office and see what I just found. Right away."

One minute later, I faced the two agents who were clearly exasperated by my refusal to give them any more details during the walk down to my office. I turned the computer screen in their direction and walked around to the other side of my desk. After a moment the NCBI genome Web browser shimmered into view.

They both stared at the screen, their eyes going back and forth between the letters on the victims' foreheads on the right-hand side and the short DNA sequence inside the ripper gene that I'd highlighted, projected on the left.

"Oh my god," Woodson finally said beside me, and then Terry gasped too.

ATANCATCANTATTAC.

I watched their faces pass through identical stages of puzzlement, incredulity, excitement, and back to bafflement.

After a sufficient period of time had passed, I spoke. "Guys, I don't know how to break this, but the message being left behind on the victims is a portion of the exact DNA sequence from the ripper gene."

They both stayed silent, still digesting the implications of what I was saying, so I continued.

"In other words, the message being left on the victims is from a portion of DNA sequence from a gene related to dopamine signaling in the amygdala, which I showed many years ago to be frequently mutated in serial killers. The very first gene ever included in what is now affectionately called the Damnation Algorithm."

Woodson sat down heavily in a chair and exhaled, for a moment sounding like she'd just run a marathon. "Unbelievable," she finally announced.

"Yeah, it is," Terry said, but then frowned. "But wait, Lucas. If this is a DNA sequence, then it should only contain *A, C, T,* or *G.* Why are there *N*s in the ripper gene?"

I leaned back against my desk. "Yeah, good point. I had forgotten that, back when I sequenced ripper, long before the next-generation sequencing of the human genome, a lot of the time you had no idea which of the four letters—*A, C, T* or *G*—sat in certain positions in any given gene sequence. Whenever that happened, the universal symbol to indicate an unknown nucleotide was *N.*"

"So you really aren't shitting us, huh?"

"Definitely not shitting you, Terry. This guy's been spelling out a region in the ripper gene on the foreheads of these poor young girls."

"So everything actually *is* about you, then?" Woodson asked.

I shrugged. "I don't know. I'm looking at this screen, guys, seeing it in black and white. We've finally broken SWK's code. But I still don't know what it means."

"At least it's safe to say the killer is acquainted with your theories on the genetic basis of serial killer behavior," Woodson observed.

"So does that make him a scientist?" Terry asked.

"Not necessarily," I said. "For better or worse, there have been a lot of lay articles on the link between ripper mutations and serial killers. A lot of nonscientists have heard about this gene and its link to violent behavior. It could be anyone."

I paused, suddenly remembering the puncture wound on the last two young girls' hands. "You know, these girls probably all had pinpricks in their fingers," I said.

"Right," Woodson said. "Which we think is an injection site for our mystery drug, right?"

"Maybe, but maybe not," I said. "It's as obvious as the noses on our faces, but I'm just realizing that our mystery drug doesn't have to be an injectable."

Woodson frowned, but then her face relaxed just as quickly. "I guess not. We had just put two and two together—unknown chemical in the blood, pinpricks on fingers—and assumed we were dealing with an IV-injectable drug. But you're right . . . it may be faulty logic."

"So it's possible, once you figure out the chemical structure, that it's in a tablet form, right?" Terry asked.

"Possible? Honestly, it's more like highly probable. Now that I think about it, a fingertip would be a strange way to inject a drug. Much more likely in the arm, or in the rear," Woodson said.

"Exactly. So what if your mystery chemical turns out to be a tablet or some other type of drug that doesn't require an injection?" I offered.

"Then I'd ask why the hell did these girls have pinpricks in their fingers."

"Maybe the question we should be asking about those pinpricks isn't whether they are sites of injection, but whether they're sites of blood samples taken for some kind of analysis," I said.

The room went silent as both Terry and Woodson considered the possibility and followed my logic.

Within minutes we'd enumerated the most logical possibilities: a doctor's office, a safety office, a biohazard lab, and a few others. We concluded that the victims most likely had blood samples taken somewhere, but the key question was why.

"In this case," said Woodson, "knowing the why will definitely help us figure out the who." She broke into a smile. "Hey, just like you said in your lecture at Quantico."

"Seems like eons ago," I said, "but you're right: the why should definitely help lead us to the who in this case."

"So let's go back to what we know. Or at least, what we think we know," Woodson said. "We're dealing with a killer who sees these women as being somehow at fault, as if they harbor something sick or deadly inside them. Why do they need samples?"

It was silent for a long time, and then it hit me.

"Holy shit," I said aloud.

"What? What is it?"

"He's taking blood to find his victims," I proclaimed. "So he must have access to samples of their DNA."

"Why?" The two queried in unison.

"He's been telling us all along. Our killer is obsessed with ripper, and he's chosen these women because they fit into his plan."

"And what exactly is that?" Terry asked.

"Actually, I'm hoping you can tell us," I said, rising from my chair. "We need one of your best people to do some real fast sequencing of those victims' blood samples."

"Sorry not to follow you, but why?"

"Because I'm willing to bet that the Snow White Killer is sampling women's DNA, and unless I'm way off the mark, I believe he's killing them because he's somehow discovered that they carry mutations in their ripper genes."

Terry and Woodson stayed silent as we all considered the possibility.

I sighed and stared at the photographs of the five young victims, still lying on my desk. If I was right, then the SWK had killed these women because they carried, at the genetic level, something I had once labeled as a genetic predisposition for creating a killer.

My skin turned to gooseflesh as I made the analogy in my mind: just like a lethal razor hidden in the soft flesh of an unblemished fruit.

TWENTY-EIGHT

The New Orleans branch contained an impressive forensics lab, complete with a next-generation DNA sequencing center. In relatively short order Terry assembled a team to isolate DNA from the five victims and sequence their ripper genes.

In the meantime I placed a call to my friend Gary Turner, at Tulane, one of the leading researchers in the field of ripper-gene research. Since my initial discovery, he'd established an entire NIH-funded program on the ripper gene's product, a dopamine receptor subtype in the amygdala. Just as I'd hoped, he possessed many sequencing primers for ripper and agreed to provide them with no questions asked, which would make a targeted sequencing approach a lot easier.

Within two hours the hypothesis that the SWK had selected his victims because each woman had harbored mutations in her ripper genes was being tested as the technicians in the FBI lab created the sequencing libraries. We'd have the genetic data for each of the victims by that night.

After the flurry of activity in the preceding days, there was nothing to do but wait.

While waiting, I called Faraday for a check-in and he assured me that everyone was fine. In fact, Katie had cooked everyone breakfast, agents included. He and Tucker were probably in for the best surveillance duty they'd ever receive.

Satisfied that Katie and the girls remained safe, I sat back down at my desk and stared at the ripper sequence still depicted on my computer screen. If I was right, the next letters the SWK intended to leave on a victim would finally be completely nonsensical: GCGAT or such. I wondered if we could stop him before we would find those letters on the forehead of another victim.

I also realized that if this really was his motivation, then we might be able to draw the Snow White Killer to me. If he was obsessed with the ripper gene, then perhaps we could lure him to focus on me and distract him from going after any other victims.

I called Woodson, who immediately picked up. "What's up?" she asked.

"I was just thinking. There has to be some commonality in the victims. Have you heard anything from Harmon or St. Clair?"

"No. You want me to give them a call?"

"Yeah, go ahead. Then swing down here. I want to run an idea by you. If you buy into it, then we'll call Raritan and see if we can get him to approve some special investigation funds for this case, now that we have a real lead."

"Okay. I'll be down in a few."

Ten minutes later Woodson dropped by. "Did you get through to anyone?" I asked.

"I got in touch with Harmon. He said they're still working on it, but nothing yet. He said they're going through garbage at this point."

"You tell them to focus on medical records?"

"They've pulled all of them. But all the victims had different general practitioners. No insurance claims link them. In fact, four of the five hadn't filed a claim for a visit to a doctor for more than a year."

"Maybe we need to consider non-physician-related reasons for blood sampling," I said.

"I think it's headed in that direction."

"Okay. We'll just have to keep working on it." I motioned her to take a seat. "I want to draw this guy out, Woodson. And it's going to be a major undertaking."

"Draw him out?"

"Yeah. Set up some sort of public event that might draw him in, something he can't resist."

"Like what?"

"I'm thinking about giving a false lecture on the ripper gene."

Woodson frowned. "It might work, but how would it not stand out like a sore thumb? Where would you do this without it being obvious that it's a trap?"

"You're absolutely right—I'd never propose this except for the fact that the Society of Neuroscience is in town next week. It's the perfect cover."

"Don't tell me you were literally invited to speak on the ripper gene at this year's meeting?"

"Hell no."

"Then how do you plan to give a lecture there? Surely the deadline has passed if the meeting is next week."

"Months ago. But I know the annual meeting organizer and he'd go along with it," I said. "I would have to tell him everything, but I'm sure I could get a slot."

"So how would we advertise it?"

"I'm thinking we could ask Jimmy for some funds for a local advertising campaign to make sure the word about a Society of Neuroscience–sponsored lecture on the ripper gene gets around. It could be titled something like 'Ten Years of the Ripper Gene: What Have We Learned?' or something like that. If we can get this sort of title out in time, hopefully it will be enough to bait SWK. We can shoot for Web, TV, newspaper, and radio. Make like we're celebrating the ten-year anniversary of the ripper gene's discovery or something."

"Honestly, I don't think he'll be able to resist. Can I help?" Woodson asked.

"Absolutely," I said. "It would be great if you could help convince Jimmy that this is all worth it. If we can get the word out, I think the chances are good that SWK won't be able to, as you say, resist it. And we could post as many agents as possible at the lecture to keep an eye out for anyone suspicious, someone with a fake name tag, anyone overly nervous, anything out of the ordinary."

Woodson smiled. "This investigation is finally starting to sound like fun for a change."

A few minutes later Raritan's voice carried over my office phone. "Raritan here."

"Jimmy," Woodson said. "I'm with Lucas here, we're on speaker-phone. You have a few minutes?"

"Sure. How's the investigation going?" The chair in his office creaked loudly, and we heard both of his boots clomp down onto the desk as he put his feet up. Jimmy was settling in to listen.

"We think we're getting somewhere. But we're going to need a little help from you," Woodson said.

"I'm listening."

"Well, you remember the message our guy's been leaving on the victims' foreheads?"

"A tan cat can't . . . what . . . attack, right? So did you figure out the message? Did Shelly come up with something?"

"No, Lucas figured it out. The killer isn't leaving behind a message. He's leaving behind letters. Letters of the genetic code."

"What? That doesn't make sense." Jimmy paused on the other end. "Genetic code? With a word like *attack*?"

"It was A-T-T-A-C, not *attack,* on the last victim's forehead,"

Woodson said. "We just assumed he'd gotten interrupted in writing *attack*. Turns out, he really did probably mean A-T-T-A-C."

"I'll be damned. Does the sequence actually mean anything?"

"Yeah," I said, "it shows perfect identity with only a single gene in the human genome."

"Which one?"

"Guess."

"I'm not going to guess, Lucas. No, wait. Don't tell me it's . . ."

"Ripper," Woodson finished the sentence for him.

"You guys are shitting me."

"No, we're really not shitting you," I said. "For some reason SWK is leaving the ripper sequence on the foreheads of his victims."

"So why the hell is he doing that?"

"Well we're not sure on that point, but we suspect at least one thing— he's obsessed with ripper. And we think we can draw him out. That's why we need your help."

"It sounds like you're about to ask for money."

"Yes. We need your money. What do you need from us?"

"It depends. What do you have in mind?"

"A sting operation. Nothing too expensive or extensive. Woodson can tell you all about it."

I sat back while Woodson walked Jimmy through the entire proposal we'd plotted earlier that day.

Raritan paused after she finished. "I like it. If you can get the word out, it just might work. Okay, here's the deal. Write up the proposal. I'll put it on Moynihan's desk Monday morning, so you have to get it to me by Sunday."

"Thanks, Jimmy," Woodson said.

"Just keep the funding request as modest as possible and still get your work done. The less you ask for, the more likely you'll get it."

"Understood."

"Good luck, then."

"Aye aye, Captain."

———

After we hung up, Woodson leaned back. "What's next?"

"What's next, you ask? Only the most difficult thing for profilers in the world."

"What's that?"

"We wait."

TWENTY-NINE

As if cooperating with us, the SWK went into a brief cocoon of inactivity for the next several days, which gave us a window of opportunity to set up the sting. When I wasn't speaking to an organizer or an advertiser, I was conferring with Faraday to hear how Katie and the girls were doing, talking to Terry regarding progress in the lab, or reviewing details of the operation with Woodson. By Thursday there were still no new victims, and I began to secretly wonder whether SWK, after such an initial frenetic pace, had finally cooled off. The potential for this sting operation to be a big bust began to gnaw at me.

I drove the doubts from my mind as best I could by focusing on my upcoming lecture, "Genetics and Violence: What Have We Learned from the Ripper Gene?" I'd easily convinced Gary Turner, my colleague from Tulane, to give me a slot in a Late-Breaking Research session that he was chairing at the Society of Neuroscience meeting. It took a little more cajoling to get it made open to the public.

After the Late-Breaking Research session was announced, many former colleagues from various universities had called or e-mailed me to welcome me back to academic research. Though I felt guilty for doing it, I played along with all of them, just to maintain the ruse. We couldn't afford to tip off SWK, in case all our efforts to publicize the event actually worked.

On the morning before my evening lecture, Woodson and I reviewed the plans with the agents assigned to work undercover with us. Harmon, St. Clair, McCloskey, and Rivera (the last two guys hailed from Homicide) would be posing as researchers at the meeting. They were to avoid conversation with the other real scientists in attendance and sit at predefined positions during my lecture, indicated on a blueprint map we handed out. They would move in controlled paths during the cocktail reception at the Magnolia Mansion, where two other agents from Homicide named Mincy and Huskinson would be posing as event organizer staff. Every detail was geared toward increasing the likelihood that at least one of us would cross paths with SWK, if he happened to attend.

After we adjourned, I walked with Woodson back to our offices. At her doorway she stopped. "So, everybody else seems ready, and we poured as much publicity into this talk as we could. The only question left is whether you're ready for your big return back into academia."

"I think so. In fact, I'm probably going to use the slides I presented up in Quantico. You may remember that lecture."

"Ah, yes," Woodson said. "I remember it well."

We both laughed, then Woodson clapped her hands together. "Okay then, Madden. I'll see you this afternoon. I'm going home to get ready." She shook her hair loose from a tightly pulled ponytail. "My starring role as Dr. Karen Waveland, neuroendocrinologist extraordinaire from McGill, is about to begin."

I was suddenly struck by the same overpowering sensation I'd had when I'd found myself hypnotized by the perfect curvature of this stranger's collarbone as she'd driven me from the hospital to my home. As Woodson's hair tumbled out of its ponytail, another jolt of desire shocked its way through me.

Woodson stared at me, and I realized it was my turn to speak. "Okay, then. I guess I'll see you at the afternoon session?"

"I will see you then. Good luck, Professor Madden."

"Same to you, Professor Waveland from McGill."

I eventually left the office early as well, finding it impossible to concentrate on anything else except the upcoming sting operation that night. I checked on Katie and the girls with a quick call to Faraday, then drove home to prepare for the evening.

A shower (run just a bit colder than usual) cleared my head. I dressed the part of Professor Madden—tweed jacket, corduroy pants, and brown wingtips. I drove back into the city and parked near the convention center.

Once inside, I made my way through the main atrium, navigating crowds of scientists dressed in suits and dresses, some carrying cylindrical tubes containing their poster presentations, others scurrying off to the next seminar they wanted to attend.

I finally found the main auditorium on the third floor of the convention center. The lecture hall was a large room with two big projection screens flanking a podium. The lecture hall was already half full of scientists.

The audiovisual guy gave me a microphone for my lapel and seated me in the first row. I couldn't help turning around to scan the initial sea of faces, but no one leaped out.

The two other speakers, Domenici Piralde from Harvard and Ruth White from Stanford, arrived together and took seats beside me in the front row. In typical chaotic fashion, Gary Turner, my friend from Tulane and the chair of the afternoon panel of talks, showed up only a minute or so before the session was scheduled to start.

"Dr. Lucas, how are you?" The Irishman's unmistakable voice boomed out from behind me as he clapped me on the back.

"Fine, Gary, fine. And thanks again."

"Don't mention it. I'm just glad to hear about this damnation signature everyone's talking about!" He patted me on the shoulder. "I'll see you on the podium in a couple of minutes; let me quickly say hello to the other speakers."

He left, and when I turned around to take one last look out across the audience, I struggled to hide my surprise. The room had filled almost to capacity, with standing room only in the back. I feared that the sheer number of people attending this lecture might ruin our chance of identifying any outlier individuals in the audience.

I shifted uncomfortably and adjusted the ultrathin flak jacket beneath my shirt and suit coat. It served as a pretty dismal reminder that I hoped my behavioral profile to date was correct, and that SWK would never use a gun in a public place. And if I were wrong, that at least he wouldn't go for a head shot.

A minute later the session started. The other speakers and I took seats on the stage, facing the audience. Ruth was the first lecturer. While she spoke, I scanned the crowd, trying to keep my gaze as professorial as possible. I located three of the five agents involved in the sting but couldn't find Harmon—or Woodson, for that matter—in the crowd. During the debriefing we'd worked out signals: an eye rub from any of the agents meant that I should leave the stage and they would make a move on a suspicious suspect. A covered yawn from any agent meant that I could stay onstage but that they'd found someone of moderate interest.

Not a single yawn or eye rub from anyone. Things were looking pretty unpromising. No need to stop the show; not even a possible suspect at this point.

After Ruth's presentation, Domenici spoke. In the interim I finally spied Harmon, sitting four or five rows behind his intended position. I made eye contact with him a couple of times, but like the other agents, he had no sign to give. All quiet on the Western front.

After Domenici's talk ended, I almost didn't hear Gary introduce me. I made one last run-through of the agents in the sea of faces, but no one made a move. I stood slowly and walked to the podium.

I hadn't anticipated the lights on the stage. They were nearly blinding, and it was difficult to see the faces beyond the first few rows. I recognized that we weren't going to find our guy in the lecture hall, and that our only chance would be at the reception. With a mounting disappointment that I struggled mightily not to portray, I launched into the lecture.

The least I could do was make good on our end of the bargain with the Society of Neuroscience.

After I finished my lecture and retook my seat beside the other presenters facing the audience, I held my breath while Gary asked the audience if they had any questions. I'd held out hope that even if we couldn't spot him in the audience, the SWK (if in attendance at all) might not be able to resist the chance to pose a question.

Unfortunately, no questions were asked. Gary thanked the attendees and looked forward to seeing everyone at the cocktail reception at the Magnolia Mansion. A round of applause went up, and I walked slowly down the steps. All of that time, all of that effort, all of that money wasted.

I stopped short as Woodson materialized in front of me at the bottom of the stage.

I didn't move, because I couldn't stop staring. I hadn't seen her for the entire lecture and had begun to wonder whether she was even there. Her long blonde hair was only loosely tied up with a black ribbon, instead of pulled back tightly the way she wore it on the job, and she wore a black working dress that exposed her muscular shoulders and lean arms. She even wore a fake pair of black-rimmed glasses that somehow made her sexier by hiding her blue eyes behind the frames. Though we were supposed to blend in, it wasn't possible for someone as beautiful as Woodson.

Her skin glittered in the artificial light of the lecture hall, and the dark mascara drew me to her eyes. I felt a sensation of heat somewhere in my chest, even amidst all the disappointment with the sting operation and the SWK investigation.

"Hey, nice talk, Professor Madden," she said at the bottom of the stairs.

"Thank you, Professor Waveland," I returned, with false cordiality. "You look amazing, to say the least."

"As do you, Professor." She stepped backwards and led me away from the last remnant of people slowly exiting the lecture hall. "I didn't see anyone out of place," she relayed in a low whisper, once we were out of everyone's earshot. "But I got caught out of position and couldn't risk a scene with the guy who'd taken my seat. Did any of the other agents signal you?"

"Nope, nothing. Looks like a bust."

"We still have the reception," she offered.

"I suppose so," I said with a genuine sigh. "So we can continue with plan B and head over, though I'm afraid at this point nothing will come of it." I looked around the empty room. "All of this time and effort. For nothing."

"Don't give up. Your own profile says this guy probably blends in . . . same as BTK. He could have been here and maybe no one would have noticed. We still have the reception," she repeated, "so don't give up just yet."

We walked slowly out of the lecture hall as the AV guy turned the lights off behind us. "I don't even want to think about what Jimmy will say about this. All this money."

Woodson intertwined her arm with my own, turning her face to look at me as we walked alone down the hallway. "Don't worry about the money. The night's still young. The glass is still half full. Let's go to a cocktail reception and try to catch a killer."

I shook my head but couldn't help smiling at her endless reservoir of optimism as we pushed open the door and walked toward our parking garages. As always, her enthusiasm was infectious, and I actually found myself looking forward to the reception. Maybe she was right; maybe we still had a chance of catching the guy. The Magnolia Mansion was across town near the Quarter, and we'd have to drive to get there.

"I took a cab here," Woodson said, as if reading my mind. "Would it be possible for me to get a ride, Dr. Madden?" She batted her eyes, asking the question with a slightly pouty smile—the kind normally meant to trick a guy like me into doing anything a woman like her might ask.

"Of course," I said simply, momentarily unable to refrain from looking into her eyes longer than usual.

She returned my gaze, and then we both looked quickly away. "Let's hope we can find this guy tonight," Woodson said, still holding my arm.

I nodded in silent agreement as we pushed open an exit door and walked out into the night.

THIRTY

Woodson and I pulled up outside the Magnolia Mansion fifteen minutes later. As the parking valets took my keys I recognized one of our agents standing on the far side of the street. He was posing as a valet but was responsible for the perimeter of the mansion. He gave me a barely perceptible nod—no eye rub, no yawn—to signify that no one suspicious had yet arrived. Woodson and I walked together through a massive wrought iron gate intertwined with ivy and made our way up the cobblestone sidewalk to the house.

Inside, the floor of the lobby was black-and-white checkerboard marble, and two staircases curled on either side of the entranceway up to the main floor. A green banner was strung between the two staircases welcoming everyone to the Society of Neuroscience reception.

We dropped our coats off at the coat check and recognized the coat checker as the final agent from our so-called sting operation. I was pretty sure this was a waste of his and everyone's time, but we'd see it through.

Woodson and I were halfway up the staircase on the right when I heard a familiar voice above the cacophony of conversation around us. A deep and sultry laugh rose above the rest of the noise, and I glanced upward, disbelieving my eyes.

"Lucas! Lucas!" Mara waved over the crowd at the top of the stairs. Woodson looked upward sharply, and I panicked for a moment.

The first thought that ran through my mind was simply to ask myself what the hell Mara was doing out in public. But then I remembered seeing her at the Society of Neuroscience meeting the previous year, accompanying my brother, who'd presented data on neuroendocrinology findings in pregnant women. I should have considered the possibility that they might be in attendance at this year's reception, and possibly my lecture as well.

The second thought was a decidedly more personal question, which was whether Mara was going to make a scene or not. I watched as she excused herself and walked down the steps toward Woodson and me. A tall man still half hidden by the crowd followed her and I felt a surprising sense of anger surge in my chest. I wasn't sure if it was some vestigial jealousy over our previous relationship, or some subconscious remnant of the protective instinct I'd never outgrown for my younger brother.

Regardless of why, I suddenly became keenly interested in making her new companion's acquaintance.

I climbed the last few steps behind Woodson and felt a sense of relief as I recognized Mara's partner as none other than Dr. James Kinsey, her psychiatrist. In fact, in a convoluted way I was slightly indebted to him: I'd conjured up the original idea for our sting operation after seeing a filled-out registration form for the Society of Neuroscience lying on his desk when we'd interviewed Mara.

"Lucas," Mara said pleasantly, using my name as a salutation.

Woodson and I did a double take. "Hello, Mara," I offered politely, still uncertain as to how the conversation would go.

Kinsey stuck out his hand. "Dr. Madden, we meet again. I greatly enjoyed your lecture."

"Thank you very much." I glanced from Mara. "Mara, Dr. Kinsey, you've met my companion, Dr. Waveland."

I watched Mara as I introduced Woodson and saw a fire illuminate in her pupils. Her eyes became watery and caught the light of the chandelier above. "Dr. Waveland," she said with a less than genuine smile, placing an emphasis on the word *doctor* that made it sound like slander rather than a title.

"Hello," Woodson said.

Of all people, Kinsey appeared oblivious of Mara's passive-aggressive salutation. "Well, it was nice seeing you all again. Please, go mingle," he said, gesturing toward the crowds. "I'm on the board of directors and I must go do some requisite mingling myself. Please enjoy your evening if I don't see you again."

Kinsey nodded, gave a final reassuring pat to Mara's arm, then faded into the crowd, leaving us alone with her.

"So, Mara," I said, "where's Tyler?"

Mara, however, continued looking at Woodson, who had by now become aware of Mara's glare and pretended not to notice. Mara stared at Woodson for a second longer, then turned to face me, a falsified smile across her lips. "Tyler's coming a bit later. He has a grant application or something. I came down alone." She looked over my shoulder, caught the eye of someone, and waved daintily. "I was just about to say hello to the Prevines, so if you don't mind," she said, offering her hand to me without looking at Woodson.

The smile from the top of the stairs was gone, replaced by a piercing stare more akin to the look she'd given me on the basement floor of her grandmother's house.

"It was good seeing you again, Mara."

She turned and walked away into the crowd without another word.

"Good-bye," Woodson called out, but Mara didn't seem to hear.

A few minutes later Woodson and I found a corner in the second-floor ballroom where we could speak in relative privacy.

"Friendly girl," Woodson murmured, popping a shrimp appetizer into her mouth.

"Oh, that's just Mara's way of saying hell—" I began to say, but stopped midsentence as a chorus of shouts and intermittent sirens split the night outside. Adrenaline surged through my body.

Without another word Woodson and I walked rapidly through the ballroom and knifed our way through the crowds on the stairs in the entryway, moving as quickly as possible toward the commotion outside.

At the front entrance a police officer was addressing a crowd of people gathered on the porch. Their attention was focused collectively across the street. Woodson and I pushed our way through the crowd, flashed badges discreetly to the unfamiliar officer, and ran to the road, where the reason for the commotion soon became apparent.

A young woman sat strangely huddled against the low stone fence on the other side of the street, facing the Magnolia Mansion. Looking more closely I could see that she held an apple, and bloody letters were visible on her forehead. It was only at that moment that I realized she was dead.

The newest victim of the Snow White Killer sat across from the very cocktail reception in which we had hoped to trap him.

And her body had been sitting there less than an hour.

Within five minutes Woodson and I and the other undercover agents had secured the area with crime scene tape. No one could raise Simmons, the homicide agent originally stationed on the perimeter, the man we'd seen from our cars when we'd arrived at the Magnolia Mansion, by radio contact.

Unfortunately, I had little doubt as to his fate.

Woodson walked back across the street to the mansion to help the local police with crowd control and then to organize the available agents to interview attendees and valets alike, to ask if anyone had seen anything strange. She also mobilized a couple of agents to fan out and begin looking for our missing agent within a five-block radius.

At the crime scene I squatted to face the nameless victim sitting against the brick wall. The young woman, just as I'd feared, possessed the next sequence of letters from the ripper gene on her forehead, GCGA. The theory that SWK was leaving a message encoding the nucleotide sequence of the ripper gene was no longer in doubt, confirmed by the nonsensical lettering in the sequence. I stared at the unfortunate young woman, forcing myself to avoid her still-open eyes.

Accusatory in death, they seemed to ask me if she really had needed to die on my behalf.

My attention was soon thankfully diverted, however, to her hands: copious residues of caked black blood sat beneath each of her fingernails. Finally, a girl had been able to fight back. I instructed a nearby CSI to wrap her hands in plastic immediately. I wondered whether the killer's blood beneath this woman's fingernails would, as we'd suspected all along, match the blood lettering left on the foreheads of all the other victims.

A light rain began to fall, and I helped the CSIs get a tarp above the body to preserve the crime scene. As we worked I suddenly couldn't shake the feeling we were being watched, and I wondered whether the SWK might be observing his handiwork. As inconspicuously as possible, I swept my head slowly through my full field of vision as we unrolled the tarp and began setting it up.

I turned my head as we secured the last corner, looking in the direction of a dark alley at the end of the block. At that moment a dark figure crossed the alleyway.

Somehow I knew it was our man. I broke into a full run as I saw the figure jerk to a stop, turn wildly at the sight of me running, and then vanish into the darkness.

THIRTY-ONE

The figure ahead of me ran full tilt, and I followed in silent, grim, maniacal determination. At one point he was only thirty yards ahead in the night, but I didn't dare to stop and shoot. If I missed, the time lost in stopping to aim would make it impossible to catch up to him again. I couldn't lose him. Finally, he turned right into an alley, and as I made that alleyway he vanished down another. All of a sudden, I felt more like prey than predator. I pulled a two-way and spoke into it between gasps for air. "Woodson. It's Lucas. I have a bead on him. He's in an alleyway off Saint Martin's Street, about seven or eight blocks south of the mansion. Bring backup. It may be a trap."

"Where the hell," Woodson voice crackled into the air. "Oh for shit's sake, we're on our way. If you really think you saw him, don't go after him. Just wait and we'll be there for backup in less than five minutes. Do you hear me, Madden?"

"Ten four," I said, even though I had already entered the smaller alleyway, turning the corner with my gun held aloft. I had no intention of waiting for backup.

The narrow alley into which the fleeing suspect had vanished was empty except for a single doorway at the end. A tiny, unreadable sign rocked back and forth above the door, creaking eerily in the night.

I walked slowly forward, catching my breath in the otherwise silent night. I walked farther into the alleyway, my heavy wingtips methodically clomping against the damp cobblestone beneath my feet. "Come out, with your hands up," I said aloud, mist pouring from my mouth, realizing that I'd never spoken that phrase in my entire life. Nothing greeted me in return. I flicked on my flashlight and held it away from my face at eye level, illuminating the brickwork of the alleyway surrounding me.

The small sign above the doorway at the end still swung slightly back and forth, telltale evidence that the person I'd pursued had ducked inside or somehow brushed against it. I looked at the sign and illuminated it with the flashlight. I took a half step backwards in grim amazement as the words became visible.

A sign announcing the Ripper Gallery greeted me. A caricature of Jack the Ripper, replete with cape, top hat, and saw, was painted beneath the title of the sign, which resembled a pub sign one might find in London or the English countryside.

Beneath the Ripper Gallery sign, my flashlight illuminated the outline of a shape at the end of the alley, a human form crouching near the doorway entrance. I trained my flashlight on the person and leveled my gun. "Don't move," I said, stepping closer until I finally recognized the face reflected in the wavering light of my flashlight.

At the end of the alleyway was Simmons, the young agent originally stationed on the perimeter. "Simmons?" I asked into the darkness, but received no greeting in return.

After another step I realized that he too was dead, a dark red ribbon of blood encircling his throat, his body crumpled against the wall where he was slain. As I extended my hand to check for a pulse, the Ripper Gallery door swung open and crashed into me. My gun went off with earsplitting intensity right beside my face, the blast echoing with a tremendous boom, reverberating down the entire length of the alley.

A hand grabbed my wrist and shoved the Luger into the brick wall behind me, sending the gun clattering to the cobblestone. Almost as quickly, a punch landed in my stomach, and I felt two hands pick me up by the front of my shirt and slam me backwards into the brick wall. An intense pain shot up my side. I realized in a split second that my still-stitched knife wound had reopened. I struggled to turn and face my attacker, but his face was lost in the shadows above me.

I felt hot breath on my face and a sick minty smell in my nostrils.

"Welcome, Madden," the voice said in a hushed whisper, then pushed me backwards so that I slumped halfway inside the doorway to the gallery, then fell onto my back on the floor. The voice continued. "Our work is almost complete."

The shadow loomed above me and I felt something unbearably cold at my neck and realized he held the blade of a knife against my throat. With every ounce of energy, I thrust upward with my right foot and caught my attacker in the solar plexus, even as he hunched above me for the kill. I drove it with all my might and felt his body lurch sky-ward and backwards, even as the air rushed from his body amidst a grunt of pain.

He landed and stumbled backwards, gasping, as sirens suddenly sounded in the distance. I grabbed his right wrist with both hands in an attempt to control his knife hand.

Suddenly fireworks of green and yellow stars filled my entire field of vision as an intense pain in my side exploded into my brain. I was only barely able to assimilate that my opponent had taken his free left hand and worked two fingers into my back, pressing relentlessly into the recent knife wound. The whispering voice breathed in my ear. "Enjoy the exhibit. I'm not finished with you yet, Madden."

I reached out for my assailant through the fireworks exploding be-fore me, but grasped only air. The figure retreated into the gallery, van-ishing amidst the vibrant, multicolor spectacular that continued to plague my sense of sight. His footsteps became echoing clacks that eventually dissolved into the night, and the only sounds left were the approaching sirens.

I pulled myself to the doorway of the gallery and tried to stand but fell backwards. From my prone position I saw a strange rectangular shape before me, illuminated by brief flashes of lightning. As the fireworks receded from my vision, I rolled over, found my Luger, stood, and stumbled forward to investigate.

The rectangle floating in midair was simply a placard on a tripod, inviting the public to an art exhibit bearing a strangely familiar name, but one that I couldn't place: The Devil's Orchard.

I stepped inside, holding the Luger unsteadily in front of me in one hand, my flashlight in the other. The interior of the gallery revealed an expansive single room with a hardwood floor. My shoes clomped against the smooth surface and my footsteps echoed in the dark interior. I focused my flashlight on the far wall. No sign of my adversary. The sirens grew louder in the distance, but were still several blocks away.

I turned my attention back to the wall and the flashlight illuminated a series of paintings before me. I swept the light across the gallery floor, surveying the entire room. There were no stairs leading to an upper level, and the ceilings extended a good thirty feet into the air. There were two doors, the one through which I'd entered, and one in the rear corner, only partially closed.

I walked toward the rear door but the paintings on the wall drew my attention. The fading circular light of my flashlight bounced along the dark walls. The paintings in the shadows were dark, mostly black, but with splashes of color: red.

The images became more discernible as I approached. The first painting on my right was of a young woman, her eyes rolling back into her head, surrounded by stars similar to the great glowing orbs of van Gogh's *Starry Night*.

The girl in the painting threw her head back, her eyebrows arched in fury and helplessness. Her face bore the depiction of suffering.

I stepped closer and blinked. Small red lines on her forehead formed the letter *A*. And then I realized I was looking at a painted image of the once-living Anna Cross. The world around me became surreal as I stared at a portrait of the Snow White Killer's first victim, captured in the very moment of her death.

In disbelief, I cut my eyes to the next painting. Another woman, with the red letters *T, A,* and *N* adorning her forehead, grimacing as if to shield herself from an attack, a bloody knife in the foreground of the painting, wielded from a first-person perspective this time, poised in midslash. From this portrait the terrified eyes of Jessica Harrison, the killer's second victim, stared back at me.

The room tilted before me. I couldn't grasp it, couldn't get my mind around it. I stumbled forward to the next painting, a young brunette with a beautiful pale complexion.

I felt sick to my stomach as I realized I'd discovered a gallery of all the dead girls left by this killer, all staring silently ahead, young women all failed by me.

I noticed for the first time, as my eyes adjusted to the darkness of the gallery, that it wasn't completely dark inside. In the rear, next to the other door, a decently lit painting sat on its own, not surrounded by other portraits. A series of muted exhibition lights sat poised around it, illuminating it in garish fashion.

It was the indubitable centerpiece of the exhibit, but I couldn't make it out.

I walked toward it, the Luger hanging limply at my side, my wing-tips slowly trudging the floor in zombielike thunks. The pain in my back and side grew worse with each step.

For some reason I was afraid of what lay ahead. The hair on my neck stood up, a preternatural warning telling me to leave, but there was no going back.

The painting, even from far away, seemed somehow strangely *familiar.* The repetitive wash of déjà vu flowing over me felt like walking into an ocean of memories, each wave a little more familiar than the next, but still unrecognizable. The painting depicted a landscape I'd seen before. Trees in this painting, unlike the others, as more and more of the picture came into view.

The artistic style in this painting was different from the rest as well. A little more crude, not as well defined as the others, perhaps. It came into view as my flashlight bobbed in the dark toward it.

I kept walking slowly closer, unable to stop myself, to get a better look at the dark canvas.

Trees, branches. A young boy's smudged white face in the background in the lower left-hand corner, in front of the main figure in the center of the painting, still covered in shadows. A boy with cuts on his body, a torn T-shirt. A boy? A blurry-faced boy I somehow recognized. From where?

The boy in the painting held the hand of a woman behind him, the central figure. As I approached, the shadows and light shifted to reveal the painting in greater detail. The young woman followed the boy, holding her free hand above her head to keep tree branches out of her face. The sleeve of her white blouse partly obscured her face, which finally came into view.

At that moment I heard Woodson's voice suddenly echo behind me in the gallery, calling for me, screaming for me to answer. I felt the vibrations of many footsteps scuttling across the hardwood floor toward me, but I couldn't hear what Woodson was saying.

I took a last look at the painting.

Right before the room went black, I registered that somehow, impossibly, confusingly . . . the eyes of my *very own mother* stared back at me from the painting, her frightened face surrounded by the dark and twisted orchard in which she had died alone more than twenty years before.

THIRTY-TWO

Eventually Woodson's face emerged from the darkness.

I tried to rise, but couldn't, as a boom of thunder broke in the distance. I focused on Woodson above me, whose concerned expression seemed consistent with the urgency in her voice. "Lucas. Wake up. Are you okay? Wake up."

"What happened?"

"Oh, thank God," she said. "Guys, he's waking up over here. Lend a hand, please?" She turned back to me. "Just stay still, Lucas. You passed out in here. You lost a lot of blood." She pulled my shirt up and away from my chest.

I looked down to find my torso wrapped in fresh white gauze, an irregular red stain spreading from my back to an area behind my left rib cage. "That's just the old cut, reopened," I murmured.

"Who did this?"

I looked past Woodson and observed my surroundings. We were still inside the dark gallery into which I'd tracked the SWK. The interior was now lit by a series of crime scene lights, and multiple silhouetted figures moved in the darkness. CSIs, I finally realized.

"Who did this, Lucas?" she repeated.

"It was him, Woodson. The Snow White Killer. I'm sure of it."

"So did you get a good look at him?" From the lack of surprise in her voice, I realized Woodson had already put two and two together.

I shook my head. "No. He surprised me. He was waiting for me in here."

"Lucas," Woodson ventured her next question gingerly, "did you happen to look around inside the gallery yet, by the way?"

"Yeah. Yeah, I did."

She blew the hair out of her face. "I was afraid of that," she said, and cradled my head in her lap and kissed my forehead. "I'm sorry, Lucas."

I started to speak, but Woodson pulled out a small cylinder with a handle and pointed it toward me. "Hold on. Before you go anywhere. If you fought him, you might have caught a little piece of him. Don't move until I roll you with a lint roller to find out if Mr. SWK actually left any trace evidence on you during the fight."

"Lots of luck," I said, but lay still as Woodson went to work. We both fell silent as I rested my head on her legs and she rolled the tape roller slowly over my shirt, along my collar, and over my chest without speaking. I felt strangely comforted, if only momentarily, amidst the bustling crime scene investigation in full swing around us.

"Okay," she said after she finished, "let's hope we find something." She unrolled the piece of tape from the roller and placed it into a small brown paper bag, which she then placed into a briefcase beside her. She gently stood, guiding my head from her lap to the floor, and then offered her hand to help me up. "Come on, let's get you to a hospital."

"No way, Woodson. I'm staying here."

"Don't be ridiculous."

"I'm staying here."

Woodson sighed. "Okay, we'll see about that. Let's see if you can even stand up first."

I took her hand. The room swam before me, but it quickly went away and left in its wake a pounding headache instead. "Damn it."

"Are you sure you don't want to go to the hospital?"

"I'm sure. What have we got?" I asked, lifting my head and looking around the gallery. I had to steady my forehead with the first two fingers of my left hand to keep it upraised despite the pain.

"Nothing but paintings."

"Did they use UV lights yet?"

"Yeah. No blood in here, Lucas. Except the blood on you. All of which appears to be yours, which is why you should be going to the hospital and—"

"So this is just an art gallery?"

Woodson sighed in resigned fashion, apparently accepting that I wouldn't be going to a hospital as long as I had anything to do about it. "Yes, seems to be just an art gallery, no other sort of purpose by day."

"I want to have a look at that painting again. The one of my mother."

Woodson held out her hand and touched my shoulder. "Are you sure? What good will it do?"

"I want to see it again, see if there's anything that might give us a clue." I started to walk back toward the rear of the gallery when my cell phone rang.

"Hello?"

"Lucas. It's Terry. You got a second?"

Woodson looked at me with a question on her face as I answered aloud for her benefit. "Not really, Terry. What's on your mind?"

"You sound like shit."

"Is that why you called?"

"No, just an observation. The real reason was to let you know we're starting the sequencing reactions to amplify ripper genes from the victim DNA samples. Thought you might want to be here when we finish sequencing the genes tomorrow morning. We're a little ahead of schedule."

"Okay. Any progress on separating the caffeine and the pseudocaffeine?"

"Yeah, a little. We've extracted it, so we should be able to run it tomorrow and get an ID." He paused. "So what's going on down there? Alan just mentioned you guys found another victim?"

"Yeah, and this girl had a lot of blood beneath her fingernails. A lot, Terry. Maybe finally one of the victims had a chance to fight back. We can check whether the samples beneath this last victim's fingernails match the blood in the messages on the victims' foreheads."

Terry replied, but I didn't hear. All of a sudden I saw two versions of Woodson looking back at me. A sound like the ocean crashed in my head as I began to sway back and forth. "Yeah. Terry, sorry, listen I gotta go," I managed to say, just before one of the Woodson twins reached for me and yelled my name. Then everything faded away to the increasingly familiar black.

"Lucas," the voice said.

Woodson stared down at me once again. Just one Woodson this time.

"Where am I now?"

"You're in my house."

"Why?"

"You fainted at the gallery, but I managed to catch you before you hit the floor. Not the world's most graceful catch, but I managed to keep you from hurting your head. I took you to the hospital, but your MRI was negative. You don't remember? You woke up in the middle of it and demanded that you be taken back to the crime scene. You wouldn't shut up. Mercifully for me, they finally deemed you well enough to receive a sedative. They gave you fluids and stitched you up in the ER and sent us on our way."

"What's going on at the gallery?"

"The gallery is secure, I promise. And the paintings are safe. Can you relax for three seconds?"

"I don't have that luxury." I tried to sit up, but a pain in my head sent me back into the pillows. "Oh shit, that hurts. Look." I squinted at Woodson through one eye. "I need to call Faraday and Tucker, check on my sister and the girls. Can I have my phone?" I closed both eyes in an effort to thwart the pain and held my hand out, palm up.

"Relax. Faraday called less than an hour ago and said everyone was fine. You're going to have to rest for at least a little bit, Lucas. You can't keep going full tilt or you're going to keel over."

I propped myself up on one elbow and winced again.

She stared at me in the ensuing silence until I opened my eyes. "You have the weight of the world on your head, don't you?" she asked softly.

"Just the weight of my world," I said, suddenly unnerved by the luminous glow of Woodson's eyes in the darkness. "What time is it?" I asked.

"Just lean back," she said, gently pushing me back onto the plush pillows and pulling a goose down comforter up over my chest. And suddenly, although I hated to admit it, I realized how good it felt to sink into the lush, cushioned mattress. I took a deep breath, the kind my chiropractor always told me to take, and it was the first one I could remember taking in a long time.

"And by the way, it's three in the morning, Lucas. So just lay back and go to sleep for a few more hours. If you feel okay, no fever, and all that good stuff, then we should be able to get back on the case before you know it. The doctor said the headache was from dehydration after the blood loss. The fluids they gave you should take care of you by morning."

I rested my hand on her arm. "I can't stop now. The guy who's killing these women . . . he killed my mother. I'm sure of it."

I heard Woodson sigh, as if she'd already come to the same conclusion and simply dreaded hearing it from me. "Who knows?" she said. "It's also possible that the killer's just messing with you; found an old picture of your mother, portrayed her the way he imagined she might have looked that night. Put her portrait in the gallery with all his other real victims, then led you there. Maybe he's just trying to screw with you."

"Impossible," I whispered back. "The setting is perfect. Those were the woods where she died. The painter of that picture was there that night. I'm sure of it."

"Lucas. It's still possible that the SWK is just messing with you. Maybe he read about what happened to your mother or painted it according to the reports in the newspapers. Just think about it. You have to stay rational with me here."

I shook my head again, even more strongly in the negative, although it hurt to do so. "Everything about that painting was real. The woods, her dress, her face, that boy leading her into the woods—that's what he looked like, Woodson. I remember it. I was there, don't forget. I saw it all myself, my own two eyes. Those details weren't in any historical news archives. Believe me, I've read them all."

"Lucas," Woodson began, but fell silent. She didn't have an answer.

"Whoever is killing these girls in the present day," I said, "is the same person who killed my mother twenty-five years ago. And I'm going to find him, Woodson. And when I find him, I'm going to kill him."

I felt the backside of her hand softly touch my cheek and suddenly became conscious that my own face was moist. Woodson spoke softly above me. "Shhh. Just sleep for now, Lucas. We'll start again tomorrow morning, I promise."

I reached up and held her wrist. I couldn't let it go. "I'm going to kill him, Woodson. You need to understand that. I don't want you to get hurt. But I'm not out to capture this guy anymore. There will be no Miranda rights. I'm going to kill him. You have a right to know."

"I hear you, Lucas. I'll pretend that I didn't. But I hear you." She pushed my head into the pillow, and descended gently upon me. "And I understand."

"I don't care about anything anymore," I said, but she shushed me from speaking further with a finger pressed lightly against my mouth. The gentle touch of her fingertip on my lips sent a quiver through my body. A sensation for which I was wholly, utterly unprepared. It instantly reminded me of the intimacy I'd felt earlier in the night, when she'd lifted the trace evidence from my body with the repetitive motions of the lint roller. How shockingly comforting that simple, methodical procedure had been.

She flicked off the lamp and the room went dark, save for a sliver of moonlight through the window outside.

"Everything will be all right, Lucas," she said, her voice echoing above me from the pitch-black darkness like that of a hypnotist.

At that same moment I felt her take my face in both hands and tilt my head gently upward. I thought she was simply repositioning my head on the pillow, but a sensual thrill passed through my belly again as I felt the bed move beneath her weight. Suddenly I felt her lips against mine, forcing my mouth open and taking my breath away for a moment. One of her hands traced my chest and came to rest on my stomach, slowly moving in a soothing circular fashion.

And then my hands were reaching upward and finding her neck, and I pulled her toward me. The pain in my head dissolved as I became aware of only her. Her kiss was warm, with a perfect degree of pressure from her lips as she continued to kiss me from above.

I ceased kissing her for only a second so that I could see her, now that my eyes had adjusted to the dark. Her long, angular face hovered above mine. And somehow, impossibly, this interesting, brilliant, and beautiful woman whom I'd known for mere days was above me, kissing me silently in the darkness. I noticed that her lips glistened in the moonlit darkness, sparkling with leftover lipstick from the Magnolia Mansion reception earlier in the evening.

Without a word Woodson lifted her silky cream-colored top above her head. It slid off and disappeared over the side of the bed.

Naked from the waist up as she swayed above me, she looked down at me with a calmness that juxtaposed oddly with the moment. It stunned me for what seemed the tenth time in as many minutes. She leaned down and kissed me again, and I relished the way she welcomed me to her.

She helped me remove my clothes, taking care to avoid the bandage on my back. Chills swept over me in repetitive rushes of pleasure, but I couldn't stop to take the time to enjoy them. A voice inside my head screamed at me to just stop and think about the ramifications of becoming involved with a colleague . . . but an equally loud voice told me to shut the hell up for a change and give in.

For once, I listened to the latter voice.

I succumbed to her, and in moments the night was suddenly full of our sounds; the bed, our breath, our skin, the deepness of our intensity—a newfound intimacy that didn't smother me but gathered me to her. My mind raced backwards through time as we moved together, a series of images spilling faster and faster like a waterfall in my head, leading all the way back to our first exchange in the auditorium in Quantico.

In the midst of it, Woodson suddenly stared down at me, an oddly quixotic look on her face. "Lucas," she whispered. "Everything is going to be okay. I promise."

I looked at her blankly as my body threatened to finish, and I had to fight to hold myself back. I strained upward toward her and buried my face into her chest. "Woodson."

She pushed me back down. "I promise it will be." And then she began to move again, and as I began to keep rhythm with her, I felt her body begin to shake, imperceptibly at first, then more noticeably, until every muscle in her body tightened simultaneously. I couldn't hold back any longer, and succumbed.

After a few moments of tremulous silence she uttered a half-broken cry and finally pushed her head backwards away from me as though she were trying to stretch herself into oblivion. A little later she collapsed beside me, my face in her hands.

I waited for a time, relishing the moment and thinking about everything that had just transpired, feeling her fingertips on my cheek. After a little while I spoke. "Woodson," I spoke her name into the night.

But the only sound that greeted me was the heavy breathing of someone in deep slumber beside me. I fell asleep within minutes after that, making sure her hand remained.

At seven the next morning the phone rang. I managed to search around on the nightstand and pick the phone up on the third ring, even as an intense pain shot upward through my back. The bedroom phone felt strange in my hands as well: too big, too oblong.

I brought the receiver to my face, eyes still closed. "Madden here."

"Lucas?"

"Terry?" I said, and felt something move beside me. I looked over, half expecting the furry body of Crick to flop beside me. Instead, Woodson flicked on the light. Her blonde hair was disheveled and her mascara had run. She still looked gorgeous amidst the chaos of her makeup. I stared at her, the night's memories swirling upward with a dizzying intensity from the bottom of a deep, lost pit, straight into the very forefront of my mind, as I recalled every last bit.

I tried to focus on the voice on the other end of the phone.

"Oh yeah, that's right. Woodson told me she let you stay there last night after the hospital, rather than having to drive back to your house. I just didn't expect you to answer her phone. Anyway, I have some good news at the lab and thought you and Woodson would both want to hear about it."

As Terry spoke I found myself negotiating a series of facts flowing like white water through my mind.

One, I wasn't at home—I was at Woodson's.

Two, I was at Woodson's because last night I'd grappled with the Snow White Killer himself, then passed out in the gallery after the pain became too great.

Three, the Snow White Killer had likely killed my own mother.

Terry's voice continued, and I became cognizant of it once again. He was speaking. "Yeah. If you're up to it, you guys better come on back to the lab. We're getting close, I think."

"Okay, Terry," I said. "We'll be there as soon as possible."

As I hung up the phone, Woodson rolled over, took my face, and pulled me back toward her in the bed. I allowed her to pull me backwards. Even though it felt good and I wanted to collapse backwards into her arms again, I dreaded it. I dreaded the reality of what we'd shared last night, fully illuminated between us in the bright light of morning.

I hated that part of it. I didn't know what to say, because after finally denying all the repressed desire for my strange and alluring partner, I hadn't had time to consider what, exactly, the consequences of
our passion might ultimately mean in our professional lives.

"Woodson," I started to say, but she breathed into my ear before I
had a chance to turn around. I'd hoped to stumble through an explanation of why it would be a good idea to keep our tryst confidential,
even though it had been memorable and I wanted things to continue,
but her low voice sent an electric thrill through my body before I could
speak further.

"Not a word to anybody, *Madden,*" she said, and quickly swept away
in a rustle of sheets behind me. She called to me from behind the closed
bathroom door. "Hey, you can take a shower in the guest bathroom
downstairs. I brought in one of the extra suits you keep in your SUV,
you weirdo, for you to change into. I'll see you in the field office in
about an hour."

Strangely, I felt both relieved and slightly peeved that she already
fully intended to keep our rendezvous a secret as well, and that
I didn't need to awkwardly suggest it myself. "Okay. See you then,
Woodson."

"And Madden?" Woodson yelled as she turned on the shower.

"Yeah?" I assumed she was going to inquire as to my physical
well-being after the previous night's sequence of events. To be honest
I was surprised at how refreshed I felt. No more headaches, and a
lot less tension in my neck. "Yeah, Woodson?" I said, a little more
loudly.

"Hey, I forgot to mention. Don't let the door hit you in the ass on
your way out."

For about half a second I was stupefied, as a sense of sheer embar-
rassment began to take hold, until I heard the cacophony of laughter
ring outward from the shower. "I'm just kidding, you big galoot," she
said. "I'll see you in a bit."

Surprised to find myself already smiling, at that moment I began to
suspect that maybe, just maybe, having someone in my life who was

able to make me laugh for a change, take me by surprise for a change . . . well, maybe it wasn't such a bad thing after all.

Downstairs, after showering and changing into my clothes, I took Woodson's advice. I left straightaway, making sure not to let the door hit me in the ass on my way out.

It was a liberating feeling, I had to admit.

THIRTY-THREE

During the ride back to work, I reentered reality. My thoughts turned to the most recent twist in the SWK investigation. My mother's eyes in the painting grew larger and larger in the back of my mind as I struggled to understand the link between the SWK, the gruesome art gallery, the victims of today, and my mother's death so many years ago.

It didn't seem so much like my own cosmically pervasive shithouse luck anymore.

I arrived at the field office a little past eight. To my great surprise, I found Raritan and Parkman sitting in Terry's office when I walked in. All three looked up.

"Aha. The agent with nine lives," Raritan said.

"In the flesh. What are you guys doing here?"

Raritan smiled. "Where's your partner, Lucas? I heard you two have been inseparable lately."

"Your guess is as good as mine," I answered.

"Terry told us you stayed at Woodson's place after you were released from the hospital last night."

"I did. She let me stay at her place last night since it was close to the hospital and they wouldn't let me drive under the influence of all the drugs I received in the ER. I slept on her couch and left this morning, before she even came downstairs." I was surprised by how easily the lie slid from my tongue.

"Okay, thanks for filling us in." Raritan spoke with just enough sarcasm that I wondered whether the untruth that had so easily slid from my lips hadn't sounded quite as believable as I'd thought.

I changed the subject. "So again, what brings the two of you down to visit?"

"You, naturally," Raritan said. "Your sting worked, even if it didn't go down the way you planned. You brought SWK out of the woodwork. You're making serious headway here. I felt it was time for Parkman and me to come down, help out directly."

In that instant I finally appreciated why local police usually abominated the FBI, at least whenever we came to an investigation under the pretense of "helping out" toward the end. Even from my perspective as an agent within the Bureau, Raritan's offer for the BAU to suddenly help out sounded a lot more like "take the credit at the last possible minute" to me.

But I betrayed no such thoughts. "That would be great," I said, looking at Terry. "Have you gotten them up to speed on everything?"

"Doing that now. I was just about to go over why we're sequencing the ripper gene in all the victims' DNA samples."

"So you think your pinprick isn't an injection site for the mystery drug, but rather a blood sample that's being taken from the victims in common?" Raritan asked.

"That's the prevailing theory. I even think the killer somehow screens the samples for mutations in ripper."

"You think SWK took the blood samples himself?" Parkman asked.

"Maybe, but not necessarily. He could just be screening a database or a blood bank rather than taking the blood samples himself."

At that moment Woodson walked in. "Hello, boys," she said, acting just a bit too casual with everyone.

"Agent Woodson," Raritan said. "So good of you to join us. Thanks for taking care of our friend Lucas here last night."

It was the same gauntlet they'd run me through, but Woodson shrugged it off like a pro. "Hey, all part of being a good partner, just like you told me when I had to give him a ride back from the hospital in Gulfport. Right?"

Raritan peered at her for a split second, then looked at me. "I suppose so."

"So what were you guys talking about?" Woodson asked, pulling up a chair.

"We were talking about the pinpricks and what they might indicate," I said. "I was just saying that it doesn't mean the victims necessarily gave their blood directly to SWK. But I do believe he somehow had access to their blood samples after the blood was drawn."

"Right. And you were saying you think the SWK is sequencing their DNA?" Raritan asked.

"Yes. For some reason, I think SWK is trying to eliminate women in the population carrying ripper mutations. I'm not sure why."

"How can you prove it?" Parkman asked.

"I hope Terry's proving it right now," I answered. "If all the victims have ripper mutations, we'll be able to figure out pretty quickly how unlikely it is that all the victims would carry such mutations in the same gene by random chance."

"And if not?"

"Then we focus elsewhere."

A knock on the door interrupted us. A lab technician poked her head inside.

"Agent Randall. The results are in."

"What's the verdict?" Terry asked. "Go on, tell us."

The young woman looked from me to Woodson, then back toward Terry and Parkman, and finally to Jimmy. "It's the rest of the women. The ripper sequence analyses we ran last night."

"Yes?"

"Every single victim carries a mutation in the ripper gene."

We reconvened in the laboratory downstairs and stared at the computer screen linked to the DNA sequencer. Just as the young lab tech had reported, every single sample harbored heterozygous mutations in the ripper gene.

An event which, a decade ago, I'd postulated would grant the unborn zygote a stronger odds ratio of one day becoming a violent offender or even a serial killer.

"Well, I'll be damned," Parkman finally snorted in disbelief.

I tapped the computer screen. "Less than two percent of the Caucasian population carries mutations in ripper. The odds that all six women would have mutations in ripper by chance? Almost impossible. One in what? Three hundred million?"

"Pretty convincing," Raritan said.

"This guy has gotten access to their blood. Or at least their DNA sequences. Somehow, he knew these women had mutations. And to find this many ripper women carrying mutations, he screened a lot of women." I calculated it quickly in my head. "He probably had to have access to at least four or five hundred women's DNA to find six women carrying ripper polymorphisms."

"And that's a conservative estimate," Raritan added.

"So forget the why for a second," Parkman said. "Let's just focus on the how. Any ideas?"

Woodson spoke up. "We've already had a brainstorming session on that. Most likely venue would be a doctor's office, or someplace where drug tests are mandatory, someplace where extra portions of a blood sample could be siphoned off for other purposes."

"Any luck?" Raritan asked.

"No, nothing yet," Terry replied. "We just came up with that possibility a day or so ago. We'll keep looking."

Woodson stood. "Well, I agree that all of this is very exciting, but I need to get down to the tox labs. They finally isolated the unknown mystery drug in the blood last night, and got a mass spectrum on the compound as well."

"Really?" I asked.

"Yep. Now that we have its mass spectral profile, we just need to screen it against as many databases as we can. It's only a matter of time, now. Even as we speak the lab is accessing every chemical spectral database around. If this mystery drug is in any of those databases, we'll find it. Unless SWK is cooking something off the shelf." She opened the office door and turned to face us before leaving. "I'll let you all know the minute we find anything." She closed the door.

Raritan looked at Terry and me after she left. "Okay. Let's reconvene at noon. You guys put all these leads together, it will be like Woodson says—only a matter of time before we catch this guy. Parkman and I can cancel our flight back to Quantico if things really heat up down here in the meantime."

As the ad hoc meeting adjourned, I mentioned aloud that I'd forgotten to discuss a peculiar property in one of the peaks in the mystery drug chromatograms with Woodson, and made my way down the hall to her office.

THIRTY-FOUR

In Woodson's office I closed the door behind me. "I'm finding it hard to concentrate here."

"Me too." She craned her neck from her seated position and looked behind me, out her office window. "But we have to be careful, Lucas. One slip and I'll be the one getting reassigned to Anchorage. Not you."

"Don't be so sure," I said. "But you're right. I'll be careful."

"Well, at least for now," Woodson said, twirling her tongue across her lips for half a second before smiling at me.

I suddenly felt a lot better about coming to speak with her in private. "So," I said, "you're serious? You really isolated our mystery drug in the victims' blood samples?"

"Yes. Well, Terry's group did. Now we just have to screen the databases."

I stared as she leaned over the computer keyboard and typed. My personal life was, for once, taking a turn for the better. I enjoyed the chill-bumps on my arms when I looked at her. I couldn't tell if they were due to the long-forgotten embers of romance, the excitement of being this close to breaking a case, or some complex mixture of the two.

"I hate to ask this, Lucas, but I have to. How do you think Mara

Bliss fits into all of this again?" Woodson asked. "With all her claims about talking to the killer, hearing the killer, seeing the killer's victims? Is she just a loon?"

The question caught me off guard. We'd been following up so many bona fide physical forensic leads lately that I hadn't thought about Mara's claims from the interview, about how she dreamed she spoke to the killer and saw the dead girls.

"I don't think they mean anything. I think she's just disturbed, that's all."

"You don't think she could have any link to the killer? Something you don't know about?"

I glanced up at Woodson to get a read on her motives for asking the question. From the sincere look on her face, the question seemed to be posed without ulterior motives. Just an honest inquiry. "No, I don't," I answered. "Don't forget, I'm the one who found her chained up in her grandmother's basement, left there by the SWK."

"Right, but one could ask whether she was put there or if she put herself there. Just to throw you off."

I laughed. "I don't think so. You're grasping here, Woodson. What's going on? Why are you asking about Mara again, all of a sudden?"

Woodson shook her head in the negative but didn't immediately speak. She paused as if weighing whether she should speak again or not. "Remember the gallery where you found the 'Ripper Exhibition'?"

"Sure," I said.

"I'll give you one guess as to who owns it."

My mind reeled as I assimilated the question and its obvious answer. "Mara?"

"You win on your very first try." She turned her computer screen around to face me.

I looked from Woodson to the computer and back again. "Have you told anyone yet?"

"No," she sighed, "I wanted to tell you first. But it's only a matter of hours before this will come out in the autopsy report. They always list owners of property involved in crime scenes."

"I know," I said, without really listening. I was too busy trying to understand how Mara could have anything to do with the Snow White Killer. And how that related to the centerpiece of the so-called Ripper Exhibition: my mother's untimely death.

I thought back. Mara had been with me in the backseat of the car that night. She certainly never saw a close-up of my mother being led to her death in the woods. Nothing made sense anymore, and the more I thought about Mara, and my mother, the less I understood anything about the present-day Snow White Killer.

By all accounts, the evidence at this point was overwhelming that Mara and the SWK were somehow inextricably linked. I couldn't deny it any longer. I just had no idea how.

"So what are you going to do, Lucas?" Woodson's question shook me from my thoughts.

"I don't know. I guess I'm going to find Mara again. I don't have any idea how she's related to this investigation anymore, but we have to bring her in. Too many coincidences ceases being coincidence at some point."

Woodson came around her desk, but walked past me to turn down the blinds and lock her office door. She sat in the chair beside me and touched my arm. "Lucas. I'm telling you this as a friend, not as anyone else." She paused. "I don't think you should have any further contact with Mara. In fact, I don't think you should have any further contact with this case at all. It's all just hitting too close to home, all of a sudden."

"What? So you don't believe I should be on this case anymore, either?"

She leaned closer. "I believe in you, Lucas. I can't trust you any more than I already do," she said, lightly touching my face. "You'd be a lot better off in life if you knew that some people really do believe in you."

"But what are you saying?"

"I'm saying I believe in you, but I also think you shouldn't be dealing with this case anymore. But if you think it's important, and correct procedure, for you to go get Mara yourself, then by all means, bring her in. I won't say anything to Raritan or Parkman about where you're going. But you better get moving and you better stay in touch with me."

"Thanks, Woodson."

She leaned forward to whisper in my ear as she stood. "And be careful," she said, brushing her lips past my cheekbone ever so slightly.

With that, she stood, walked over and opened the blinds, unlocked the door, and returned to her seated position behind her desk. When she looked up at me again, it was with feigned surprise. "You're still here?"

As I assimilated the question, a tremendous sense of gratitude welled up inside. Against her own better judgment, Woodson was letting me go deal with Mara on my own terms. I stood to leave, just as a knock on the office door sounded from the hall.

"Come in," Woodson called. Another young technician poked his head into the doorway. "Dr. Woodson, Dr. Madden. We've chemically identified the compound in the victims' blood. Terry told us to find you so you can come take a look."

Woodson and I exchanged glances. Though I desperately wanted to find Mara, now that we knew she was the actual owner of the Ripper Gallery studio, I couldn't leave the office just yet. Not with something that could break the case wide open—finally establishing the identity of the mystery drug in the victims' blood—only a short distance away from us down the hall.

"By all means," Woodson said to the young technician. "Lead the way."

I followed them down the hall. Mara could wait another half hour until we found out what drug or chemical was floating around in the bloodstreams of all the Snow White Killer's victims at the time of their deaths. It was a lead that was too good to pass up.

Downstairs a different technician sat on a stool and pointed to another computer screen in the laboratory, around which all of us had reconvened: Raritan, Parkman, Terry, Woodson, and myself. We peered over the seated man's shoulder and regarded a split screen. The mass spectrum on the top panel was labeled "SWK Victim 3 Unknown," while an identical spectrum on the bottom was labeled "Marihypnol."

"Marihypnol?" Woodson asked as she read it. "I've never heard of it."

"None of us had, either," Terry said. "So we looked it up. It's an investigational drug on file at the FDA. That's why we didn't find it when we initially searched the database of approved drugs. Marihypnol isn't an approved therapeutic yet, so it's not in the FDA database of known drugs. It's still an exploratory drug. It's undergoing a phase three trial for Arrow Pharmaceuticals."

"What does it do?" I asked.

"It's undergoing evaluation in clinical trials as a nonteratogenic antianxiety drug for women of childbearing years. If approved, it will be one of the few depression-related drugs that pregnant women could safely take. Could be a billion-dollar drug, for obvious reasons."

Woodson cut her eyes toward me, but I didn't speak.

Terry continued. "But that's not the kicker. There's a serious side effect—sedative hypnosis, as the 'hypnol' would imply. To the point of incapacitation, if the dose is too high, such that the subjects can't respond to stimuli. Even painful stimuli."

"You're kidding me," I said.

"I'm not. This is definitely our drug, guys. Rodents given Marihypnol don't respond to pain. No one understands the mechanism—the nerves are still responding, sending whopping signals to the brain to cease the pain-causing activity. But for some reason, when subjects are on high-dose Marihypnol, they can perceive pain but can't respond to it. They know it's there, but they're unable to do anything about it."

"You've got to be shitting me," I said, struggling to keep my jaw in place as everything we'd proposed regarding the modus operandi of the Snow White Killer clicked into place.

"This explains why the victims never struggled. If they were pumped full of Marihypnol, they couldn't." I let the words fall onto the rest of the group as they assimilated everything. It was an unsettling thought; the victims had still felt the pain, they just couldn't do anything about it. The SWK had probably watched his victims like an entomologist watches an insect pinned to the foam of a collection board.

The young tech's voice snapped me back to the present. "As Dr. Randall was saying, they've already done tolerability studies in humans. So we know what's acceptable and what's considered toxic."

"And?"

Terry spoke up again. "And we've done a rough calculation—every single one of the victims had circulating levels of this drug well above the maximum tolerated dose."

Woodson spoke. "So they were drugged intentionally with high-dose Marihypnol."

"Looks like it's time to find out which clinical sites in this part of the United States are involved in that phase three trial of Marihypnol," I said.

We all went back upstairs. I walked to my office, while Raritan, Parkman, and Woodson set up a teleconference with Arrow Pharmaceuticals to find out more about their clinical studies. I desperately wanted to bring Mara in and follow up on the link to the gallery, but we were so close to an even more tangible break in the case with the Arrow Pharmaceutical lead that I forced myself to stay in the office until we knew the locations of their clinical trial sites in case we got a lead.

As I sat at my desk, I couldn't shake the memory of my mother's eyes in that portrait gallery. It all came back. I tried to steer my mind away from it. I tried to think about the geography of the kill sites, about the killer's access to blood samples, about the ripper sequence as a road map, about the killer's obsession with me, about the killer's link to Mara.

On the surface, in the onslaught of facts and evidence, everything kept boiling down to one person, and I refused to believe it. It had to be someone else.

A few minutes later I heard footsteps coming down the hall. My colleagues hadn't called ahead, which meant they wanted to talk to me face-to-face without giving me time to prepare.

One pair of heels, a pair of boots, and a pair of wingtips: each of them made a characteristic clack on the tiled floor, a trio of sounds I hadn't heard since I'd been released from the hospital in Gulfport so long ago.

Woodson, Parkman, Raritan.

I wiped my face with my hands, opened my eyes, and gathered myself. I closed my eyes and took a final deep breath before they made it to the door.

"Come in," I said, as soon as I heard the knock a few seconds later.

No one looked me in the eyes as I searched each of their faces, not even Woodson. She finally spoke, after Parkman closed the door. "Lucas. We found out the names of the principal investigators running the clinical trials for Marihypnol."

"Oh? Good." I pushed myself back from the desk and started to stand.

Raritan stepped forward. "Just stay seated, Lucas."

"Uh, okay," I said, feeling my legs go numb beneath me.

Raritan gave Woodson an imperceptible nod, and she sat in one of the chairs across from my desk. "It's time for you to be off the case, Lucas," she said.

"Why?" I asked, but the only image filling my mind was the face of my mother in that painting.

Woodson took a deep breath. "There are five investigators leading the clinical trial for Marihypnol. One of the centers is in Hattiesburg."

I felt a tear coursing over my cheek and struggled to quell it. "I see."

"The principal investigator in the Marihypnol trial is Dr. Tyler Madden." She put her hand on mine from across the desk.

I looked up at her face, saw the strain and the sadness in it. I looked up at Jimmy, then to Parkman. I gazed at them all, helplessly, and only found grim visages in return.

"It's a no-brainer, Lucas. I'm, I mean, we're all very sorry."

The words registered, but still I refused to believe them. "No. You're all wrong. It's not Tyler. It can't be."

Jimmy held out his hand, and cut me off. "You're off this case, Lucas. End of story."

I ceased speaking and simply nodded.

"If you're up to it," he said, "you can stay here and help Woodson round up the case files and take them over to the Jackson field office while we find your brother." He looked at me. "If you can't handle that, we'll just have Woodson stay here with you and send somebody over for the case files later."

"I can handle it."

"Okay. Agent Woodson," Raritan spoke her name in good-bye fashion, but the implication of the unfinished statement was clear.

If he tries anything, stop him.

THIRTY-FIVE

Raritan and Parkman called the police department in Hattiesburg and left to meet several members of the local force at Tyler's offices.

After they left, Woodson simply sat and waited across from me in silence, allowing me the time I needed to recover from the shock.

"Woodson," I finally said. "I know how bad this looks. But it's not him. Somehow, he's being framed for this." Even as I spoke the words, I realized the fallout that would inevitably come. How was I supposed to explain this to Katie? Or my father?

Woodson shook her head. "Let's just see what he has to say."

I picked up my phone and dialed a number.

"Lucas, you can't call him. Raritan said—"

"I'm not calling him. I'm calling my sister, to make sure she's okay. I'm not calling my brother and telling him to make a break for Mexico."

"But you can't say anything to your sister, either."

"Woodson, I'm checking on her. I won't say anything to her about Tyler. After I talk to her I'll ask for Faraday and get him up to speed, just in case Tyler should happen to show up over there. Okay?"

Woodson peered at me for a couple seconds. "Okay."

I resumed the dial, and my sister's voice answered. "Hello?"

"Katie. It's Lucas. Just checking in. How's everything going?"

"We're fine," Katie said. "Just fine. But how about you? You sound like you have a cold; you're all stuffed up."

"Yeah, a cold. Okay, I won't keep you. But before I go, can you put Faraday on the phone?"

"Sure. Take care, Lucas."

"Will do. You do the same."

Faraday's voice came over the phone. "Agent Madden?"

"Hi, David? I need you to listen carefully, and I need you to do me a favor. Just in case. I can't answer any questions you'll have, but this is of the utmost importance. You can't let my sister know about anything we talk about here. Okay?"

"Yes, sir."

"Okay. Keep your eyes out for my brother. You remember what he looks like from the stadium, right?"

"Yes, sir. What's the matter?"

"Just keep an eye out for him. If he shows up, arrest him on the spot. Don't let him near Katie or the girls. Okay? Let Tucker know, too. And this is just between the three of us for the time being."

"Agent Madden, I'm not sure—"

"I'm not sure about much of anything, either, but I'm certain that I'm the agent in charge and you're supposed to follow my orders without question. Are we clear?"

"Yes, sir."

"Okay. Just do this if Tyler shows up. I want you to arrest him on sight, then call me immediately."

"Yes, sir."

"And David?"

"Yes?"

"Just be careful."

"Yes, sir."

I hung up and looked defiantly at Woodson, who still regarded me with sad eyes. "It's not Tyler, Woodson. I just don't want anybody shooting him just because he might go over to visit Katie and the girls. Do you see how crazy this is? It's not Tyler."

"Lucas. These things are always difficult."

"Oh yeah? Well, I have news for you. This isn't one of 'those things.' So it's not difficult at all. Except for my jackass colleagues in the FBI, unwilling to listen to reason."

"Lucas, if you were being objective here, you'd probably be amazed that Jimmy didn't put you in a jail cell until this is all over. I essentially talked him out of it. But we need to round up the evidence and take it to Hattiesburg. Are you ready for this?"

I started to tell her to take it herself and to shove it up Jimmy's ass when she got there. But then I envisioned having one last chance to sift through the evidence during the ride to Hattiesburg, and possibly find anything that might exonerate my brother. The wheels were in motion, and I couldn't stop them. If I continued to fight the Bureau, I'd find myself on the outside looking in. It would work better if I could do it from the inside. "Absolutely, I'm ready. Let's get that evidence rounded up."

Woodson eyed me suspiciously. "Really? You're sure? Just a second ago . . ."

"I'm sure."

She kept looking at me and said, "Okay, then. Follow me." I followed her out of the office, down the hallway, and down the elevator, without another word. In the basement we walked through a maze of overstuffed, dusty shelves of cold case files until we came to the room where we stored the case files for all ongoing investigations.

"Here it is," I said, pulling a box from the shelves. "Evidence files for case four-four-three." I was struck by the lightness of the cardboard box and its contents. I'd expected it to weigh a hundred pounds when in actuality it only weighed a few.

"Is this everything?"

"Yep."

"Okay then. I'll drive," Woodson said, waiting to see if I would agree to it.

When I didn't protest, she turned and walked back toward the elevator. Hefting the box under my arm, I hesitated a moment longer, then followed her.

A little later we were driving along the bridge toward I-10. It was hot and humid, but the clouds bore a dark, angry, gray color, and the radio stations warned of an evening of tornado watches and flash flood warnings. It was going to be a rough night.

I reached into the backseat and lifted the evidence box into my lap just as a few scattered raindrops began to plunk the windshield. I opened the lid of the box and began to flip through the manila envelopes and folders inside.

"What are you looking for?"

"I don't know. Something . . . anything, I guess, that could clear my brother."

Woodson didn't reply, but her silence was deafening. I pulled out a stack of brown paper envelopes and continued flipping through the folders stacked in the box. I noticed a folder bearing my own name that I didn't recognize. Opening it, I saw the letter that the presumed Snow White Killer had left for me at the football game. A white flash of lightning crackled down on the horizon, and a second later a tremendous boom of thunder rattled the inside of the car.

I refocused on the SWK's note to me in the plastic bag and reread it. The question "A TAN CAT CANT WHAT, DR. MADDEN?" still mocked me from the page. He'd posed a question to me, addressing me as Dr. Madden. As I looked at the paper from the unknown printing press I also remembered that Terry hadn't gotten any further with finding the paper's origin based on the strange watermark we'd examined in the lab that day.

I looked at the page with the certainty only a brother, albeit an estranged brother, could possess. Tyler hadn't written this note. I couldn't articulate exactly how I knew, but I knew my brother hadn't written it. Maybe it had to do with the appellation. Tyler would have never sent a letter to me addressing me as "Dr. Madden."

At least I didn't think he would. Unfortunately, at the very same moment, I was rapidly coming to the conclusion that I for one definitely did *not* know what to think anymore.

I closed my eyes, took a deep breath, and then opened my eyes, willing myself to think clearly. I fished around in my jacket to remove a penlight and held it over the note with the watermark to illuminate it better, since the dark clouds had darkened the afternoon sky all around. The watermark bore an oval shape with squiggly lines inside it. Strangely, as Terry had pointed out, this watermark was almost the size of a nickel, whereas most watermarks were closer to the size of a half dollar.

I stared harder. The letters *TAK* sat in an arc above a second T shape, with a series of barely discernible loops surrounding the base of the bottom *T.*

I studied the *T* beneath the three-letter word. Something about the overall shape reminded me of something I'd seen before.

After a few more moments I realized what the bottom *T* was—it wasn't a *T,* but rather was the caduceus, the symbol of the medical profession. The bottom *T* was a light impression of the crosslike object bearing snakes twisting around it.

A medical school? A press?

But something was still wrong. The indention was so small—perhaps it wasn't a watermark?

I took a moment to rub my eyes, and I laid the letter on my lap. When I looked back down, I focused on the three letters at the top of the mark. TAK. It made no sense.

I looked more closely. There was a small indention just to the left of the *T,* near the bottom.

Perhaps not a *T,* but a *J*?

And when I considered *JAK* as the potential three letters of the watermark, I almost screamed aloud as the reality of who'd written the letter slammed into me like a fist.

"Woodson," I spoke as calmly as I could, fighting the urge to scream it, "I need to share a theory with you, and I need to ask you to just listen, okay? Pull over up here, just for a second."

"Are you kidding me? I'm not pulling over."

"Woodson, please. I'm begging you. It'll take two minutes, I swear. No more. Please, Woodson."

She looked at me again, and this time her annoyance was clearly conveyed.

"Please, Woodson. Just hear me out. One last time."

I felt the car decelerate and heard the gravel on the roadside begin to crunch. I knew I had less than two minutes to make my case.

Ten minutes later we were driving up I-10 as quickly as possible. I started to call Raritan, but Woodson touched my arm.

"Don't call Jimmy. He won't believe you. The idea that it's a cuff link impression on that note, rather than a watermark? It just isn't going to cut it for him. The circumstantial evidence against your brother is still enormous. If you call him, Jimmy's just going to be pissed at both of us and tell us to turn around and go back to the field office and wait."

I was all too happy to oblige. "Thank you, Woodson."

"Don't thank me yet," she said. "I wouldn't be doing this if I didn't think you really are on to something there." She paused. "The least we can do is check it out."

I would have kissed her if I could. After we'd pulled over, I'd taken her through the letter, shown her the watermark, shared my theory about a cuff link impression, and then relayed how I remembered the expensive cuff links that Dr. Kinsey, Dr. James Allen Kinsey, had worn on the day we interviewed Mara. Although initially skeptical, she ultimately couldn't dismiss the JAK as sheer coincidence. She had agreed to stop in Slidell, on our way to Jackson, to speak to Dr. Kinsey before resuming our trip. It was all I could ask for.

Fifteen minutes later we found ourselves once again winding through the lush landscape of Memorial Oaks. After parking in the same parking lot as before, we ran through the rain, up the sidewalk to the front entryway. Inside the marble-floored foyer we shook the water from our clothes and flashed our badges to the security guard at the desk. We explained we were with the FBI and needed to speak with Kinsey.

"And no calls ahead," I said. "You don't need any obstruction of justice charges ruining your life at this point. It's not worth it."

The old guy only nodded. "No problem, sir."

Woodson and I took the elevators to the third floor and walked down the red-carpeted hall until we came to Kinsey's door. I pulled my Luger out, silently signaled one, two, three to Woodson, then we walked quickly inside.

Dr. Kinsey's secretary stood behind her desk when we entered. "Excuse me?" she said, but fell silent as I brought my finger to my lips and she saw our guns.

I swept around, stood beside the closed door to Kinsey's office, and again gave Woodson the one, two, three signal. In the background I saw Kinsey's secretary motion toward me, but I ignored her. The element of surprise was still on our side.

On the silent count of three, I burst through the door, only to find an empty room sitting before me.

Behind us, his secretary finally spoke. "The doctor's not in today. He left earlier and said he wouldn't be back today. Could you please tell me what's the matter here? And could you please put those guns away?"

Woodson stepped forward. "Did Dr. Kinsey say where he was going?"

As Woodson questioned the secretary I stepped back into Kinsey's office and my eyes swept up toward one of his hanging paintings, *The Creation of Adam* by Michelangelo, the one where Adam twists and touches the hand of God.

A torso, twisting, pointing . . . something wasn't right. Then I realized it.

A cruel gash severed the middle of the painting, where the finger of Adam grasped toward the hand of God.

At that moment, Kinsey's secretary's voice became audible in the outer office as she spoke with Woodson. "He was going to the fertility clinic in Hattiesburg. For the genetic study he's coordinating over there."

I heard Woodson ask the secretary to repeat herself, even as I turned toward them, my own amazement causing me instant vertigo. But I stopped as another painting, hidden behind the half-closed office door, caught my eye. I closed the door to the office to get a better look.

The painting on the wall bore the same color-splashed style as the portraits in the Ripper Gallery. It was a portrait of Kinsey himself.

The bronze tag on the frame beneath the portrait bore a caption: "Dr. James Allan Kinsey II: Self-Portrait, 2012."

THIRTY-SIX

An odd mixture of horror, joy, exultation, and fear gushed through my veins all at once. He'd been right under our noses the whole time.

Beside me, Woodson entered the office and stood momentarily speechless as she took in the painting and recognized its style from the paintings in the gallery.

I pointed. "Meet the Snow White Killer."

Woodson shook her head in disbelief. "His secretary just told me he's out of the office because he's in Hattiesburg of all places."

I started to suggest that we go there immediately, but Woodson continued.

"He's in Hattiesburg collecting samples for a trial his laboratory is analyzing here."

"Okay, so let's go."

"Don't you want to hear the punch line?"

"What's the punch line?" I asked.

"The trial he's supporting is for something called Marihypnol, according to his admin. She says his laboratory here is screening every single blood sample from every woman enrolled in the Marihypnol trials that your brother is overseeing."

A few minutes later Woodson and I were driving—or flying, would be a better description—up the highway on our way to a certain fertility clinic at the University of Southern Mississippi in Hattiesburg. Armed with nearly irrefutable evidence that James Allan Kinsey, not Tyler Madden, was the Snow White Killer, I tried to raise Raritan and Parkman on the phone, but couldn't. Nobody at the office knew their whereabouts. I explained everything we'd found out about Kinsey to Terry in the New Orleans field office, then Woodson called the Jackson field office and did the same.

As Woodson relayed the breaking evidence to one of her colleagues there, I went over everything in my mind.

Kinsey was the Snow White Killer. While we didn't know the location of Kinsey's residence, his place of work, Slidell, fit with the geography of the kill sites, according to Terry's jeopardy surface. And the modus operandi I'd proposed, that the killer selected his victims by screening for women carrying mutations in the ripper gene, suddenly seemed perfectly plausible, since Kinsey's lab was screening the DNA of all patients enrolling into the Marihypnol drug trials.

Ironically, the Arrow Pharmaceuticals link, based on Woodson's discover of the mystery drug, had taken us in the right direction, just to the wrong suspect. Before we left his office, Kinsey's secretary had showed us the clinical protocols for the Marihypnol trials. Kinsey was listed as the genetics consultant, not a principal investigator, which is why his name didn't show up when they'd searched the databases for investigators running clinical trials of Marihypnol. Kinsey was supposed to be screening patients for certain polymorphisms in the serotonin receptor that might be linked to adverse reactions to the sedative hypnotic.

But for some reason that was still unclear to me, Kinsey had also undoubtedly been screening the women's DNA samples with his own genetic test, searching for women carrying mutations in a certain dopamine transporter in the amygdala as well.

The ripper gene.

But the most important question still remained: Why? Why was Dr. James Kinsey a murderer? Even more specifically, why was Mara's psychiatrist, of all people in the world, the infamous Snow White Killer?

A ring of my cell phone made me jump. I snatched it. "Hello?"

"Lucas? It's Harmon. I'm sitting here with the computer forensics team at Memorial Oaks and you need to know something."

"What's that?"

"The CSIs have already done a quick forensic search of Kinsey's computer."

"And?"

"They found some MapQuest directions."

"To where?"

"824 Birch Street, Crossroads, Mississippi. Your father's—"

I hung up.

Ten minutes later, following my frenetic directions to my father's house, Woodson had exited onto Highway 43 and headed east, averaging nearly eighty miles an hour despite the conditions outside. The rain had let up momentarily to a steady drizzle, and Woodson took advantage of being able to see in the remaining gray light as we barreled toward the small town of Crossroads.

Less than a half hour later, we pulled to a screeching stop in front of my father's house. His car still sat in the driveway.

I withdrew my gun as we emerged into sheets of rain, and ran up to the porch. My stomach dropped when I found the front door slightly open.

Woodson touched me on the shoulder. "You want me to go in first?" she asked over the downpour on the roof.

"No. I'm okay," I yelled. "Cover me to the right."

I pushed the door open to find the foyer in order. To the left, the living room was also well kept, except for a lamp lying broken on the floor. I glanced backwards at Woodson and signaled to her. We walked through the living room quickly and turned the corner into the next room.

My father's study, as opposed to the rest of the house, was in complete shambles. The chair at the desk lay tipped over on its back, and papers from his desk and filing cabinets were scattered all over the floor.

No sign of my father.

We walked back through the rest of the house, checking every closet, underneath every bed, behind the shower curtains and inside the bathtubs. I didn't have time to think about questions like why Kinsey was the Snow White Killer. Instead I was just trying to keep up with him, trying to keep him from hurting the people closest to me.

With each pull of a curtain, with each creaking door, I felt my heart give way, the blood ringing in my ears as I feared what we would find.

But after a complete search of the house, we never found my father. Or his body.

One thing was certain, however: there'd been a struggle. We returned to the office to investigate the site of the altercation, and Woodson gestured toward the floor. "These papers. They're all outlines of some sort."

"I recognize them. They're my father's sermons."

Woodson held one up. "This one's from 1983."

I shrugged, glancing about, desperately trying to think of our next move. "Maybe he was just looking through old sermons, trying to get some ideas for his next one."

"They're *all* from 1983, Lucas."

"All of them?"

"Yeah. Check for yourself."

I glanced at the papers on my father's desk and shuffled through them. "What the hell?" Underneath a Christmas paperweight full of fallen snowflakes, I noticed that one of the sermons had some scribbled pencil writing on it, which was odd. From what I remembered as a child, once my father typed a sermon, it was finished. He would place the typed sermon like a printed poem in his Bible on Sunday morning, preach from it, then file it away, forever preserved in pristine, un-marked form.

I peered at the pencil writing and did a double take.

"Captain Courageous" sat scribbled in the upper margin.

The words took me rapidly back through time.

A long time ago, when my mother was still alive, our entire family came up with a code word one night at the dinner table. My mother and father had just finished watching a CBS News special about John Wayne Gacy. That night we'd decided that our family needed a code word, in case anything ever happened, a code word that would let us know that something was wrong. Or, if a stranger ever claimed that he'd been sent by our parents to pick us up and he didn't know the code word, we were supposed to "scream bloody murder," as my mother always used to say, and run away as fast as we could.

The code word was *Captain Courageous.*

A scraggly arrow pointed from our family code word to the top of the sermon outline, to the title. My father titled every sermon.

And the title of this particular sermon, one from 1983, literally took my breath away for several seconds: "The Devil's Orchard."

I noticed additional penciling at the bottom of the page, in big block letters.

LUCAS, DO YOU BEGIN TO SEE? COME TO THE CHURCH OF OUR YOUTH AND YOU WILL FINALLY UNDERSTAND EVERY-THING. COME ALONE IF YOU EVER WANT TO SEE HIM ALIVE AGAIN.

YOURS, SWK

THIRTY-SEVEN

When Woodson looked over my shoulder, she gasped. "Oh my God. That's where SWK got the name for his exhibition in the gallery? One of your father's old sermons?"

"I guess so. I don't remember it, though."

I scanned the rest of the outline. A tiny, barely visible penciled check mark sat next to the name of the church at the top of the outline. My father always listed the title, date, and location of every sermon.

The checkmark was next to Farview Baptist Church, my father's second church, where my mother was buried.

I stared down at the paper in my hand—a sermon, "The Devil's Orchard," dated 1983. The code, *Captain Courageous*. A check mark beside Farview.

And then I realized: my father was trying to tell me where Kinsey had taken him, before Kinsey left his own note on the sermon outline title page.

I grabbed Woodson's arm. "Let's go. I know where they are." We rushed out of the messy room, but at the last second I stopped. "Wait. Do you have a cassette deck in your car?"

Woodson frowned momentarily. "No," she answered, without understanding.

"Let me see if there's one inside." I led her back to an old dresser in the corner that I recognized from my childhood and pulled open the top drawer.

"Wow. That's a lot of tapes. And a tape recorder."

I started scanning through the ordered rows of audiocassette tapes as I lifted the recorder out of the drawer. The tapes were arranged chronologically, one for each Sunday, just as I remembered. "When I was young, my father started taping his sermons to keep an ongoing audio library."

I scanned tapes from 1985, 1984, and finally 1983. Within the span of a minute I'd found the tape labeled "The Devil's Orchard, 1983."

"Let's go, Woodson. You drive. We'll listen to this in the car on our way."

Farview was only twenty-five minutes away. I called Faraday and confirmed that my sister and the girls were okay.

I was still unable to reach Raritan or Parkman by phone.

Woodson urged me to call the local police departments in Farview.

"No way."

"What do you mean, no way?"

"Kinsey's in a 'final gambit' mode now," I said. "We're talking about my father, Woodson. I have to try and save him. If a squad of police cars arrives at the church, Kinsey is going to simply pull the plug, play his endgame. I can't risk it. You saw the note he left me."

Woodson narrowed her eyes, weighing the validity of my argument. Finally she spoke. "What do you propose we do, then?"

"I'm not sure yet. All I can hope to do is get to that church before it's too late. Beyond that, I don't know." I held up the tape of my father's sermon. "Maybe this will give us a clue of what the hell is going on here."

I inserted the tape into the tape recorder just as big drops of rain began to once again pelt the window. As the tape played, warbling organ music came over the speakers, playing a gospel hymn I hadn't recalled in twenty years. The notes pulled me instantly back in time. In my mind's eye I could see my father walking to the pulpit to face the congregation. I could see my mother in the choir behind him, seated with the rest of the blue-robed Sunday morning singers.

I could recall Tyler and Katie sitting quietly beside me in the second pew, waiting for the sermon to start.

I remembered how I could look over my right shoulder and always find Mara sitting with her mother on the other side of the church, a few rows back, usually casting me a furtive smile.

I let myself go back. How could I have forgotten this sermon? My father's disembodied voice came over the tape recorder, sounding far off and muffled, as if preaching from the bottom of a pit.

"Someday there's going to be a resurrection. Many people think that only those who are saved will be resurrected to everlasting life. But I'm here to tell you, everyone will be resurrected. The good, the bad, the followers of God, the haters of God."

The vision in my mind's eye became even clearer. I could remember how my father, preaching to the congregation in his white robes, would use his hands, pointing at the parishioners, pointing down to the Bible for effect. I had forgotten how much he pointed, for how long I felt that finger bearing down on me over and over in my youth, always pointing at me, pointing out my own endless fallibility.

On the tape I listened to my father speak of the resurrection of the body, when the end of the world would come. He said that most people only thought about the resurrection of the elect.

My father envisioned another resurrection, a resurrection of the damned.

"Everyone. For some, those who believe, those who follow in the footsteps of Christ, it will be a resurrection to life everlasting, a return to the Garden of Eden. But for the rest of us, the ones of us who sit here and listen, let the message, the good news, the gospel go in one ear and out the other, the ones who don't believe, the ones who reject the good news, the ones who stare at a suffering Christ and turn their faces, there will be another resurrection. Yes, another resurrection."

My father paused long enough to take a sip of water at the pulpit as a number of amens lifted from voices in the crowd.

"But this is an unwelcome resurrection, friends. It's a resurrection you want no part of. It's a resurrection to pain everlasting, the torment of hell, separation from God and the ones you love. If the believers in God, the followers of God, are to find eternal life in paradise, in the re-created Garden of Eden, then the haters of God, the liars, the murderers, the betrayers, will find banishment to the devil's orchard. An orchard of eternal death. Don't be part of it. You only have a short time to choose. It's your choice. Life everlasting, or torment everlasting. You decide. Will you join the son of God, or the son of perdition?"

I suddenly remembered the way my father could become lost during a sermon, a faraway look in his eyes as he stared up into the heavens then back down at the congregation, sweeping his hands across them all.

"Children. Come to God. He doesn't wish anyone to come to harm. Your sins are in the past. That's what God is. He's love, the Bible tells us." He paused, and I could hear through the tape that he was smiling as he spoke. "Yes, folks! The Beatles had it right, my friends!" A loud chorus of laughter arose from the church, then died down.

"Honestly friends, they did. He is love. And He's forgiveness. Love is all you need. Whatever you've done, God will forgive you. He only asks that you repent, that you come clean, that you desire to do those hurtful things no more. Hurtful to you, hurtful to others, hurtful to God himself."

There was another pause on the tape as I assumed my father looked out at the sea of people before him. "The heat of hell is evident all around us. A kitchen stove, a soldering tool, the flame from a match. That's only a taste of the pain everlasting. Will you be like Lazarus, the wicked man who died, went to hell, then begged God for one drop of water, just one drop of water, to cool his tongue? How he begged and pleaded with God—to just let him tell his still-living brothers that they may avoid the searing flames of hell! The fires of hell; they're so real!"

His voice had risen to a fevered pitch, a loud and thundering oration that held everyone in the congregation transfixed. I closed my eyes, still recalling those kinds of sermons. I remembered how during those types of sermons I would always look back at Mara, but she would no longer be looking at me and instead would be focusing on my father, the fear in her eyes. Tyler and Katie would sit paralyzed beside me, silent as lambs. During those kinds of sermons I put my arm around them both, tickling Katie's shoulder, trying to keep her comforted.

My father's voice on the tape descended again. "The bad you've done. It can all be washed away. White as snow. It's gone. God promises He'll forget. But you have to ask for His forgiveness. You have to reject your own pride and ask for forgiveness. Can you?"

After a brief prayer the entire church congregation sang the closing hymn.

I knew that my father would have been standing with his head bowed and eyes closed, facing the front of the congregation. On the tape he extended an invitation to belief, an invitation to salvation.

Suddenly there was a discordant note on the piano as the entire congregation seemed to stumble in unison during the hymn "Just as I Am," the same song that ended every Billy Graham crusade. It was as if the entire church, like a single organism, was suddenly perturbed all at once.

On the tape a heavy pair of boots could be heard walking along a creaking wooden floor, and suddenly I remembered this specific sermon with complete and utter clarity. How could I have forgotten? At that moment in the car with Woodson, I suddenly remembered it as though it happened yesterday.

A large shape sweeps past me, walking toward my father. A man, a hulk of a man, in navy blue work pants and a light blue short-sleeved shirt. Tattoos on both forearms. Not typical dress for a church down South; the man is an outsider. A sensation of fear passes through me, until the gargantuan man collapses against and down with my father, his tremendous broad shoulders racked with heavy sobs.

The congregation continues to sing, and sing, and sing.

The long brown hair belongs to a man known as Mean Jim, a two-time penitentiary convict for armed robbery and assault with a deadly weapon and intent to kill; a man who frequented the bars and was always getting thrown out; one time beat a prostitute so badly that she died a few days later, but nobody could ever prove it was him; knifed two black men, but said it was self-defense and got off. A man who used to make fun of my father and the other preachers in town when they'd come out of the Holiday Inn after prayer breakfasts on the first Monday of every month, up in Pontotoc. A man who'd call out to God in front of them and ask if God was out there, then why didn't He strike him down dead with a bolt of lightning. *Go ahead, God,* he'd laugh.

I hated him, and I didn't even know him. I'd only heard about him when I overheard adults having conversations. No wonder the church had trouble keeping its collective voice in rhythm when Mean Jim had walked down the aisle that day.

Woodson shook me. "Hey. Which way?"

I stared up at her as she materialized in the car seat beside me and the terrifying clarity of the memory receded. "What?" I ejected the tape momentarily.

"Which way, Lucas? I've already asked you twice."

I looked outside and struggled to see through the rain. I became cognizant of everything in the real world again. The pouring rain, the driving wipers on the windshield, the headlights illuminating the forest all around. Finally I recognized our location.

"Left, Woodson. Left ahead. It's about another three or four miles up Hickory Road."

"Got a plan, by the way?"

"Not yet."

Woodson turned left, and the car moved off the paved road and onto gravel. "You might want to start thinking one up," she said, as she straightened out the wheel and kept driving forward.

My mind, however, traveled back to Mean Jim.

Nobody ever thought that his "conversion" that day, into the ranks of Christianity, would last. But everyone had been wrong. He never reverted to his old ways. Never again a scrape with the law, never again touched a drink. He became a deacon in my father's church and remained there faithfully long after my father moved our devastated, motherless family on to a new church a few years later.

Mean Jim experienced a rarity, in my estimation: a conversion experience that stuck. He was a modern-day Saint Augustine in small-town Mississippi.

Mean Jim remarried afterwards. One of the reasons he later testified that he came to God that night was because his wife finally left him, filed for divorce, moved to the next county. Wouldn't put up with him anymore; last straw sort of thing.

I tried to remember his wife.

Back then he was married to a skinny little lady . . . Flora, that was it. Flora McKinsey. A tiny lady, as I remembered. They had a kid, a little boy, about four or five years older than I. I only saw him a couple of times. My mother had once confided to me that she thought Jim McKinsey used to beat that boy.

What was that boy's name? Jamie?

Jamie Mc—

My thoughts, the sum total of my brain processes, froze. Jamie McKinsey.

"Woodson," I said, out of the blue. "We have to hurry."

"Don't worry, I am."

"But we have to hurry. Kinsey hasn't been using my father to get me."

"What are you talking about? Of course he has."

I shook my head, still stunned by the realization myself. "No. He hasn't."

"Then what has he been doing?" Woodson asked.

The flow of blood seemed to slow in my veins as I said it, as I finally understood what everything had been about all along. Not me. Not me. "He hasn't been using my father to get to me, Woodson. He's been using *me* to get to my *father.*"

I peered through the window a few minutes later and realized we were close. The old pond where my father had baptized Jim McKinsey rolled past on our left as we ascended the long hill leading up to the church. We drove another mile or two through the kudzu-smothered landscape, and our old church finally came into view, perched atop the hill on the left-hand side. The white steeple glowed in the stormy night, the lightning every few seconds illuminating the building and the cemetery landscape beyond as bright as day.

My father's face filled my mind, and I wondered if he was still alive.

THIRTY-EIGHT

I had Woodson cut the lights halfway up the final hill, as lightning illuminated the church in the distance and we pulled into the driveway of my childhood home. It hadn't been inhabited for decades, and the desolate building at the end of our driveway looked more like a forgotten crypt than a home anymore.

Woodson shifted into neutral and cut the engine as she turned into the driveway, and we coasted into the carport without a sound. Emerging from the car, I batted a cobweb from my face. "Here's where we split up," I said.

"We're not splitting up."

I pulled my Luger free of its holster. "Yes, we are. I have to go in there alone. Kinsey said he'd kill my father otherwise. There's no way I'm risking it."

"And I have strict orders from Jimmy Raritan to never let you go into any situation alone again since what happened to you in Mara's grandmother's basement."

I shrugged. "At this point, technically, you're under strict orders to take me to the Jackson field office with the evidence box from the SWK investigation for my brother's arraignment, and you aren't doing that, either."

"There's no way you're going in alone, Lucas. Sorry." She stared at me defiantly. "Unless you're going to shoot me."

I knew it was no use. "Okay, okay. But you have to give me a head start. I have to show up alone, at least at first. I don't know what Kinsey's planning, but he has to believe I'm alone." I saw her begin to protest and made a final plea. "It's my father, Woodson."

Her lips tightened, but she relented. "Okay. Five minutes. If I don't hear from you, I'm coming and I'm bringing the entire Mississippi police force with me. You understand?"

"Ten, Woodson. It'll take me five minutes just to get up the hill to the church."

She stepped close, and I thought she was about to bargain further. Instead, she reached up, took my neck in one hand, and kissed me with force. When she pulled away, she looked at her watch. "Nine minutes and forty seconds," she whispered.

I gave her one last look of gratitude, then ran into the night to find my father.

I ran up the last half mile of road and crunched my way through the white gravel parking lot in the pelting rain as I approached the church. The lightning illuminated the entire night for seconds at a time, leaving me completely exposed. I still didn't know exactly *why* Kinsey was the killer, but I didn't care.

I couldn't help glancing to my right as I ran across the parking lot. I wiped the rain out of my eyes and looked over the cemetery where Mara and I had shared our first kiss. A cemetery I hadn't visited for a long time, and the same cemetery in which my father had buried my mother over twenty years ago.

I knew I had no time for such recollections, and kept running.

I continued toward the front steps of the church as the rain and wind continued, and another protracted flash of lightning crackled overhead. For a moment the face of the church reminded me of a skull, the two oval windows in the upper balcony and the dark glass doors reflecting the night like a gaping mouth. I walked up the steps and pushed open the sanctuary doors, scanning the vestibule. The outer chamber was immersed in darkness, and I slipped inside the foyer.

A muffled voice emanated from within the church, and I peeked through a small circular window in one of the doors leading from the outer vestibule into the dimly lit sanctuary. The church hadn't changed much; three separate rows of pews still stretched into the dark front of the church, toward the altar area. The only difference was that the floor had been carpeted, in contrast to the hard, wooden floors of my childhood.

My eyes traveled toward the end of the sanctuary. Two lights at the base of the large pulpit were glowing. And there, atop the pulpit, stood my father. His head tilted awkwardly, his arms at his sides. He mumbled what sounded like a sermon.

I pushed the middle doors open and cautiously entered the darkened sanctuary.

I swept my eyes constantly to the sides and walked rapidly toward the pulpit, my gun drawn. As I came closer, I could see two ropes ascending into the night above my father, twisting garishly like a gallows, illuminated by the lights at the base of the pulpit. Both ropes were looped as a double noose around my father's neck.

I walked rapidly toward the pulpit and whispered harshly, "Dad!"

My father stopped murmuring as a second head appeared behind him in the shadows, and a flash of metal suddenly appeared beneath my father's chin.

"Dr. Madden? A little early, but we've certainly been waiting for you." Kinsey emerged from behind my father, holding the cruel instrument of the Snow White Killer against my father's throat.

"Don't, Kinsey."

Kinsey kept the hunting knife tight against my father's throat as he spoke in a calm voice. "Drop your gun, and remove your ankle gun, too."

I considered my options, which quickly boiled down to none. The steel blade of the knife glinted against my father's neck, reflecting the moonlight streaming through the stained glass windows. I accepted the cold reality that I could never reach them before Kinsey could draw the blade across my father's throat. A tremendous crash of thunder rang out and lightning lit the entire sky for a few seconds.

"Agent Madden," Kinsey said, "you, of all people, should believe that I have no problems with killing people. Drop them in three seconds." He pushed my father forward roughly. "Three, two . . ."

"Okay, okay!" I dropped my Luger to the floor and removed the snub-nose from my ankle holster. I kicked both guns down toward the altar, where they tumbled to a stop on the carpeted floor.

In a matter of mere seconds, my best-laid plans had been ruined. I stood weaponless before Kinsey, unless I counted my father's pocket-knife in the inside pocket of my jacket. In the shadows, I slipped my hand inside and retrieved the small knife.

"Raise your hands and come up here into the light. Slowly."

I did as he commanded, instantly fearing that even the pitiable pock-etknife I'd just grasped would be detected. I held my hands up as casually as I could, hiding the pocketknife between my thumb and the fleshy part of my hand. I walked up the steps and toward the two men behind the pulpit.

"Not too close. Stop right there."

I paused only four or five feet away. Kinsey still held the jagged blade of his knife tightly against my father's throat. He removed one of the two nooses from around my father's neck and swung the free end of the double noose toward me.

"If you'd be so kind as to put that noose around your neck." He tilted his head, regarding me curiously. "As before, you have three seconds to do as I say, or I'll toss you your father's head."

I slipped the noose around my own neck, feeling the rope pull slightly taut. I looked upward and saw that, as I feared, it looped over a rafter in the ceiling of the church and connected to the other end of the rope around my father's neck.

"Much better. Now turn around and put your hands behind your back."

I turned slowly around, facing the entrance to the church. I couldn't think fast enough, but I needed to do something before I was incapacitated for good. It had only been five minutes; I needed to stall him until Woodson showed up, then pray that she could stop him. I instantly regretted bargaining with her for a head start, but it was too late for hindsight now.

As I lowered my hands behind my back I rotated my palms to shield the jackknife, and an instant later my wrists had been cinched tightly together with a plastic cuff. Too late, I whirled around and tried to pull them free. With cinched hands behind my back and a noose around my neck, I wobbled unsteadily in the darkness. For a moment I imagined falling backwards off the altar and hanging both my father and myself with one misstep. Though I'd feared Kinsey would push me off the precipice of the pulpit immediately, he didn't. Instead, he simply retreated to a position near my father, staring at me in silence.

The adrenaline surged through my frightened body and made me impatient, angry, and desperate. Another blast of thunder shook the rafters and split the night. The wind picked up outside, and the stained glass windows shuddered slightly around us. "What do you want, Kinsey? What exactly is it that you want?"

Kinsey didn't answer, but rather smiled and walked down the altar to where I'd kicked my guns. He picked them up, never taking his eyes off me, and then walked back up the altar and on into the choir loft behind us. He withdrew the curtains and dropped both guns into a newly installed baptismal. The guns plunked as they hit the water and quickly sank to the bottom.

Kinsey stepped back down out of the choir loft and took up his position beside my father. He smiled. "What I want? I want you and your father to watch each other die."

The sanctuary fell silent, save for the sound of the wind outside.

"Why are you doing this, James?" my father whispered.

"Because of you, Pastor Madden. Or maybe because you presumed that my own piece-of-shit father deserved the so-called forgiveness you were selling."

Kinsey turned toward me, looking about the sanctuary. "Yes, Lucas, good Pastor Madden brought the good news of salvation to my own piece-of-shit father, good old Jim. I believe it was a certain sermon entitled 'The Devil's Orchard'?" At that point he opened his eyes wide toward me. "Is it maddening to realize that if you'd only listened to your father's sermons, you might have put two and two together sooner?" He smiled. "All these innocent women sacrificed on the altar of an object lesson designed just for you and your father." He paused as he let his words sink in. "All those innocents could have been saved, if only you'd paid attention to your father so long ago."

"James. Please don't do this." My father breathed the words. "We never knew that Jim did anything bad to you."

Kinsey started to respond, but I spoke up first and cut him off. "Don't bother, Dad. *James* has a little problem, I bet. He can't help himself. Right, *James*?"

The smile left Kinsey's face. "Please, enlighten me."

I was baiting him, hoping that he'd become distracted as I continued to saw the pocketknife ever so gently back and forth across the plastic cinch binding my hands together. It was slow work, but within a couple minutes, the knife was already gliding into a small groove I'd cut into the plastic. "I bet you have a tiny little genetic alteration in one of your genes, don't you, James?"

Kinsey laughed. "And so the famous profiler finally begins to profile. Yes. I sequenced my own DNA a few months after your first article on the ripper gene appeared, in fact. *Madden, Madden,* I remember thinking as I read your article in the seclusion of my office in Atlanta. *How utterly ironic.*

"So yes, I carry your little ripper mutation, Dr. Madden. Both copies." He paused. "Leave it to the son of Madden to come up with the truth. A biological basis for behavior that, for centuries, had been ascribed to an imaginary devil by men of the cloth."

I tried to distract Kinsey from focusing on my father. "So why go around killing innocent women?" Even as I spoke I felt the groove in the plastic cinch grow deeper, but when I tested the ligature behind my back, my hands were still bound tight. I returned to the painstakingly methodical work of drawing my pocketknife back and forth, as Kinsey answered.

"They were simply object lessons," he shrugged. "Your discovery—the biological basis of deviant behavior—inspired me. The same way your father's words had tortured me, all these years. His predestination rhetoric doomed me to hell before I was even conceived, and I could do nothing about it. And then, twenty years later, you came right behind him and proved it, Lucas, with science. Even if all that Biblical tripe your father preached to us in our childhood was false, I was still condemned by my own genetic code, over which I had no control."

At this point his eyes grew wild. "Don't you see? You can't escape predestination, whether you're predestined by a God or by your own nature. Which one doesn't even matter anymore. Now, nothing matters." He touched the tip of his knife with his finger, and his teeth broke into a threatening smile. "I'm blameless. We're all predestined."

"Your father changed his ways, James. You could change, too." My father spoke the words from the pulpit as though a challenge.

"My father?" Kinsey's voice suddenly trembled with an uncharacteristic fury. "You embraced my father, the same man who used to hold me underwater if I cried during my bath. Or cut me with his hunting knife if I missed a shot while hunting."

"Oh. I get it," I said, in an innocent voice that belied my condescension. "So it was *your father* who is to blame. Not God. Not the ripper gene. Your father." It was a calculated risk. If he could just focus his anger on me, perhaps I could save my father—if Woodson showed up in time. "You're in a win-win situation, James. It's everybody's fault except your own. You can't be blamed. You're the only one who's golden."

He wanted to come at me, I could feel it; the way his entire angry being, all of his focus, concentrated on me. He stepped toward me, flipping the knife back and forth in his hands. The nick in the cinch where I'd been gently sawing the pocketknife felt even deeper, but still the cinch held when I tested it. I decided that if he came at me before I could free my hands to remove the noose from my neck, I'd kick straight forward into his knee and try to shatter his shin, then kick the toe of my boot straight up into his throat and hope for incapacitation.

And I had to hope that I wouldn't fall off the altar during the scuffle, hanging my father and myself in the process. It was a sadly deficient plan, to say the least, but it was all I had.

I steeled myself for the final confrontation as Kinsey's twisted features emerged from the darkness and he staggered toward me.

THIRTY-NINE

However, as quickly as he'd begun to advance, Kinsey stopped. His anger dissipated and he addressed me as if we'd been carrying on a pleasant conversation. "Wait a minute. I can't kill either of you just yet. I have a secret, and I haven't yet told you what it is."

I let out a breath, and suddenly felt how tired I really was. Tired of all the deduction, guesswork, strife, games—tired of everything. I needed to stay focused and try to keep him distracted, but it was so draining. I just wanted everything to be over. "So what's your big secret?" I finally asked, continuing to saw the pocketknife's blade back and forth behind me.

Kinsey smiled affably. "The secret? Oh, the secret. Yes. Well, for starters, I killed your mother."

My stomach went sour. I almost dropped the pocketknife as the blood swirled in my head. I struggled to assimilate his last statement in my mind. Having tried so desperately to protect my living family in the last twenty-four hours, I'd completely forgotten my original theory, that the Snow White Killer of today was somehow linked to my mother's murder more than two decades ago. Could it really be him? Once I'd accepted that Kinsey, and not my brother, was the present-day Snow White Killer, I hadn't given my previous theory another thought.

Kinsey continued. "I killed her that night. You want to know what really happened? I didn't even plan on it."

My mother's face filled my mind; not the way I remembered her that final night, leaning into the car and reassuring me with a smile that everything would be okay. Instead, I could only recall her terrified visage in Kinsey's painting from the art gallery. My heart filled with a black poison, and I knew that Kinsey was telling the truth. He was the last person to see my mother alive; the last to see the look of terror, the wild-eyed searching of her fearful eyes in the last moments before she died; the painter of her final portrait.

Kinsey kept talking, and I struggled to listen. "My friends and I had a motorcycle wreck that night on Halloween. They left to get help. And then what to my wondering eyes did appear, but Pastor Madden's bitch wife? You could imagine my surprise. That was only a few weeks after Mean Jim's baptism, wasn't it, Pastor?"

I looked over at my father, but he looked dead. As much as the sick revelation hurt me, I could only imagine what it had done to him. My father was wholly unprepared for the revelation. His knees sagged and the noose was the only reason he stayed standing. His face had gone a sickly white, which glowed eerily, pathetically, in the darkness.

Kinsey kept talking, reliving the night aloud. I managed to remind myself that if he became completely engaged in the retelling, I might still have a one-shot chance. I went back to work on the sawing of the plastic cinch tying my hands, even as I dreaded to hear any more of his story. Another white sheet of lightning illuminated the stained glass windows above, followed by a tremendous blast of thunder that rattled the pews. The wind outside howled even harder, shaking the glass in the windows.

I momentarily wondered where the hell Woodson was, but I knew I didn't have time to lose focus. I went back to my work on the cinch, and steeled myself to hear the rest of Kinsey's story.

His voice became once again audible over the wind. "Those other two boys and I collided in the dark on that motorcycle trail. I wasn't hurt as badly as I thought. But then, through the forest they came, leading a beautiful woman by the hand. And I couldn't believe my eyes; the very woman who'd led the brigade to accept my piece-of-shit father into their church with open arms."

I closed my eyes. My mother's killer. All along. Suddenly it made a sick and disgusting sense. He'd been a few years older than me. He'd come to our church a couple of times with his mother. It all fit.

I looked across at Kinsey and saw him breathing heavily, a twisted smear of anger across his face as he relived the memory. He hated her even to this day. Kinsey held the knife in his hands and looked at me. "I killed her with this very knife. My own father's hunting knife, the knife from the belt he'd whipped me with just a few hours before because I forgot to feed the dogs that day." He looked backwards toward my father for a moment. "Did you catch that, Pastor? He beat me because I didn't feed a goddamned dog." He turned back toward me. "And then your mother, of all the fucking people in the world, traipses into the clearing to help me? Miss Holier-than-Thou, arriving to help? And before I knew it, I was killing her with that knife of my father's, slashing her, over and over and over."

"No," my father said, the single word weeping out of his throat.

"And I had to kill those other two boys, after that. Just like I heard you say one time, Pastor Madden. One lie begets another. And another. And another. That night the true, gruesome killer inside me came out."

My father groaned again in the darkness.

Kinsey glanced at him but continued, undaunted. "I walked my motorcycle back along the trail, dumped it in Old Moss Pond. Ironic, wouldn't you agree?" At this point he looked at me. "I mean, ironic that I dropped the evidence linking me to your mother's murder into the very same pond in which your father had baptized my own daddy only a few days before."

Nausea assaulted me. My brother and I had swum in Old Moss Pond, even fished it with our father, and the whole time, the evidence that could have possibly led to our mother's killer lay underneath its dark surface. That could have ended all the pain and uncertainty so long ago.

Another wave of nausea hit me as I considered the sheer irony of it all, even as Kinsey gloated over it. I couldn't believe my father had baptized the father of my mother's eventual killer in the very same water that Kinsey would soon use to hide his role in her murder.

"Eventually it was like nothing ever even happened." Kinsey murmured the words, staring above our heads, not focusing on anything. "You keep telling yourself something never happened, and it approaches an asymptote, so close to truth. Pretty soon, maybe it never really did happen."

I stopped listening to his attempts to rationalize his repression of my mother's murder. Instead I focused more furiously on moving the pocketknife back and forth, back and forth, finding myself once again trying to calculate a way I might stop him or kill him. Once I sawed through the plastic ties on my hands, I'd only have a few seconds to reach up and work the noose free. If I could do that quickly enough, both my father and I would be out of danger. But even if I succeeded, I'd still need to deal with a man holding a ten-inch locking hunting knife, who wanted me dead more than anything else in the world.

I suddenly thought that if I got that far, I would probably be doing pretty well. I continued to saw the pocketknife back and forth, but I had to stop for a moment as the muscle beneath my thumb cramped up. In a moment I started again.

Kinsey walked over, but stopped a good five feet from me. "I could have been you. I could have had your life or your brother's life." He glanced toward my father.

I whispered in reply, "You chose your own path."

He breathed heavily. "No. It was chosen for me. By my father, by my mother. By my DNA. By the ripper gene. By the Damnation Algorithm."

"Everyone but you."

Kinsey sneered at me. "You self-righteous piece of shit. You have no idea. You don't have a clue because you never had to endure a life without a father."

"James." My father's voice was hoarse and weak, but he spoke deliberately. "Neither I nor my son understands what you went through. Your father's supposed to love you. It's one of the first places you understand the true nature of a God who cares about you." My father paused. "And despite everything you've done, God still loves you. I swear to this."

Kinsey recoiled from my father's words like a wary, rabid animal. I wanted to scream at my father and shake him, make him stop talking to Kinsey and redirecting his attention. But there was nothing I could do. Kinsey kept his eyes on me as he addressed my father.

"None of what you say is the truth, old man. You sell snake oil. There is no God, there is no love. It's just a sickness inside me, inside my genetic makeup." He cut his eyes toward me. "I'm a killer and there's no escape. Your son knows it."

"No, James. Forgiveness is real. And I can forgive you. Even knowing that you killed Mary . . ." at the sound of her name, my father's voice broke, but he gathered himself and kept speaking. "Life is all about love, James, not hate. All hope isn't lost. You can still find your own path to salvation. But do it while you still have the option, son. Don't do this. Don't hurt my boy just to get back at me. How does that resolve anything?"

I watched as Kinsey's face, for the first time, frowned momentarily in doubt. Then the uncertainty left his face, and anger once again creased his brow.

"One last question, before you both die," he said loudly, in a voice that reflected a renewed level of commitment after what may have been a momentary doubt. "Tell me. Is a serial killer made or born? Is the ancient idea of spiritual predestination nothing more than modern-day genetic predisposition, where our eternal destinies are simply wrapped up in the DNA you inherit from your father and mother?"

He paused and let the questions sink into the air of the sanctuary.

My father mumbled incoherently, so Kinsey turned to me. "What do you think, Lucas? Do you even believe in anything anymore?"

I hesitated to answer him. I flexed my arms one last time, but the cinch still held tight. I looked up and realized that this might be the last time I'd ever communicate with another human being. I resolved to answer his question truthfully, and in so doing, answered a question that had dogged me since the night my mother died.

Kinsey smiled and raised his eyebrows encouragingly, urging me to speak.

"You kill because you think you have the right to kill," I said. "And it's a conscious decision on your part. Your genetics had precious little to do with it, you piece of shit. Every bit of the blame falls squarely on your head. You, Kinsey, are absolutely to blame, and no one else."

Kinsey's face fell into a mock smile of barely bridled anger as he realized I'd grant him no reprieve with my dying words. He stepped toward me and I instinctively retreated. "Well then, off you go," he said with complete nonchalance, dooming me to death in an instant. He reached out to push me over the edge.

"Stop right there."

Woodson's voice rang out into the sanctuary from behind all of us as she emerged from the curtains behind the baptismal in the choir loft. "Nobody move."

For a singular second, relief washed over me, but in the next moment, Kinsey rushed me anyway, his face twisted into a visage of maniacal rage. His final gambit.

"No!" he screamed, even as the report of Woodson's gun went off and his body jerked violently as the bullet slammed into his back. He crashed into me, then fell off the altar to the right, spinning me around and knocking me backwards. As I stumbled toward the edge, I watched Kinsey tumble off the altar and fall hard and awkwardly, landing sprawled out and unmoving on the sanctuary floor below.

I couldn't gain my balance. I tried desperately, to no avail. I pulled my arms apart until they felt like they'd pop out of their sockets, but the cinch still wouldn't break. I felt the rope grow taut around my neck as my left foot missed the edge of the altar.

At that point, everything around me blurred into slow motion. I looked across at my father, who watched me with a calm sadness as I fell, knowing full well that the weight of my body would instantly lift him into the air as well.

In the next moment the pressure in my head soared to a skull-popping limit as the small amount of light in the sanctuary faded and my father vanished before my eyes. Everything blotted out, and blackness filled my vision. My brain stopped trying to make me breathe, and a calmness suffused me. A voice in my head, not at all cynical but simply observant, informed me that *this* was how you died.

I closed my eyes and succumbed to the black. But a different tiny voice inside my head whispered, *It can't end this way.* I opened my eyes, and a few holes of light poked through the black curtain in front of my eyes.

And suddenly a tangle of arms gripped my chest and waist and pulled me backwards, back onto solid footing on the pulpit, back away from the void, back from the darkness.

As the hands clung to me, I looked on my rescuer as if detached from my body, watched as Woodson struggled to hold me aloft, holding me around the waist with one arm while desperately working her other hand between the rope and my neck.

When she succeeded in loosening the noose around my neck, the pressure in my head finally released. As Woodson pulled the noose away from my throat and lifted it over my head, air rushed into my gasping mouth, filling my lungs and slowly permeating my torso, my legs, my arms. Thin streams of fire raced into my heaving lungs, and a million needles of pain fired on every patch of skin as I drank the oxygen in great, ravenous gulps.

I fell to my knees. I opened my eyes, and darkness gave way to specks of light. I watched my father fall as the rope between us fell slack, and Woodson ran over to tend to him in similar fashion. I still clutched my pocketknife, so I sawed back and forth vigorously until the cinch binding my hands finally gave way. I struggled to my feet to join them, but needles of pain shot through my legs and I fell back down on all fours. I rested a moment as the feeling came back and looked down to my left to check on Kinsey's body.

Nothing but a small, oblong bloodstain remained on the sanctuary floor where he'd fallen. An erratic series of blood splatters led back through the sanctuary, toward the exits, and into the darkness.

FORTY

I debated whispering across the altar to inform Woodson that Kinsey was gone, as she continued to care for my father. Thankfully he was still moving, but he seemed incoherent.

I knew that Woodson would never let me go after Kinsey in a million years.

"Woodson," I said, rising to my still-needling feet and limping quickly across the altar to kneel where she tended my father. "Thank you. How is he?"

"Amazingly, he seems okay. He's out of it, but I think it's the Marihypnol. He's moving his neck and limbs on his own. He should be fine."

"Thank God. Hang in there, Dad." I touched him gently on the shoulder and glanced back toward the altar. I realized that from this position on the floor, we couldn't see where Kinsey's body had landed. The pulpit obstructed the view.

"Listen," I said to Woodson. "I'm going to the front of the church. Did you call the police?"

"Yes, right before I came inside. They should be here any second."

"Great. I'll go outside and flag them down when they get here," I lied.

"You sure you're up to it?"

"Absolutely."

"Okay, I'll sit tight and take care of your father in the meantime." She looked over my shoulder and tried to peer around the pulpit. "Is Kinsey dead?"

"Dead as a doornail," I lied. "Finally, after all this time, it's all over."

"You're sure?"

"Absolutely. I'm indebted to you forever, Woodson. You saved me and my father."

"Then go get those cops and let's be finished with this fucking case once and for all."

I smiled and she smiled back. With one last look at the two of them, I nodded. "I'll be back as soon as I can."

"Be careful," Woodson said, as a matter of course.

She didn't realize how relevant her simple admonition really was.

I hurried through the darkness of the sanctuary, cursing myself that he might have already gotten away. Kinsey's blood trail led out of the sanctuary, into the vestibule, and stopped at an entry door to the church. I pushed the door open just as a spectacular flash of lightning lit the entire landscape for a full three seconds.

And then I saw him. He was staggering across the parking lot in the distance, making his way toward the entrance gates of the Farview cemetery. I ran after him, instantly drenched by great torrents of rain sweeping over me.

Lightning flashed all around, illuminating the erratic course that Kinsey followed as he made his way toward the old iron gates of the cemetery. He walked like a drunkard, probably weak from the loss of blood. But I could tell he was going to make the gates before I caught up to him.

I knew the single destination inside those gates that I dreaded, and I was equally sure Kinsey intended to lead me directly there.

A minute later I slipped through the gates and into the cemetery. Dark tombstones floated all around and a flash of lightning revealed Kinsey only thirty or so feet away to my left, bobbing in and around the shadowy shapes of mausoleums, grave markers, and statues scattered about the graveyard.

I hadn't been inside these cemetery gates since I was twelve years old, yet I knew exactly where he was headed. I assumed he believed he could muster some psychological advantage by leading us to my mother's grave.

I somehow found an extra reserve of energy and cut a diagonal path through the graveyard, dodging tombstones and grave markers in an attempt to cut Kinsey off before he could reach his destination.

The rain pounded down all around, and I caught glimpses of Kinsey as he ambled along the far side of a row of mausoleums between us in the middle of the cemetery. His head jerked back and forth as he walked, and I realized he was searching.

"It's over, Kinsey," I yelled above the howling wind, rounding the corner of the final mausoleum to face him. "Give up. The police are already on their way."

Though caught off guard initially, he recovered quickly. He glared at me, then smiled and pointed over my left shoulder. "There she is."

He said it so convincingly I turned to look, and my eyes fell upon the very place I'd avoided since I was twelve years old. The face of a modest tombstone glowed white in a lightning flash, and the engraved black lettering was plainly visible in the light of the storm.

HERE LIES MARY MADDEN

LOVING WIFE OF JONATHAN MADDEN

ADORING MOTHER OF LUCAS, TYLER, AND KATIE

The words registered within a second, but a second was all Kinsey needed.

I turned back around to find him barreling toward me. I saw the glistening steel of the hunting knife in his right hand, reflected by a brief flash of lightning.

I clutched his right wrist with both hands, but he carried us both crashing backwards toward the ground. I lifted my foot to keep him from falling on top of me, driving it into his chest. The entire encounter took place without sound, save for the elements around us. As I fell backwards, locked in a deathly embrace, I realized no more words would be exchanged between us. One of us would die tonight. As I landed in a puddle on the wet ground, I kept my foot in Kinsey's bloody chest and used his own momentum to flip him over me.

As he flew through the air, I was startled by the look on his face as he passed above me, a blatant expression twisted with hatred.

Only then did I realize that I felt the same fuming hatred toward him, and probably cast the same expression upward to him.

I rolled over as a loud thud sounded behind me, and a single groan slid from Kinsey's throat. I gained my footing and stood to face him, only to find my attacker lying still in the wet mud. A great gaping gash covered half his forehead and blood flowed freely from it. He lay upon the muddy earth without moving, staring up into the night sky as rain fell all around, his head resting crookedly against the base of my mother's gravestone.

He wasn't saying anything, just staring into space. He was looking past me. I'd seen people die before, and I knew it was finally over.

When I heard the sirens in the background I looked up and saw the shadowy shapes of Woodson and my father illuminated in the blue and red lights, making their way toward me in the cemetery, calling my name. I had no idea how long I'd been standing there above Kinsey.

I turned away and left him there, then staggered back through the cemetery to embrace the motley pair of people approaching me, people in my life who, I suddenly realized, meant more to me than anything else in the world, and whom I loved very deeply.

I fell into their arms, and we sank into the mud as the police ran around us, guns drawn, carefully approaching the Snow White Killer's lifeless body in the distance.

EPILOGUE

Three days later my father, brother, sister, and I stood at the edge of the murky waters of Old Moss Pond. We watched in silence as the recovery crew worked steadily in the afternoon sun.

I glanced behind us, wincing as I turned. The doctors were amazed that neither my neck nor my father's was broken during Kinsey's final play. There'd been just enough tension in the line to constrict my airway, but enough slack to keep our spinal columns intact. Divine intervention seemed the most likely explanation, along with Woodson's rapid response. To this day, she couldn't explain how she'd found the strength to lift my body with one arm and undo the noose with the other. My father claimed that he knew, and no one argued with him.

In the distance, Raritan and Parkman stood in the trampled-down grass of the pasture, talking to members of the local search and rescue unit.

Woodson stood to the side, playing with my nieces as Mara looked on. Mara seemed a lot better already, now that Kinsey had been exposed for who he truly was. She still needed more therapy—much more therapy, after what he'd put her through—but it was clear she was seeing a light at the end of a tunnel that had been dark for many years until recently.

When Woodson saw me looking, she waved in a single, slow gesture.

I waved back with the slightest motion of my hand, my thoughts drifting to Kinsey.

In the days after Kinsey was killed, a team of computer forensics experts and other FBI analysts had reconstructed his life and motives, thanks in large part to a manifesto he himself had prepared. Apparently Kinsey had killed my mother and those two boys and then, just as abruptly, returned to a normal existence and continued as a normal contributor to society for almost twenty-five years, living with a dark secret that only he knew.

Six months after my article about the ripper gene was published, however, Kinsey quit his psychiatry practice in Atlanta and moved back to set up a hometown practice in Mississippi. Within six months both Flora McKinsey and Jim McKinsey had passed away—his mother of an accidental overdose, his father by a violent suicide.

Kinsey had snapped. He originally planned to kill my father and then kill me right after he killed my father, but he stumbled across Mara while trailing me, and realized Mara provided a perfect cover. Mara's psychiatrist committed suicide under suspicious circumstances soon thereafter, and at the funeral Dr. James Kinsey introduced himself to Mara as a dear friend of her deceased therapist. He offered to begin seeing her, free of charge, and she became his patient.

His plan then became to kill all of us—my father, Mara, and me—but Mara and I went our separate ways. Soon after our breakup, Mara became attached to Tyler, and Kinsey, through his psychiatric sessions with Mara, became aware of Tyler's clinical trials of the wonder drug Marihypnol.

On one of his tapes he actually described the young women in the Marihypnol trials as the perfect "object lessons" to throw into my face and my father's. To draw me into the investigation, he decided to select the victims based upon their DNA and then leave the genetic code for the ripper gene on the foreheads of his victims, knowing that at some point I would figure out the code. He also made sure that the victims were left at crime scenes in counties and parishes to which I'd be summoned in my role as the profile coordinator of the New Orleans field office. The game began in earnest when he kidnapped Mara, his own patient, and pretended to be me while she was blindfolded, telling her to kill him when he (actually I) returned.

When that didn't work, Kinsey devised a scheme to kill us both and pin the blame on Tyler. Tyler told interviewers later that Kinsey had once insisted on taking a vial of Tyler's own blood to run as a negative control. Tyler had found it strange, but had chalked it up to the eccentricities of a quirky psychiatrist–research scientist. Little had Tyler known that Kinsey would smear that blood sample of his all over the final female victim at the Magnolia Mansion in an attempt to frame him for the murders of all those poor women, and eventually, for the killings of our father and me.

Upon hearing everything, I didn't know if it was the profiler in me who was able to identify with a serial killer's distorted logic, but some small part of me empathized with the tortured question James Allan Kinsey had ultimately been asking—why bad things happen to good people, and vice versa.

I'd been asking it all my life. I didn't have the answers, but I realized with great regret that I'd willingly followed Kinsey into the devil's orchard that night. My father, brother, and sister had all moved on and *lived,* but I'd lost some small part of my soul the day I'd decided to never permit myself to believe in something—God, love, anything— ever again.

All at once, I was struck by how incredibly lonely that belief system had made me feel all those years.

And just as suddenly, it didn't feel right anymore. It felt like an absurd grudge against the universe, rather than a bona fide belief system, to deny the existence of something or someone greater than myself. The final understanding of my mother's demise had sprung some dark lock inside me. I found myself considering the possibility that we were more than just piles of DNA stumbling around a random, chance rock in orbit after billions of years of evolution. I couldn't shake the feeling that my mother already knew the truth, and was inexplicably comforted by knowing that I would know, someday, too.

Whatever the answer.

Down in the pond one of the men in hip waders pulled on the rusty chain leading from the crane into the water and gave a shout, snapping me to the present. He gave the operator the thumbs-up signal and stepped away.

The engine sputtered to life, the chain went taut, and the entire mechanism began moving slowly backwards. The surface of the pond roiled and bubbled as the weight on the end of the chain moved to the surface.

I put my arm around my father and sister, and I felt my father place his hand across his chest to hold on to mine. A few seconds later, rusted and covered in branches and mud, the handlebars of an old dirt motorcycle appeared above the water.

When the gas tank emerged, I shut my eyes and Katie moaned beside me. Beneath the mud and leaves, I caught sight of an emerald-green plastic fender.

My mother's favorite color.

We stayed until the motorcycle was completely extricated and the officers ran the twenty-five-year-old license plates against the database.

It took a few phone calls, but eventually Raritan and Parkman came over with the news, told us, and left us to our thoughts. Registered twenty-seven years ago to a Mr. Jim McKinsey. Otherwise known as Mean Jim McKinsey.

Katie cried, and Tyler did, too. My father and I, however, were all cried out.

He turned to me. "We finally can lay her to rest, Lucas. Now we can all let her rest in peace."

I nodded, but my mind was elsewhere. I realized that my clearest memory of my mother was the one of her kissing my father in the church parking lot as the three of us stared up at them from our childhood perspectives, backlit by an intense sunrise above the church itself.

It was a masterpiece painting in my mind, a scene of perfection, a momentary utopia . . . and I would never relinquish it.

I missed her still.

And yet, now, having understood exactly what happened to her that night . . . somehow her memory was more lucid, more real—and easier on the heart. I hugged Katie and my father once more, then turned to Tyler.

"I'm sorry, little brother. I'm sorry for every—"

Tyler put his hand on my shoulder and shook his head. "No more regrets, Lucas. No more."

I nodded without words and hugged my brother for what felt like the first time in eons.

As we embraced, I found that I still had tears left inside. Through tearstained eyes, I caught sight of Woodson in the distance, still staring in my direction like a watchful guardian. She'd never looked more beautiful, almost angelic in the dusky haze. The woman who'd saved my life more times than I cared to remember, the woman who had made tremendous breakthroughs throughout this case, and the woman who'd believed in me when no one else had. I kissed my brother's cheek, patted his back, and made my way over to her.

I couldn't wait to pull her into my arms, thank her, ask her to come with me, and go home.